DEMONS

Sara glanced back. She was about forty feet from the tip of the crane, directly above the rolling lift unit or skyhook. She couldn't fly. She didn't know what the Witchblade could do if she took a dive. She'd never tested it that way. She had a feeling it wasn't designed for high-altitude bailouts.

The one on top of the crane got down on his belly and reached for her hair. The Witchblade shot up, index finger poking through the kid's thorax like a leather punch, hooked around a floating rib, and yanked it loose like a car door handle. The kid gave a little sigh and slumped. Blood poured from the hole in his torso as from a faucet.

Chango got his head in her stomach and his arms around her waist, and bulled her down on the single horizontal beam. The Witchblade dug for his eye with a thumb. Chango sprang back, shoving her violently, and she slipped off the edge of the beam.

And as she flew toward the ground, her last thought was, *Why doesn't the Witchblade do something?*

ABOUT THE AUTHOR

MIKE BARON broke into comics in 1981 with *Nexus*, his groundbreaking science fiction title co-created with illustrator Steve Rude; the series garnered numerous honors, including Eisners for both creators. A prolific creator, Mike is at least partly responsible for *The Badger, Ginger Fox, Spyke, Feud,* and many other comic book titles. Baron has also written numerous mainstream characters, most notably DC's *The Flash*, Marvel's *The Punisher*, and several *Star Wars* adaptations for Dark Horse. He lives in Colorado with his wife, dog, cat, and wildebeest.

DEMONS

MIKE BARON

ibooks

new york

www.ibooks.net

DISTRIBUTED BY SIMON & SCHUSTER, INC.

An Original Publication of ibooks, inc.

An ibooks, inc. Book

Distributed by Simon & Schuster, Inc.
1230 Avenue of the Americas, New York, NY 10020

ibooks, inc.
24 West 25th Street
New York, NY 10010

The ibooks World Wide Web Site Address is:
http://www.ibooks.net

ISBN 0-7434-4520-1
First ibooks, inc. printing January 2003
10 9 8 7 6 5 4 3 2 1

Edited by Steven A. Roman

Cover design by Mike Rivilis

Printed in the U.S.A.

PROLOGUE

Thaddeus Bachman's antique shop was the crown jewel of Worth Street, a renovated and gentrified slice of the Village dedicated to separating the upscale from their money. Bachman's famed brownstone rubbed elbows with Lubitsch Rare and Hard To Find Books on the west and The Estelle Gallery—featuring "Outstanding Western and Wildlife Art"—on the east. Bachman's four-story brownstone had been built in 1898 by a shipping heir, and had been equipped with a ballroom on the top floor. Bachman renovated the joint stem to stern, turning the first floor into his main showroom.

Four broad steps led to his generous red granite stoop, a double wrought-iron gate protecting his Italian hand-carved oak doors from the depredations of the hoi polloi. At ten A.M. on a Tuesday morning, those gates should have been open, allowing ingress to Bachman's loyal customers, who included several members of the House of Saud as well as a Baldwin or two.

In particular, they should have been opened to admit Robert Hotchkiss, Esq., an investment banker facing a messy divorce. Hotchkiss was 5' 11", thin on top and round in the middle. He had one of those bland middle-aged faces that gets less memorable as it ages, marching toward anonymity. He wore a black Fedora to hide his bald spot. He glanced impatiently at his Tag Heuer and cursed his soon-to-be ex-wife for putting him in this position—forcing him to sell a Japanese sword she didn't know he owned—to pay his lawyer.

Where was Bachman? Worth Street was chock-a-block with cabs, delivery vehicles, tourists, bike messengers, and immigrants with portable stands hawking everything from fake Rolexes to Viagra. Hotchkiss leaned on the bell. Inside, he could hear a faint trilling. He went down the steps and stood on the sidewalk, trying to see in through the large display window on which the words THADDEUS BACHMAN ANTIQUES was written in Gothic gold-leaf script, with black accents. In the corner was the blue-and-white rectangle of Panther Security Systems. Behind the glass were two Ming Dynasty vases, a jade dragon, a freestanding silk screen, and an immense, hand-carved mahogany Balinese wedding scene that must have weighed a ton, complete with dancers, firewalkers, and elephants. Bachman specialized in Eastern art, had perked right up when Hotchkiss told him about the sword. The banker's father had smuggled the sword home from Iwo Jima after World War II.

"Hang on to this Bob. You never know. It might be worth big bucks someday."

A frisson of panic crawled down Hotchkiss' spine. He was hanging by a thread at the Bloare Agency, the investment house where he worked. If he missed the 11:30 meeting, it would only give his boss the excuse he needed to give Hotchkiss the sack. It was a warm June morning and as usual, Hotchkiss was overdressed in his wool worsted suit and London Fog overcoat. A bead of sweat crept out from under his hat.

He returned to the stoop. The nerve of the man! In frustration, the banker grabbed Bachman's elegant wrought-iron gate handles and shook them. The handles swiveled freely. The gate opened.

2

Peculiar.

Hotchkiss folded back the gate, which swung silently on oiled hinges. He tried the heavy brass latch on the split Italian doors. It swiveled, too, and the door swung inward.

"Bachman?" he said. Investment bankers didn't bellow. "You in there?" The darkened foyer beckoned.

Hotchkiss ventured further, searching for a light. He found one. He stood on a parquet floor beneath a domed twelve-foot ceiling from which hung a Tiffany chandelier. On his left was a glass case featuring Bachman's announcements, an intercom system, and an alcove holding a jasmine-scented candle in a jade bowl. Directly ahead was the closet-sized elevator. To Hotchkiss' right was the heavy door leading to the shop itself.

Hotchkiss turned the knob. If the place were unlocked, he would leave Bachman a note. It didn't occur to him that something was amiss. His primary emotion was irritation that the famed Bachman had stood him up. The door to the shop swung inward, revealing utter blackness, and emitting a peculiar coppery smell. He stepped through the door and felt along the wall for a light switch. His hand swept something small, which fell to the floor with a tinkling sound.

"Crap," he muttered, venturing further into the cluttered room. He was assailed with the comforting odors of antiquity, all our yesterdays stacked and polished with lemon wax . . . and something else. Something metallic and dangerous. Hotchkiss recalled that Bachman kept a goose-necked lamp on the counter opposite the door. He took one step toward the counter.

His feet shot out from under him, as if he'd stepped on ice.

3

Hotchkiss went down, instinctively shoving out his hands to break his fall. He slipped on something slick and sprawled on the floor, feeling ridiculous for one nanosecond—until his reptile brain clicked that all was not normal in the antique shop.

The strange smell, the sticky slickness added up to animal panic. Demons lurked in the shadows. Gasping, Hotchkiss scrambled to his feet, hanging on to a hand-carved Indonesian table, spilling expensive doodads to the floor, where they landed with a muted clatter. He scraped, bumped, and turned into the heavy drape separating the display window from the shop. Like Jerry Lewis flubbing an entrance, he twisted in the drapes, admitting sunlight into the shop. He looked down. He was standing in a sea of crimson. He stared at his blood-soaked hands and found himself sobbing. He began to shake.

His first thought was to call the police. He hesitated. His soon-to-be ex-wife knew nothing about the sword, or certain other assets he'd kept hidden. If her vampiric lawyer learned about this attempted sale, it would go even harder on him, if that were possible.

Breathing in little shrieks, Hotchkiss decided to let himself out the rear. If he hurried, he would just have time to stop at his condo, shower, and change. He looked toward the front of the store. The height of the floor and the forest of objects insured that no one in the street could see in.

Shambling toward the rear, Hotchkiss glanced once behind the counter.

He immediately wished he hadn't.

P ezzini!" Lieutenant Joe Siry yelled from his redoubt at the end of the detectives' bullpen, on the second floor of the Eleventh Precinct.

Detective First Grade Sara Pezzini paused at her keyboard. Since discovering she could type seventy-five words a minute, Lt. Siry had found no end of work for her.

"What?" she yelled back. No intercoms in the Nineteenth. It was a miracle they even had computers, and what few they had had been purchased with forfeiture money from a drug kingpin Sara had helped bring down.

"Would you come in here please," Siry shouted back without a trace of self-consciousness. He'd been born screaming, and he hadn't stopped since.

Sighing, Sara saved her work and stood, tucking her gray cotton sleeveless turtleneck into her Versace jeans. "Like a hog-calling contest around here," she muttered as she strolled toward the lute's office, aware of but not intimidated by the sex-hungry eyes of two male detectives.

Sara looked like some coke-crazed casting director's dream of a detective. At thirty-three and 105 pounds, she looked ten years younger. But no one would ever mistake her for a pushover. Not with that swagger. Her auburn hair hung straight down her back. She wore her detective's badge on her belt.

One detective hummed the theme from *The Twilight Zone*, in reference to Sara's caseload. Even before acquiring the Witchblade, she'd been the go-to guy on weird. Every bizarre killing or ritualistic murder fell in her lap. Initially, this was because the overwhelmingly male hierarchy got a kick out of watching this perfect "10" get down and dirty with the guys, just to see if she could do it. Being a woman in the police force was a lot like being gay or a Quaker, in that she was constantly being called upon to prove herself. No matter how many cases she closed or perps she brought in, there would always be a gaggle of cops standing around saying, "Yeah, but what have you done for me *lately?*"

Baltazar, the cop who was humming, even looked like Rod Serling. He had the dark good looks and the voice. Baltazar was a Portugese-American. Cops spent more time studying each other's genealogies than hagiographers for the House of Windsor. If it were up to New York cops, there would be no plain Americans, only hyphenated-Americans. Actually, Sara mused, if cops were free to speak their minds, many hyphenated Americans would become politically incorrect. The police force drew its recruits overwhelmingly from blue-collar strata, from tribes clinging fiercely to their tribal identities. You had your Sons of Hibernia. You had your Black Police Officers Coalition. You had your Puerto Rican cops, who did not necessarily groove with the Cuban-American cops.

"Submitted for your approval," Baltazar said, dropping each word like a perfectly formed platinum billet. "Sara

Pezzini, mild-mannered homicide detective for the Nineteenth Precinct, innocently answering her lieutenant's come-hither..."

Sara had to smile. It really was a perfect Rod Serling. "That's great, Manny. Leave your number with the secretary, would ya? We'll call you."

She went into the lieutenant's office, shut the door, and planted herself in the middle of a deluxe office chair. It was adjustable for rake, lumbar, height, and castor—more fruit of the confiscatory tree. The chair slid six inches on its balls.

"What's up, Joe?"

"Decapitation in the East Village. Big-shot antiques dealer named Thaddeus Bachman. Anonymous informant over the phone. I got two greenies guarding the place. Here's the address."

"Come on, Joe. I'm up to my eyeballs, my partner is on vacation..."

"Shift your caseload to Baltazar. If he gives you any grief, tell him to talk to me."

Sara took the slip of paper. "Does this mean I don't have to continue typing your report to the Equal Opportunities Commission?"

"Come on, don't bust my chops. Murder investigations take priority over chicken scratch. Get your butt down there before the *Daily News* beats you to it."

Breathing a sigh of relief, Sara left the office, snagged her jacket, crime kit and open-face Arai helmet off the coat tree, and headed out the open door of the detectives' bullpen. Behind her, Baltazar's words echoed faintly, "...a mission that will take her...to The Twilight Zone..." He wasn't bad, actually. Kind of cute. And at least he had all his hair and no gut. But if Sara were looking for romance, and she wasn't, she wouldn't look in the detectives' bullpen. She'd learned the hard way not to find romance on the job.

Toting her helmet like a bowling bag, she took the rear stairs to ground level, exiting into the fenced-in motor pool, a tiny lot that, because of its location and the plethora of police vehicles, was jammed tighter than a bus at rush hour. It only held a dozen vehicles, fitted together like parts of a puzzle; to get one out, you had to move at least two others.

Not Sara. Her Yamaha RZ1 took up little more space than a ten-speed bicycle. She kept it snugged tight against the building in an odd little enclosure protected from cars by huge concrete posts, designed to keep trucks from careening into the rear door. There were two bikes in the enclosure, hers and a spanking new silver and copper Hayabusa. Whose was it? Another biker cop? Only cops were permitted to park personal transportation in here. She paused to admire the Hayabusa, a sleek Suzuki with a thirteen hundred cubic centimeter engine, and allegedly, the fastest stock production motorcycle you could buy. One ninety, as if any sane person would ever go that fast on two wheels. The owner had glued a pair of *Powerpuff Girls* decals to the miniscule instrument display. Charming.

Sara pulled on her red Joe Rocket jacket, her backpack, then the silver Arai. Straddling the Yamaha, she turned the key, thumbed the ignition, and the four-cylinder engine hummed smoothly to life. The Yamaha only weighed four hundred and thirty pounds, less than her Buell. Brave cops, who wouldn't hesitate to run into a darkened alley after an armed assailant, blanched in terror at the thought of riding a motorcycle in Manhattan. What they didn't realize was the unbelievable mobility it gave her. She could be anywhere in the city in literally one-half to one-third the time it took others to get there by more conventional methods. If she ran into gridlock, she could roll right down the dotted line between stalled lanes. If anybody gave her any grief, she flashed her badge.

Given an opening, she could accelerate from a dead stop to one hundred miles an hour in eight seconds. Worth Street was a mile southeast of the station house. As she cruised down Center Street, the gaping hole in the sky that used to be the World Trade Center stared at her like a baleful god. She would never get used to it. It was like losing a leg, but the nerve endings remained alive, constantly reminding her that there used to be a living thing from which those phantom feelings spring. The One-One had lost eleven men and women on September 11. Had Sara not been involved in a hot investigation at the time, she may very well have been among them. There were a lot of new faces around the precinct, which would account for the Hayabusa.

Worth Street was virtually impassable most weekdays. No one noticed the two Crown Vics double-parked in front of Bachman's. Yellow police tape sealed off the entrance, and a uniformed kid with the café latte complexion and brown wool hair of mixed parentage stood nervously behind the tape, sipping from a Styrofoam cup. Sara swerved onto the sidewalk at a service entrance, rolled the bike in front of Bachman's, and set the sidestand beneath the display window. She removed her helmet, locked it to the bike, took off the jacket, and draped it over the seat.

Ducking under the tape, she went up the steps. "Patrolman Sosa," she said, reading, the kid's tag, "I'm Detective Pezzini. What have you got?"

"Some sick stuff, Detective. Someone cut the owner's head clean off."

"You positively ID the vic?"

"We're trying to locate next-of-kin now. It's hard to tell. I mean, Jesus! You wouldn't think so, but when you cut a guy's head off, it changes his looks. The face goes all saggy and stuff." He grimaced. "Sorry."

Sara batted the kid in the arm. "Hang in there." She entered through the propped-open front door, hung a right in the foyer, and stopped short. The floor was a stinking, sticky mess of blood, smeared and marked with hand and footprints. Someone had taken a pratfall.

"Yeah," said the cop standing at the end of the counter. "Watch where you step. If you circle around the perimeter of the room clockwise, you can get over here without stepping in anything. Put some bags on, willya?"

Sara recognized the cop. "Hi, Leary. Great way to start the day, huh?" She took a pair of clear plastic baggies out of her backpack, pulled them on over her black leather Nikes, and fixed them in place with rubber bands.

"I'm glad I had breakfast two hours ago. That's all I'm gonna say."

Picking her way carefully around the crowded showroom, Sara noted where someone had knocked over several small tables, spilling expensive gee-gaws across the hardwood floor. She reached Leary, who stepped back, permitting her to stand in a dry spot and look. The antique dealer's body lay on the floor, a dark lake of blood extending from the surgically cut neck. The white spine protruded like the wire in a meat cable. She looked up. The head sat on the lower part of the counter, staring at them over a crimson clutch of leaves. On closer inspection, she saw they were invoices. The killer had mounted the head on the bills spindle. Blood completely covered the part of the counter not visible from the entrance. Bachman had had a lot of blood.

Sara swung out of her backpack, laying it carefully on the seat of a wicker chair. "You touch anything?"

"Come on, Detective. You know me better than that."

"You call the coroner?"

"Ain't had time. I'll do that right now. You okay in here?"

"I'll scream if I need you."

Digging in her backpack, she found a pair of latex gloves and slipped them on. Balancing precariously on a patch of dry floor, she hunkered down next to the headless corpse and shone a penlight on the cut. The vertebrae had been severed cleanly, leaving a faint wave pattern in the bone. The crime techs might be able to suggest the type of instrument the killer had used. Carefully, plucking at the dealer's white cotton cuff, she raised his left hand from where it had fallen. At first it did not want to come loose from the floor, to which it had been glued with dried blood. Rigor had set in, making the whole body feel like badly set plaster-of-Paris. Sara succeeded in prying the arm loose; it made a dry sucking sound. She examined the palms and fingernails for signs of struggle. Nothing. She carefully lowered the arm back into place.

A number of flies had found their way into the feast and were skating across the sticky, black sea of blood. Breathing shallowly through her mouth, Sara rose and forced herself to get up close and personal with Thaddeus Bachman. The antiquarian had an expression of surprise on his face. At least it was quick. But what kind of assassin lops a man's head off with a single blow? She was reminded of Zatoichi, the fictional blind swordsman of Japanese films. Well, a samurai, of course.

It was then that she noticed the empty sword display on the credenza behind the counter. Bachman specialized in Oriental antiquities. His head had been removed with a single blow. Here was a pair of missing swords. Sara did the math in her head. Someone had been after some swords. And if they had been given so prominent a display, surely there had to be some recent paper record of their existence.

Which brought her back to the red salad poking out from under the severed neck. If the record were among the invoices on the spindle, she would not be able to touch it. The crime lab would get those papers, and it would be their job to provide her with a complete account—by which time, the killer would be on the French Riviera.

Gingerly, standing on tiptoes so as not to dip her shoes in the blood, she picked up the sword display stand. It was made of black-lacquered wood, and resembled a pair of antlers. It had been mass-produced in China. No help there.

There was a heap of papers on the credenza next to the stand. Carefully, Sara gathered the whole pile and tiptoed out of the sea of blood. Finding a spot in the light from the street, she sat cross-legged on a Persian rug and went through the magazines and papers. A third of the way down, past Christy's catalogs, dealer magazines, and a phone book, she came to an old office copy of a paper reprinted from *Oriental Antiquarian*: "Master Sword-makers of Sixteenth Century Japan."

Placing the article in a plastic sleeve, she put it in her backpack. Next, she spied an old-fashioned Rolodex on a wooden rolltop desk tucked in behind the counter, beyond the credenza. Come to think of it, she realized, there were no computers in the shop. A single black-and-white monitor showed the front stoop. She looked up. A camera mounted over the shop entrance stared at her. Good. Maybe the killer was on videotape. The Rolodex went into a plastic bag and into her backpack. Next, she went through the cubbyholes. There were bills of lading, receipts, and customs forms in languages she didn't recognize. All of it went into plastic envelopes.

She heard a shuffling in the hall. A moment later, Gerhard Koenig of the New York City Medical Examinerr's Office, entered followed by his assistant, a moon-faced Korean girl. "Kim" something. Or maybe it was something "Kim"; she couldn't remember—they'd only met a couple of times before. Koenig wore his characteristic mechanic's coveralls, a fashion accessory he'd pioneered for coroners up and down the East Coast.

He paused just inside the entrance. "My stars and garters, what happened here? I haven't seen this much blood since the Rangers played the Bruins. Is it safe?"

"Watch where you step, Gerhard. The body's behind the service counter. The head is *on* the counter."

Stepping gingerly in plastic-wrapped shoes, Koenig made his way across the room. His assistant remained behind, setting her plastic crime scene kit on an antique chair. Koenig stood at one end of the counter and looked down. He emitted an admiring whistle. "Someone has been very naughty. And what have we here? An empty sword display case."

"Yup. We're looking for a samurai killer. You go ahead and do your thing. Holler if you need me."

Koenig nodded and went to work. He would bag the antiquarian's hands to preserve any evidence, search the

13

body, preserve the head, and ultimately separate it from the stack of bills on which it had been impaled. Sara took the plastic bags off her shoes, then went out onto the stoop, where Sosa slouched with a cup of hot chocolate.

"Patrolman, you and I are going to go up and down the street asking merchants if they heard or saw anything unusual. We want to know the last time anyone saw Bachman alive."

"What do you mean by 'unusual'?" he asked.

Sara shrugged. In the East Village, you had to go some to be unusual. "You figure it out. You go west, I'll go east. When we get to the end of the block, start down the other side and we'll meet in the middle."

She questioned a gallery and a green grocer, the next two shops. The proprietors barely knew Bachman, had seen or heard nothing out of the ordinary. A florist had seen Bachman the previous evening, as the antiquarian exited his brownstone on his way to dinner. They had exchanged greetings. That, at least, confirmed what Sara surmised from the body's condition—that Bachman had been alive the previous evening. Koenig would be able to establish time of death more accurately once he took the body's temperature.

Other antique dealers took notice. The rumor that one of their own had fallen had swept up and down the street, was probably racing through galleries on West Broadway and Chelsea as well. Mildred Oxnard, who had operated her fine art gallery on Worth since '89, remarked that Bachman frequently visited the Far East in search of booty, and perhaps had run afoul of some Asian warlord. Sara thanked her and moved on.

She was a third of the way back on the other side of the street when she saw the wrought iron sign hanging discreetly beneath a larger sign promoting THE FELDSTEIN GALLERY: SPECIALIZING IN THE ART OF THE CZARS! It belonged to the shop beneath Feldstein's stoop, a shop accessible by a wrought iron stair, protected by a wrought-iron gate, now open. The little iron sign beneath said:

TOGI

SWORD POLISHING

Sara walked down the stairs and tried the green metal door with an eyehole in the middle. It was open. A pair of chimes tinkled as she pushed the door inward.

"Hello?" she called out.

"Just a minute," someone called from a back room.

She was in a carpeted foyer, with an aquarium gurgling softly beneath the barred sunken window. The aquarium was large, at least a hundred gallons, and contained a dazzling display of coral, sea cucumbers, spiderlike crabs, and other colorful denizens. The floor was covered with thick, charcoal-colored nap. The room had been furnished with a comfortable old leather sofa, a teak coffee table, and an overstuffed chair. Examples of Japanese brush painting adorned one wall. Another wall was covered with swords—dozens of them nestling in hand-finished padded oak arches. A beaded curtain separated the foyer from a hall.

The beads parted and a man came through, bringing with him the fresh chill of the outdoors, as if he'd just stepped in from the Colorado Rockies. He was about five-nine, late twenties/early thirties, with close-cropped, dense blond hair, wire-rimmed glasses, and green/brown eyes which went from Sara's face to the badge on her belt and back again. He grinned disarmingly.

"What can I do for you?"

"Detective Pezzini, Eleventh Precinct. I'm investigating the death of your neighbor, Thaddeus Bachman. You are . . . ?"

The man's mouth opened, and he stalled as he clearly tried to digest the news. "Thad is dead?"

"Yes, sir. We received an anonymous tip this morning. May I have your name?"

"David Kopkind. I can't believe it. What happened?"

"We're not exactly sure yet, Mr. Kopkind. That's what we're trying to determine. When was the last time you saw Mr. Bachman alive?"

Kopkind slumped in the chair. "Last week sometime. He used to send me clients. He phoned me Friday, said he was sending me a client, and begged me to move him up the list."

Sara sat on the sofa, removed her note pad and a pen. "What list?"

"I'm a sword polisher. It takes about two weeks to polish a sword, and I'm currently booked through August 2005. I rarely make exceptions. Nobody likes a linecutter."

"You actually make a living at this?"

"You bet. There are enough collectors in Manhattan alone to keep me busy for the rest of my life."

"So you know something about swords."

Again, the disarming grin. Sara stifled an impulse to grin back.

"A little. I'd be happy to tell you anything you want to know."

The curtains parted again, and a large Siamese cat came through, snarling and yawning. It made a beeline for Sara, and jumped into her lap before she had a chance to move.

"Yoshi, no!" the sword polisher hissed, getting up from his chair and reaching for the cat.

Sara resisted an impulse to pet. She liked cats. But she

was on the job. And the damned thing was covering her jeans in hair. She allowed Kopkind to lift the cat off her thighs, his fingers just brushing.

"Sorry," he grinned. "Yoshi's on patrol." He shooed it back behind the curtains.

"No problem. Did Bachman have any enemies?"

"Maybe other antique dealers who were jealous. Thad was famous for obtaining rare Japanese swords, particularly the work of Masamune and his top rival Muramasa, both of whom were active in the fourteenth century. Those swords are virtually priceless."

"Hmmm," Sara mused. "I guess if people are willing to cut each other up for ten bucks' worth of crack, a priceless sword is good a reason as any."

"That's a beautiful bracelet," Kopkind suddenly said. "Where did you get it?"

Sara looked down with a touch of alarm. He was staring at the Witchblade, resting like a piece of platinum rococo around her wrist.

"Old family heirloom," she said, trying to sound casual.

"May I see?"

She permitted him to examine the strange band, holding her slender wrist, feeling his heat for one second before shaking him off. "Mr. Kopkind, this is a murder investigation. Please sit down and answer my questions."

The sword polisher resumed his seat. "Sorry. Would you like something to drink? A cup of tea?"

She *would* like a cup of tea. But she refused to let down her professional guard. "Some other time, perhaps. Are you aware of Mr. Bachman acquiring any valuable swords recently? Something that might prompt this crime?"

"Well, he did phone me, and when I asked him who

the client was he said he couldn't tell me, just to get ready 'cause the guy would make it worth my while. That's another thing. I try not to let money sway me. I would have had to tell his client that I won't move him to the front of the line. My only exceptions are for humanitarian reasons."

Sara set down the notepad. "What possible humanitarian reasons could there be that would cause you to alter your routine?"

Kopkind leaned forward and touched his fingers together between his knees. "Last year, a big-time industrial Japanese player was forced to downsize. They had to lay off twelve hundred workers—workers to whom they'd promised employment for life. The CEO who made this decision realized that there was only one way for him to atone for his shame. I made an exception for him."

Sara paused for a second. "Do you mean he used the sword to commit suicide?"

Kopkind nodded.

"You bumped his sword to the head of the line so he could kill himself?"

Kopkind spread his hands. "You can't judge him by Western standards. Suicide is not a form of mental illness in Japan. Often, it is the only honorable course of action. He did not actually wield the sword himself. That was done by a subordinate. He used his short sword, his tanto, to disembowel himself while . . ."

Sara held up a hand. "I get the idea. Here's my card. Gimme one of yours. Are these swords valuable?"

"They're priceless. Sotheby's sold an authenticated Masamune last year for three and a half million dollars."

Not that it mattered. Sara had learned that people will kill for any reason, or no reason. Greed just helped her make sense of the crime. The nature of the crime precluded gangbangers and other low-level criminals. "Does it take extraordinary skill to behead a man like that?"

Kopkind nodded. "You can't just pick up a sword and start slicing. If an ordinary man picked up a katana and tried to cut someone's head off with one blow, he wouldn't get very far. He may kill the guy, but it would be a mess. It takes incredible strength, focus, and training. The ancient samurai used to train on the occasional live criminal. Once you dipped your sword in a person of low station, you had to purify it. All the great swords were baptized in blood."

"Are you aware of Bachman taking possession of any extremely valuable swords recently?"

Again, the shrug. Sara decided Kopkind had an aw-shucks demeanor, and might have originated on a farm upstate. "That's what he did for a living. I imagine his inventory is worth maybe fifty million."

"That's a pretty informed guess."

"I'm a pretty informed observer. We were friends. We visited each other's shops, although I wish I'd stopped in recently. I don't know—not that I could have made a difference . . . You don't expect these things to happen in your own neighborhood."

Sara stood. "Nobody does. Thanks for your time, Mr. Kopkind. If you can think of anything else, you have my card."

Kopkind sprang to his feet. "You bet. Maybe I can ask around, too."

"You do that."

Sosa was back on duty, looking anxiously down the street when Sara returned.

"Any luck, Patrolman?" she asked.

"Nobody saw anything. It's a circus down here. You got green-haired hermaphrodites on unicycles selling Girl Scout cookies. Nothing's out of the ordinary. What about you?"

"Maybe a motive."

Two crime techs came out of the brownstone, wheeling a gurney with collapsible wheels. Atop it rested Bachman's remains, encased in a rubber body bag like a big blood sausage. She waited until they passed, then went into the foyer and stood in the shop entrance. Koenig was peeling off his latex gloves and packing up his kit. Kim Something waited patiently, her plastic toolbox held in front.

"Find anything, Gerhard?" Sara asked.

"Nothing beyond what you've already seen. For the amount of blood, it was a remarkably clean killing. Whoever did it left precious little of himself. No hairs. No fibers. No fingerprints. Didn't step in any blood. I got crime techs dusting all the doorknobs, but I doubt they'll find anything. I think the dealer let his killer into the shop."

Sara thanked him and booked.

Weaving in and out of traffic, Sara headed back to the Eleventh. She zipped into the motor pool cage and worked the bike into the odd triangle between the loading dock and the rear entrance. Hers was the only motorcycle.

Someone had planted a rubber Godzilla on her desk with a word balloon stuck to it. The balloon said in crude block lettering, "PEZZINI CAN HANDLE WEREWOLVES AND MUMMIES—BUT IS SHE READY FOR GODZILLA?"

Sara couldn't help it if she was a weird magnet. She hadn't chosen the Witchblade.—it had chosen her. She glanced at the Art Deco-like band of silver enclosing what appeared to be a large garnet. You'd never guess it could expand in a nanosecond to enclose her entire body.

Sara grabbed the Godzilla. It was glued to the desk. "Very funny, guys," she said, getting a good, two-handed grip. The two other detectives in the room buried their noses in their work. With an unpleasant sucking noise that reminded her of Bachman's arm, she pulled the atomic dinosaur loose and set it aside. She opened her backpack and set out the plastic envelopes filled with receipts, notations, and the Rolodex. Sitting, she pulled her dog-eared Manhattan phone book out of her lower desk drawer and thumbed through until she found Panther Security.

She dialed the number. "Welcome, and thank you for calling Panther Security!" a hearty male voice boomed. "Please listen carefully to the following menu, and make your selection when you are ready. This call may be monitored for quality purposes."

Impatiently, Sara stabbed zero. A phone rang. A female answered, "Panther Security, this is Doris speaking."

Identifying herself, Sara asked to be put through to a supervisor. Moments later, a male voice answered. "This is Norm Hansen. How can I help you?"

Sara identified herself again. "Mr. Hansen, I'm investigating a homicide that took place at Thaddeus Bachman's antique shop on Worth Street. Do you know it?"

"Very well. I installed that set-up myself, about twelve years ago. Who died?"

"Mr. Bachman was murdered in his shop sometime last

night. I'm hoping we can review those security tapes as soon as possible. They're not stored on-premises, are they?"

"Nope. Everything's here at central. We revised the entire system three years ago. Completely digital. How about I messenger those tapes over to you?"

"Mr. Hansen, that would be very helpful."

"It's my pleasure, Detective. I can't believe someone killed Thaddeus Bachman. He was a real gentleman. Give me the address and a phone number."

Siry came out of his office, unlit cigar in his mouth like an unexploded bomb. No one had ever seen him smoke one. In fact, no one had associated Siry with tobacco in any way until the City Council passed an ordinance forbidding smoking in public buildings.

"Where are we?" he asked.

"Thaddeus Bachman, a noted antiques dealer. Head lopped off with a single blow. Maybe by a samurai sword."

Siry worked the cigar like a six-speed transmission. "A samurai killer, huh? Well, why not. With you, it couldn't be an ordinary homicide."

"This case was assigned to me on a random basis, Joe. But we may have caught a break. Panther Security's sending over their tapes. We may have caught the killer on tape."

The cigar downshifted into four. "Ha. We should be so lucky. Keep me posted. Don't talk to the press. You leave that to me."

He turned to go. "Hey, Joe." He paused. "Any idea who owns that Suzuki Hayabusa in the vehicle pool?"

"What is that, some kind of car?"

"It's a motorcycle."

"Might be that new guy Sharpe, from the Bay Area. Started this week." Siry picked up the Godzilla. "Nice." He stomped back to his cave.

Sara began with the Rolodex. There were over a hundred names that she removed, one by one, and placed in three stacks: unlikelies, possibles, and likelies. The "unlikely" pile quickly grew with service firms, auction houses, the deceased, etc. The "possibles" included a long list of clients, about which Sara knew little or nothing. There were no candidates for the likely pile.

Her telephone buzzed. "Detective Pezzini."

"Sara, it's Ben Weiskopf."

It grooved her off-track. While on the job, she had a cop frame of mind. Ben Weiskopf was the retired accountant who lived across the hall from her in Brooklyn. She took a minute to shift gears.

"Ben. What's up?"

"Sara, I hate to bother you, it's not even your problem. It's those kids, those Puerto Rican kids who hang out on the front stoop. They're charging us a dollar to get in or out of our own homes. Mildred Gribble can't afford to go shopping."

"Ben, that's terrible! I had no idea. Did you phone the Brooklyn PD?"

"Yeah, yeah, phoned 'em a bunch of times. Every time I phone, they send a cop car to cruise slowly by the building. Once. That had a big effect. They scatter like flies, and five minutes later, they're back."

"How about I phone them? I might be able to get some different results."

"Yeah, sure, that would be a big help," Weiskopf said dispiritedly.

"Well Ben, what do you expect me to do? I'm on duty in Manhattan, not Brooklyn. Let me talk to them. I'm sure we can do something. People shouldn't have to live in fear in their own houses."

Weiskopf thanked her and hung up. He did not sound optimistic. They weren't best friends, but they were closer than most apartment dwellers. Ben looked after Sara's cat when she was out of town. She had brought him groceries when he had the flu. He helped her with her taxes, not that there was much to it. Weiskopf was retired, a widower, with grown children: a son in Florida, a daughter in California.

A bike messenger appeared at the end of the bullpen on the other side of the rail, carrying his thick-tired mountain bike over one shoulder. In blue and black spandex, gloves, and helmet, he looked like a participant in some new-wave extreme sport. Jan Pooley, the office secretary, pointed at Sara and held the swinging wooden gate open for the messenger, who headed her way with a brown-paper wrapped package under one arm.

"Detective Pezzini?"

"That's me."

"I have a delivery for you from Panther Security. Sign here, please."

She signed the form and took the package, which was sealed with scotch tape. When she opened it, there were three videocassettes inside, each labeled BACHMAN GALLERIES with the time indicated. The three tapes were for the hours from six P.M. Tuesday to noon Wednesday, encompassing the period during which Bachman was last seen alive, and when he was discovered.

This was going to take some time. The only videocassette machine on the floor was in Siry's office, and she could hardly commandeer that for eighteen hours. Nor could she watch the tapes straight through. The smart thing would be to divvy them up among the detectives. She badly wanted to watch them all herself, to be the one who saw the killer first. But she knew she could use help. When she looked at her watch, she saw it was twenty minutes past quitting time.

Sara took the cassettes, knocked on Siry's door and went in.

He didn't look up. "What?"

"These are the video tapes from Bachman's shop. Can you get someone to watch these, someone we can trust?"

Siry glanced at his watch in annoyance. He was making notes on a legal pad, sheer torture for him. Like most bureaucrats, he was at war with the English language. "I'll ask Raj when he comes in. Go on. Get out of here. Go home and relax. I'll see you tomorrow."

One more task. She phoned the Sixteenth Precinct in Brooklyn, eight blocks from where she lived. She spoke to a desk sergeant named Hannity, who promised that he would step up the patrols in her neighborhood. She thanked him, hung up, and methodically stored her belongings in her leather Skechers backpack.

When she went outside, the Hayabusa was back.

CHAPTER

TWO

Sara lived at Waubeska Place on St. Mark's Avenue,
state-of-the-art luxury in 1959. Today, the building was a
five-story, red brick, U-shaped apartment block, the two
arms embracing a tidy little garden, lovingly maintained
by the residents, who, until recently, had fought a win-
ning battle against graffiti. But the neighborhood was
changing. Section Eight had assumed control of part of
the building through a complicated judicial arrangement
based on the previous owner's alleged crimes against
groups traditionally considered to have been marginal-
ized. In other words, discrimination. Since the previous
owner was now serving ten to twenty at Ossining for
RICO violations, no one wept for him. One wept for the
honest tenants left behind.

The present owner was a retired entrepreneur in the
garment industry who'd acquired the property when his
consortium took over the property management company.

Sara seldom used the main entrance, because she

stashed her bike in the underground lot of the Neame Medical Center, directly behind St. Marks on Prospect Place. The medical center was happy to accommodate her, because she was a cop. Wheeling down the ramp, she waved to the security gal and found her spot on the second level down, in a yellow-striped rectangle adjacent to the elevators. After she had secured her helmet to the frame, she ran a kryptonite bike lock through the front wheel. You couldn't be too careful.

It was 6:30, still bright out, a gentle breeze playing off the East River. Instead of ducking in one of the rear entrances, for which she had a key, Sara shouldered her backpack and headed around the block, noting the young tea and mulberry trees planted in squares of soil like devotionals, held in place by guy-wire. The soil was barely visible through the layers of discarded crack vials, trash, and cigarette butts. At least the dog crap had disappeared. For some reason, Brooklynites took that ordinance seriously.

Walking now in the shadow of one of the wings, she passed a couple of homeboys working on a '67 Chevy Impala, one bending over the open hood, the other with his feet sticking out from below. A wolf whistle emitted from beneath the car.

"I'm ugly on top, *ése*," she said without stopping.

"No, she ain't!" sang the other one.

Around the corner to St. Marks Avenue, off which Waubeska Place sprung like an extra head. The street was a genteel mix of residential and retail, mostly restaurants, neighborhood markets, and laundry. As usual, the broad boulevard was parked up on both sides. It was a warm evening, and many residents were taking the stroll or

cruising the boulevard. Skaters, skateboarders and bicy-
clists swooped around her, even though it was illegal to
operate any of those devices on the sidewalk.

As Sara came into view of the main entrance, she saw
the problem. A cement walk extended straight back from
the street to the broad stoop and arched main entrance,
framed on both sides by narrow strips of flowers surrounded by lawn. A half-dozen kids, five boys and a girl,
were draped around the stoop passing cans of malt liquor
and listening to bad rap on a portable boom box. The
noise was intolerable. Sara's apartment faced the back, so
she'd never heard it.

As she approached the stoop, the youths stirred. You
couldn't really call them kids. They'd forfeited their
childhoods on the altar of machismo. No, these were
homies, a tribe of feral youngsters observing gang rule.
The men began making comments when she was a hundred feet away.

"*Qué guapa!*"

"Hey, missy! You look sweet in that jacket!"

"Hector, let her through."

"No way. Everybody's got to pay. But she don't got to
give me money!"

They laughed. She spotted the leader at once, the hulk-
ing Hector, a cruiser-weight at least, in his white muscle
shirt and black jeans that were so baggy they could have
supplied the main sail for a schooner. Hector had limpid
black eyes over an eagle beak and a hairline mustache.
His black hair was slicked straight back with either Vase-
line or axle grease. He wore a red bandanna around his
forehead, and a gold chain around his neck, his name in
big block letters. The other three were negligible.

Sara started up the steps. Hector stood on the stoop directly in front of her. She moved to go around him. He moved with her.

"Huh-unh-unh, *guapa*! Is a dollar to get in, a dollar to get out. But you know what? You and me, we can strike some kind of deal . . ."

Sara lowered her head and kept on moving. Hector had to move aside lest she butt him in the groin. When she had obtained the top step, she pulled out her badge.

"I'm a police officer. It's illegal to consume alcohol on a public ingress. It's illegal to throw your trash in the flowers. And it's illegal to extort money from people going in or out. Now get out of here."

Five heads turned grinning toward Hector, who grinned at Sara. "You ain't no cop. Lemme see that badge, wild thing."

Sara flashed the briefest grin before her left hand shot out and snagged Hector behind the neck, followed immediately by the right. Boosting herself up, she slammed her right knee into Hector's solar plexus with enough force to crack a brick. She let go and stepped back as Hector sank to the stoop like a collapsing skyscraper.

"Hey!" one of the guys said. "She smoked Hector."

Another one gave a long, low whistle.

The third said, "Are you really a cop?"

"In Manhattan. But this is where I live. And you do not, repeat, do *not* want to mess with a cop where she lives. I want, I can have half the Brooklyn police force hassling your asses twenty-four/seven. *Comprendé*?"

One of the girls looked familiar. Sara turned toward her. "Do I know you?"

"I live here," the girl said.

"That makes us neighbors. I'm Sara Pezzini. What's your name?"

"Lupé. Lupé Guttierez. I live here with my mother and little sister."

"See you around, Lupé."

Lupé said something snarky that Sara didn't catch, because she was through the double glass doors and into the marble-floored foyer. Using her key, she unlocked her mailbox and removed several bills, and the latest issue of *Sunset: The Magazine of the West*. Someone had propped open the inner security door to bypass the lock. Sara took the chunk of wood with her as she let the door click shut behind her. She really was going to have to talk to the landlord.

The trouble was he didn't know she was a cop. She'd inherited the apartment from a friend who got a job in Colorado. If the lease had formally changed hands, the landlord would have at least doubled the rent. It was an awkward situation. The management company to which she paid rent never noticed the shift in accounts. They only noticed the bottom line. Technically, she was in violation. But if the police tried to enforce every violation, it would simply choke the court system to death.

Rather than wait for the elevator, Sara took the marble steps, still elegant, to the second floor balcony. She passed an apartment that had been unoccupied since the previous tenant flipped out on ecstasy and bashed in the walls. The door was covered with faded DO NOT ENTER—CONSTRUCTION ZONE tape. Unoccupied apartments were bad news—magnets for trouble. Something else she couldn't tell the landlord.

She entered the regular stair. She couldn't help but notice the fresh gang graffiti littering the stairwell. "Romeros,"

"Brooklyn Romeros," and "Hector" were among the more legible scrawls.

Sara emerged on the fourth floor and proceeded to her apartment, 427, opposite Ben Wieskopf's, which faced the inner courtyard. As soon as she put her key in her lock, Weiskopf's door opened.

"Did you see them?"

"Hello, Ben. Good evening to you, too. Yes, I saw them, I spoke with them, and I don't think we're going to have any more trouble."

"I know you saw them. I watched you coming up the walk."

"Did you see what happened?"

"No. I don't want to remove the screen so I couldn't see straight down. You talked to them?"

"I talked to them."

"One of them lives in the building. That's why they're here, picking on us. Even jackals know not to crap where they live."

"Ben, don't worry. I took care of it."

"What about the graffiti in the stairwell. Did you see?"

"Ben, I can't do everything, and I've been working for nine hours straight. Call the management company about the graffiti."

"The management company! No, you're right. You're right. I'm sorry. And thank you. Thank you, Sara. I'm just a querulous old man."

Sara got her door open, swung her backpack inside. She turned around and went up to Ben. He was about her height, with a slightly protruding belly, and wild white tufts behind each ear, like some exotic bird. He wore rectangular horn-rimmed glasses and had a mustache.

"Ben, let's you and me get together later in the week

for some java and I'll tell you all about it. I'll even let you put brandy in your coffee." She winked. The old man brightened.

"Okay. Okay! And thanks again. I think Shmendrick is hungry. He keeps meowing. I was going to feed him, but I figured you'd be home soon."

Sara nodded with good-natured weariness and gently closed the door. Shmendrick immediately began twining between her feet. She knelt and picked up the longhaired Himalayan. He was one big cat. Blue eyes and a folded back ear.

"Meow!"

"What else?"

"Meow!"

"And?"

"Meow!"

"Very good!" Sara poured the cat back on the floor, picked up her backpack and set it on her dining room table, which served as her desk, and removed the sacked stack of invoices and notations she'd brought from Bachman's. She'd left the Rolodex at work under lock and key.

She peeled off her clothes while the tub filled, poured some lavender bath oil, adjusted the temperature so that it was almost too hot to bear, and lowered herself into the water. Fifteen minutes later she emerged in a floor-length terrycloth robe, hair wrapped in a beige towel, and famished. She went to the freezer. Genuine Palermo Microwave Chicken Cacciatore beckoned, with an olive grove and quaint skyline on the package.

She grabbed it. "Father, forgive me," she muttered, glancing toward the heavens.

While she waited for Palermo's Pride to cook in the microwave, she turned her attention to the stack of papers on the dining room table, an old oak circle she'd bought on Mulberry Street and shipped home in the "Black Mariah"—what they used to call the prisoner transport vehicle, back in her father's days; today, it was a black Ford van. Shmendrick sprawled, a furry centerpiece, tail whipping the occasional paper into the air and onto the floor.

"Shmendrick!" She flicked a dishtowel at him. He looked at her with catly disdain. As if! She'd never done anything like that to the cat before, and she wasn't about to start now. She had to physically lift the twenty-pound cat off the table. Only then did she see on what he'd been lying. A Xerox copy, bastard child of a twelfth generation twice removed, as if the article had been copied and re-copied in clandestine circumstances so that by the time it got to her, the faded gray letters were barely legible.

MURAMASA-TO, it said.

Not just sword lovers, but people in general regard the swords of MURAMASA as bad swords with evil powers. This is simply a failure of imagination on the part of the public. Originally, the sword was a divine object filled with fire, water, iron, wood, and earth—in other words, the five elements of energy. And even though it is a tsurugi that is protected and pacified the country, or a tsurugi that is a living person, it is not something that can be expected to bring evil or calamity upon the owner.

The legend of Murumasa's evil swords began after the emergence of the Edo Jidai, and is something that was born because ill fortune followed ill fortune upon the Tokugawa Ke. The grandfather of Ieyasu, Jirosaburo Kiyoyasu, was slain at the age of twenty-five by a katana made by Muramasa. His son Nobuyasu also received a

33

serious wound by a drunk with a wakizashi made by Mu-
ramasa. Finally, Ieyasu himself cut his hand at Miyagazaki
in Suruga with a ko-gatana made by Muramasa. For
Ieyasu, this meant that the death of his grandfather, the
maiming of his father, and his own cutting were all done
one after the other by works of Muramasa. It is not un-
reasonable to surmise that the swords were evil, and it is
not unreasonable that during the Edo Jidai, when the
Tokugawa Ke was all powerful, that the story of the Mu-
ramasa swords became popular.

This was very unfortunate for Muramasa's heirs, who
were unable thereafter to find buyers for his swords
among the daimyo who curried favor with the Tokugawa
Ke in the Edo Jidai. It is understandable that many pop-
ular novels and Noh plays dealt with the legend of the
evil swords, and the circumstances were that the feeling
of the evil swords of Muramasa permeated the public
consciousness.

Inevitably, among the daimyo and buge (military fami-
lies) who harbored animosity towards the Tokugawa Ke,
there was a tendency for them to like and keep swords
made by Muramasa. These were, beginning with the
Sanada Ke, the Fukishima Ke, and such, the people who
had a feeling of deep obligation to the Toyotomi Ke of Os-
aka, and included the patriots of Satsuma and Choshu of
the Sonno Ha (Restore the Emperor Faction) and Tobau
Ha (Anti-Tokugawa Faction). In their attempt to over-
throw the Tokugawa Bakafu, they favored the Muramasa
swords, which were said to have an evil influence on the
Tokugawa Ke, and tried to use them.

In the fourth month of Meiji Gannen (1867), Katsu
Yasuyoshi came to Satsuma Yashiki in Mita to discuss
the surrender of Edo Castle. Saigo Takamori, who sat op-

posite him, held a heavy gunsen (war fan). Inside this gunsen was a moroha zukuri tanto by Muramasa. The gunsen is made of iron, inlaid with silver iro-e where the fan paper is inserted in the fan; on the back of the omote and ura is a Chinese poem sketched by Fujita Toko. This Chinese poem is probably based on the tradition of a song sung by Keika when, in the vicinity of Ekisui, he assassinated Shikotei (First Emperor of the Chin Dynasty, China, 221–206 B.C.). The contents of the Muramasa and this poem were together a very positive statement of his opposition to the bakufu, and are articles left behind which graphically show the honor and dignity of Dai-Saigo.

However, in reality, the reputation of the swords made by Muramasa for being exceptionally sharp is an actual fact. The yakiba epitomizing keenness, combined with the terrible clarity of the ji and ha, may in themselves have given rise to the stories about them being evil. It is said that they cry in the night for blood, driving the owner to murder.

Moreover, Muramasa's terrible end, and the murder of his four assistants, provide further proof, if any were needed, that his blades were cursed. In 1368, the swordsman Udo, contending with the swordsman Oji for the hand of a young lady of the Gozen family, commissioned Muramasa to forge for him a remarkable blade . . .

The page, and the narrative, stopped there.

Sara woke up on the sofa when her cell phone started beeping. She'd fallen asleep reading about the art of swordmaking. Shmendrick lay curled up contentedly next to her belly. She grabbed the cell phone off the coffee table and flicked it on.

"Pezzini."

"It's Joe. We got another one."

"Another what? What time is it?"

"Another homicide by decapitation. It's 11:45. Sorry to disturb your beauty sleep, kid, but that's why they pay you the big bucks."

"Riiiiight. Where do I go?"

Siry gave her the name and address. Sara whistled. "Scott Chalmers? I've heard of that guy."

"He's a Page Six regular—charity balls, Democratic fundraisers, feed the children. Also a big time collector."

"Of what?"

"Wives, lawsuits, and Oriental art. I've cleared it with the captain at the One-Two—they'll be waiting for you."

"I'm on my way."

Throwing on her Joe Rocket, she drummed down the stairs, raced out the back entrance, and dashed across the street to the medical center. Minutes later, she zipped out of the underground garage and headed for the Brooklyn Bridge.

She was at the Park Avenue address within ten minutes, the denunciations of Pakistani cab drivers hanging in her wake. There was a Channel Six news van at the curb, a blow-dried producer arguing with a cop. Six or seven cop cars were double-parked at the curb and a small crowd had gathered. This was a big deal. People knew who Scott Chalmers was.

Also, a second samurai killing. Wouldn't the press have a field day with this? She wondered if they already knew. Sara pulled onto the sidewalk. A cop came to chase her away until she showed her badge and tugged off her helmet.

"Pezzini, from the One-One. I'm doing the headless

36

killings. Hold this." She handed the cop her helmet, got off the bike, tucked it next to the glass entrance, took the helmet back and locked it to her bike.

The cop trailed behind her as she headed for the revolving glass doors. "He's on the penthouse. They can tell you more, I just got here. Nice bike!"

She waved, went through the doors, beelined past a homicide detective interviewing the security guard. Chalmers' penthouse was on the fifty-second floor. Two cops stood in the round marble foyer, guarding a Greek fountain whose gentle gurgling belied the carnage inside. Sara introduced herself and showed her badge.

Sara let herself through the double, hand-carved teak doors leading to the living room, where three cops were standing around an incredible scene: Chalmers' decapitated body lay spread-eagled in the middle of a white shag rug. His head lay about five feet away, staring toward the patio. At first glance, it looked as if the swordsman had lopped and run. No planting of the head on a makeshift pike this time. She heard quiet, steady sobbing from down the hall.

"I'm Pezzini," she said. "I caught a similar case in the Village yesterday. Who's in charge?"

A plainclothes raised his hand. "McVickers, Homicide. We've been waiting for you. The wife found the body about an hour ago, when Chalmers didn't come back to bed. Her screams alerted the maid, who phoned 911."

Sara scrunched up her forehead. "There was a wife and a maid in the house when the murder was committed?"

"Apparently."

"Guy must be some kind of ghost. How'd he get up here? Did you talk to security?"

"Security swears no one entered the building after ten
P.M. We have videos of the main entrance, entry hall, elevators, and stairwell. We're going over them now."

Sara looked around the room. It was constructed on
two levels, with a broad sunken area, at least eight hundred square feet, filled with glass display cases and priceless objects. The top of one had been pried up on its
hinges. Inside, what was obviously a display frame for a
sword was empty.

"Anybody know about the sword?" she asked, pointing.

"That's what we figured he used for a murder weapon.
We got a call into the insurance company."

"Mind if I talk to the widow?"

"Be my guest."

Sara followed the sobbing down a hall lined with
Japanese and Chinese prints and brush paintings, past
plinths topped with Chinese pottery, past a life-sized
terra-cotta warrior, to a sitting room in which a plump
police matron tried to soothe the inconsolable widow.

Sara put a hand on the widow's shoulder. "I'm Detective Pezzini. I'm very sorry for your loss, Mrs. Chalmers."

The cop got the message and stood. A moment later,
they were alone. The grieving widow appeared to be in
her late twenties, with the leggy good looks of a Rockette.
Her long blond hair slumped shapelessly over her satin-
clad shoulders as she sniffled into a handkerchief.

"Ma'am, I'm very sorry to intrude on your grief, but if
we act quickly, we have a better chance of apprehending
the killer. What is your name?"

"Grace."

"You found your husband how, Grace?"

"We were asleep last night. We'd been watching Leno.
Scott leaned over and said he thought he heard some-

thing. I wasn't really awake, but a few minutes later I heard a noise, a swooshing sound, and voices. And when I went to investigate, there he was . . ."

"You have a maid?"

"Yes, Giselda. She called 911. She knows what to do. She's not afraid, she's perfectly legal. She's from Nicaragua."

"Did you notice the missing sword?"

"Oh, no . . ."

"What?"

"That damned sword! I should have known! He beat some other collector out in an online auction, and the other collector sent threatening e-mails. Scott had to put a block on him. Then, when the sword arrived, the deliveryman slipped on the stoop and ended up suing the association. When Scott opened the sword, he cut himself very badly."

"Was it a Muramasa sword, by any chance?"

Grace looked at her with wide-eyed astonishment. Her eyes were green. Sara recalled from somewhere that this was Mrs. Chalmers number four. "That's right. A very rare collector's item. How did you know?"

"Just a hunch. I would appreciate seeing anything you might have about the sword, including history, a cancelled check, how Mr. Chalmers learned of it, anything like that."

"All right."

"We'll have to take Mr. Chalmers' computer, the one he used to purchase the sword."

"Of course. I'll show you where it is."

Sara thought the woman's grief was a little showy. What the hell. So what if she'd married Chalmers for his money? She hadn't killed him. Sara made a mental note to check up on the three prior Mrs. Chalmers, to see if any held a grudge. It was a long shot, but cases were made on less.

Mrs. Chalmers showed Sara to Chalmers' office. Sara ordered the computer boxed up and brought in. When she returned to the living room, Koenig and Kim had arrived.

"We've got to stop meeting like this," Koenig told her.

"I agree. Did you take a look?"

Koenig nodded. "Just like the other one. A clean cut. I have an enlargement of the striations, by the way. We should be able to match the cuts. Something tells me this killer is not going to great lengths to disguise his modus operandi."

It was nearly three by the time Sara returned to her apartment, where she switched off all the phones in defiance of regulations and fell into a deep sleep.

THREE

She was in the court of the Tokugawas ... and she was a man. He was kneeling on a cotton pad on the polished mahogany floor of a castle, wearing a white silk kimono displaying the family crest—a crab superimposed on a peony. Two samurai stood on either side, wearing *kabuto* of varnished leather, their hands resting on their long swords. Immediately in front of him knelt his son, Genzaburo, eighteen—until the past week, an up-and-coming officer in the shogun's army. Genzaburo wore a white silk kimono, also with the family crest. His topknot had been unceremoniously severed moments earlier. He knelt now, facing a slab of sandalwood atop which lay a simple sheathed tanto. Directly behind Genzaburo, feet at shoulder width, arms crossed behind him, stood the Captain of the Guard Kamo Atsutane wearing the double swords of his office.

"Shigeyoshi!" barked Grand Superintendent Mizuno Kawachi no Kami Morinobu, in Japanese. The dreamer experienced the language both inside and outside. She could hear it as Japanese—harsh, indecipherable. At the same time, she heard its meaning clearly.

"You have betrayed your shogun by collecting forbidden swords! When ordered to deliver these swords to the magistrate to be destroyed, you distributed them among your retainers! Most infamously, you gambled your future on the failure of your shogun! For this most heinous crime, you and your son, Genzaburo, a party to your betrayal, are ordered to commit seppuku."

Shigeyoshi looked up, from under his hedgerow brows, and saw his son, his pride and joy, face so young he had not yet begun to sprout facial hair. He looked beyond his son, out the open door to the garden outside. It was overcast, and he could just see the branch of a gingko tree. Even in the pale autumn light, the leaves glowed luminescent.

The breeze stirred through the great hall, bringing with it the scent of jasmin and horse manure.

"Grand Superintendent!" Shigeyoshi declared in a firm voice. "Permission for my son and I to compose our death poems!"

The Grand Superintendent, a squat, powerful man with a mustache like a swallow's tail, nodded curtly. He motioned for the guard to provide paper and brushes. Moments later, these were given to Genzaburo and Shigeyoshi.

Shigeyoshi had been working on the poem in his head for some time. The peculiar thing was, he felt no shame for betraying the shogun. He never liked the man, anyway. He felt instead a transcendent calm, a satori that he'd never studied, but somehow, on the knife edge of death, achieved. He saw in his mind a long line of glittering blades extending back two centuries to their creation.

Extending far into the future, into a land that was as much straight up and down as horizontal, a place where life exploded in an unstable mix of barbarism and high culture.

The universe tilted, with Shigeyoshi in the center. It was as if he could suddenly see all the way to the sun. All those glittering blades, extending far into the future, much farther than their origin in the past. The magistrate had always known he was destined for greater things. His own rise through the bureaucracy had been meteoric; he'd been hailed as one of the most talented of the Shogun's administrators, and marked for great honors and responsibilities.

Vanity, all, in the face of the purity represented by the Murmasa blades. Particularly the Blade. Which even now, had escaped the shogun's wrath.

The Grand Superintendent shoved him with a boot. "Go on! We don't have all day! Do you have a poem in mind?"

Taking brush in hand, Shigeyoshi wrote:

> As it flies into the sun
> How piercing the swallow's song
> Feathers turn to dust

Pleased with the steadiness of his hand, the casual but controlled line of his script, he handed the paper to the Grand Superintendent who held it before him like a proclamation, then rolled it tightly into a cylinder to be delivered to Shigeyoshi's widow.

Shigeyoshi was pleased to see that Genzaburo, too, had finished his poem and handed it to one of the guards.

"May I know my son's poem?" Shigeyoshi asked.

"No," the Grand Superintendent replied. "Proceed."

Shigeyoshi watched as Genzaburo let the front of his kimono fall open, revealing his flat belly over a knotted white loincloth. Composing himself, the boy gripped the tanto, removed the blade from the lacquered hardwood sheath, and, holding it in both hands, plunged it into his belly. The curved arc of his body jerked, once, then the boy regained control and drew the blade horizontally across the lower part of his abdomen to free his intestines. At a nod from the Grand Superintendent, the samurai to Genzaburo's left drew his long sword, held the blade over his head for one heart-stopping instant, then brought it down in a killing stroke that severed Genzaburo's head from his shoulders, and sent it rolling across the sandalwood base, trailing blood.

How unnatural for a father to see his child die, Shigeyoshi thought. The thought was cool, as if he had not just seen the flesh of his blood forced to destroy himself. Beneath the cool, buried deep as within the heart of a glacier, a white-hot kernel of rage flickered. He had cut himself on the Blade, let his blood seep into its soul. He and the Blade were one now. Even if he were destroyed, his soul would live on. In the Blade.

The Grand Superintendent nodded in satisfaction. "At least your son conducted himself like a samurai. Can you do less?"

Shigeyoshi took in three long breaths and let them out. Untying the knot of his kimono, he let it fall open. His belly, too, was flat as the Hokkaido Road, despite his forty-plus years. He was samurai, and had not failed to practice his skills on a daily basis.

Feeling an immense calm settle over him like the fog in Edo Bay, he grasped the natural finish honoki wood sheath of the katana before him and slowly removed the blade.

He almost gasped. But years of Bushido had taught him to control his emotions, and he gave no sign. How could they make such a mistake? Or was it a mistake? Had the Emperor deliberately ordered the Muramasa placed there as a form of ironic punishment?

No. Nor was it a mistake. It was a sign—a sign that he, Shigeyoshi, was correct and the emperor was wrong! Freeing the blade entirely, he rocked forward on his knees, got the balls of his feet under him, rose in a twisting motion and plunged the blade forcefully through the Grand Superintendent's belly an instant before a guard rushed forward and killed him with a single blow, albeit not as artful as that which had dispatched his son.

Sara woke with a piercing pain in her neck and shoulder. The bedclothes were twisted and drenched with sweat. Shmendrick was purring loudly and licking her cheek with his sandpaper tongue. Sara lay there for a minute, gasping, wondering what she'd done to cause such pain, until it gradually subsided. She tried to connect it to the dream she'd been having, but it was one of those dreams, so utterly vivid while you dream it, that disappear like cotton candy in the rain the moment you wake.

Thank God the pain subsided. She must have twisted something working out the other day, and this was a delayed reaction.

By the time she had stretched, showered, and eaten something, it was noon. She turned on her cell phone. It immediately began ringing. She thumbed the button.

"Pezzini."

"The crap has hit the fan," Siry said.

"Give me a minute, Joe. I just woke up."

"Yeah. I know you were out late and I'm sorry to bother you," he said sarcastically, "but somehow Channel 6 got wind of the two decapitations, and they're beating the drum about a samurai killer. Turn on the news."

Sara thumbed on her remote and the small Sony flared into life. She switched to Channel 6, and there was footage of her arriving on her motorcycle and taking off her helmet. She turned on the sound.

". . . homicide detective Sara Pezzini, who has been involved in a series of high-profile cases with bizarre elements." She turned it off.

"What do they know?" she asked Siry.

"They know two prominent Manhattanites, one an antique dealer, the other a collector, have had their heads lopped off. And even though we ain't said one word about it, they're speculating that in each case something was taken."

"Did they mention swords?"

"No, and thank God for small favors. I want you to come down here and give a statement."

Sara sighed. "Oh, Joe . . ."

"Yeah, yeah, I know you hate this p.r. bat guano. I hate it, too. But you do it so well. So hop on your Yamaguchi and zip on down here, will ya? Oh, and by the way, got anything new?"

"The killer took a sword made by a famous swordsmith named Muramasa. And I suspect the same was taken from Bachman."

"Well that's something. I'll need a report."

"Before, or after I meet the press?"

"Don't bust my chops. I scheduled a conference for five P.M. That way, we can at least make the bastards sweat a little. Come on in—you'll have the space you need to compose your report and whatever you're gonna tell 'em. We'll work it out together."

"Thanks, Joe. You're a pip."

Sara showered, dressed, inhaled a yogurt and a banana, fed Shmendrick, packed her kit and split. As she opened her front door, Weiskopf opened his with the swift moves of someone who'd been waiting a while.

"They're back," he declared.

"Who's back?" Sara asked, knowing full well, and wondering how she was going to get out of this.

"Those juvenile delinquents! I can hear 'em right now down there, playing that crapola music."

"Okay, Ben. I'll go talk to them."

"Yeah, that's right," Weiskopf said with an air of defeat. "Go talk to them."

Sara took the elevator to the lobby. As soon as the doors opened, she could hear loud salsa music emanating from the front door. At least it wasn't rap. She briefly considered shooting the boom box, but then she'd have to file a discharge report, and they'd put her on suspension. If anyone complained.

On the other hand, sad to say, she could hear gunshots occasionally at night, and no reports were ever filed. She looked out. It was relatively gloomy in the marble lobby, and bright outside, so she doubted the *pachucos* had detected her presence. She counted five of them, including the girl Lupé, and a smooth new player wearing wide, pleated cotton trousers with suspenders over his muscle shirt, revealing a sinewy torso covered with tattoos.

Making sure her badge was visible, Sara strode out the front door, took one look at the boom box and froze. The *pachucos* watched with amusement as she dug in her backpack for a piece of paper. They stopped smiling when she shut off the boom box.

"Hey, what for you do that, cop lady?" said one of the lesser fish, a kid whose hairline mustache did little to conceal the acne constellations stretching across his face.

Sara turned the boom box around so she could read the serial number, ostensibly matching it to a slip of paper she held in her hand. "Guys, you may not believe this, but this boom box is stolen. I'm going to have to confiscate it."

"You can't do that!" acne constellation wailed. "I pay my man Roberto twenty bucks for that box!"

"Would you be willing to testify to that in court?" Sara asked earnestly. Acne constellation was silent. Suspenders grinned wolfishly.

"'Ey, *guapa*," he said. "Yesterday you told me *ése* Hector off pretty good. Jorgé Candido, El Presidenté for life of the Brooklyn Romeros." He held out his hand.

Sara took it. "Sara Pezzini, Eleventh Precinct. Pleased to meet you, Jorgé. Could you and me maybe have a little talk?"

"Whoah," said acne constellation.

"Look out," said another.

Lupé knotted her pretty little face into a scowl.

"Just you and me, officer?"

"Just you and me, Presidenté. Walk with me around the block." She turned back toward acne constellation. "The rest of you are loitering, except for Lupé. Take off, and I won't bust you for receiving stolen goods."

"Yeah? Bust th—" acne constellation snapped. Almost instantaneously, Jorgé's hand shot out and clipped him on the chin.

48

"Do as the police officer says, Eddie. Come on, officer. Let's you and me take a walk."

Sara could feel Lupé boring holes in her back as she and Jorgé headed for the street. "Jorgé, I never met you before, so this is a chance for you and me to get off to a good start. I don't know if you have any friends on the force, or if you ever thought about it. But it's better to have friends on the force then not, don't you think?"

"Yeah I do. An' I want to apologize about today. When Lupé tol' me what you did to Hector yesterday, I 'bout bit the sidewalk. I mean, Hector is our numero uno soldier. He's our enforcer. So I come to see for myself this bad lady cop, and I got to say, *guapa*, that you are everything I could have imagined."

"Don't let your imagination run wild. You seeing Lupé?"

"Lupé and I have an understanding, but I'm not tied down to any woman, place, or thing. What about you? You seeing anyone?"

"I'm married to the job."

"You give Jorgé a chance, he lure you away."

"I'll bet. You work for a living?"

"Jesus was a carpenter and so am I. When I gets the work. I can't get in the union 'cause I don't got no sponsor. I do after-hours stuff, get paid under the table."

"The people who live in that building, a lot of them are old, don't get around so well. The last thing they need is a gang of *pachucos* hassling them as they go in or out. I want you to keep this block safe. I want you to help these people, not hassle them. In return, you got a friend on the force."

"I can dig it. Okay!"

"You need to get in touch with me, here's my card."

They did a multi-faceted soul clasp and Sara headed on down the block to the medical center. When she was at the end of the block she turned around. Lupé was walking angrily toward Jorgé, who stood with his hands spread at his sides, like Alfred E. Newman.

A truck driver gave Sara the finger and leaned on his airhorn as she went around him on Canal Street. In New York, that was like being serenaded by a bluebird. The station house was a mad zoo, reporters bumping into perps and cops at the entrance. Sara stashed her bike in the motor pool. The Hayabusa was back.

She could sense the tension going up the stairs, and her worst fears were confirmed when she pushed open the door to the detectives' bullpen. Deputy Commissioner McElroy, with the physique and disposition of a nose tackle, was in Siry's office, taking up most of the space and talking in a loud voice while one of his lackeys took notes in a pad. As if the fat blowhard had something to say. Everyone knew McElroy was gunning to be the next Commissioner, and was mainly concerned with covering his ass and making sure he made no mistakes.

As she headed toward her desk, trying to look inconspicuous, Raj hissed at her like a spitting cobra. Raj was a two-year veteran, originally a citizen of New Delhi who had emigrated several years ago, become a U.S. citizen, and joined the police force. He had dark, delicate, almost feminine features, hair the color of fresh-poured tar, and thick, black, horn-rimmed glasses.

"What up, Raj?"

"The captain asked me to review those tapes. I have been watching night and day."

"And?"

"And I have found the killer on the tapes."

A nova pulsed through Sara's nervous system. "Where is it? Have you got it cued up?"

"In the break room."

They went to the break room down the hall, where three detectives were stuffing their faces at the thrift store table. The break room contained a counter, cabinets, a sink, a refrigerator, a micro-wave oven, a wild collection of ugly furniture, and the "audio-visual center," more fruit of the busted drug dealer tree.

Raj cued the fifty-two-inch TV, and a grainy black-and-white—blue-and-white, actually—image began to roll. Like crows sensing carrion, the three detectives rose or turned their chairs to watch.

"Watch—you will see," Raj said softly.

The timer in the corner of the screen indicated 11:30 P.M. The room was empty, light coming from the banker's lamp on the counter, and from an overhead source. Movement. A slight, balding figure in a dark sport jacket, probably navy blue, entered the picture from the shop door and went behind the counter. He seemed agitated. He was fumbling for something beneath the counter—a gun? Another figure entered the room. The second figure was clad entirely in black, even his head, and seemed to flow into the room like a cat stalking prey. He erupted like a geyser in front of the old man—it was difficult to tell from the camera angle. He delivered a series of blows with his gloved hands, subtly, delicately, as if he were playing a harp. Then he seized the sword off its rack, plainly visible in the video, and in one graceful movement, flicked the blade through the old man's neck as easily as if he were cutting a cheese log. The head fell heavily to the floor and rolled. A tingle ran up Sara's arm from the costume bracelet.

"Jesus Christ," one of the detectives said softly.

"There's your samurai killer."

"Raj, can you freeze the frame?"

Raj ran the tape backwards, searched in slow-mo for the best angle on the assailant. There was no good angle. You couldn't even tell how tall he was. Black cloth covered his entire body, including his hands. Everything but his eyes, which were exposed, but impossible to make out.

"What is this ninja crap?" one of the detectives asked.

"Pezzini's on the case," said Barley Carruthers, the size and shape of a restaurant freezer. "Freak of the week."

Baltazar stuck his head in the door. "Hey, Sara—Siry wants you in his office like five minutes ago."

"Keep working on that tape, Raj," Sara said. "There's gotta be a computer geek around here somewhere who can tell us something. And you guys—please don't mention this to anyone. The boss'll have a cow."

Deputy Commissioner McElroy was beet-colored and sweating as Sara entered Siry's office. This was not unusual. The Deputy Commissioner maintained a state of high dudgeon. That was his pose: the perpetually indignant public servant, fighting for the commonweal. Sara thought it must have been exhausting, but apparently it worked. McElroy had risen through the ranks without spending time on the street. If he could do it, more power to him, Sara thought.

"Detective Pezzini, you know Deputy Commissioner McElroy. Have a seat."

Sara nodded and sat. Siry didn't offer her anything to drink.

"Detective," McElroy wheezed, "Scott Chalmers was a

close friend of the mayor. There's no way we can keep this out of the papers, but we can try to minimize the sensationalism, so-to-speak, if we can assure the press that these killings are not related."

Siry tried not to roll his eyes. He had witnessed many futile attempts at spin control over the years, but this was the dumbest. "Of *course* they're related, Hank! The coroner's already confirmed that."

McElroy regarded Siry through little slit eyes, as if he beheld a snake. "The last thing the mayor wants is for this to become a media freak show. The public spooks easily."

"Sir, I respectfully disagree," Sara said while Siry made a throat-cutting motion with his finger and tried desperately to signal her. When she refused to look at him, he retaliated by sticking the cigar in his mouth. "New Yorkers can handle anything this freak throws at them. I think they've proven that. Not that I'm suggesting you publicize this, but it's hardly a terrorist attack. These men were specifically targeted for something they had: ancient Japanese swords."

McElroy turned his gun slits on her. He appeared to be chewing his tongue. "Why is it you attract bizarre criminal elements, Detective? Why are you a freak magnet?"

"Sir, this case was assigned to me. I think if you'll check, you'll see I was miles away from either crime scene when the killings occurred."

"You're right, I apologize. The city's lucky to have you. So. You're obviously making progress. We're looking for a murderous thief?"

"So it would seem. We have the killer on videotape, but it doesn't tell us much. He's just a blur dressed in black. We may be able to get more details from a computer enhancement."

"All right. Now we're getting somewhere. Anything you need, give me a call. The mayor wants you to know he's behind you one hundred per cent. What're you going to say at the press conference?"

Sara shrugged. "Sir, I haven't had time to catch my breath since I woke up. If you'll give me a few moments . . ."

"Please emphasize that these are not terrorist incidents."

"I'll make it clear the killer only targets rich white men."

Siry grunted and tossed his cigar over his shoulder.

"Are you trying to be funny?" McElroy asked heatedly.

"I was. I was out of line."

McElroy glared at her with his knockwurst face. He heaved himself to his feet. "No jokes! Short and sweet. The mayor is watching."

Siry and Sara got up, too. They all shook hands, and McElroy rumbled out the door like a hay bailer and headed for the stairs.

Sara held her hands up, trying to suppress a smile. "I know! I'm sorry."

"Sara, why do you do this to me? Putting me on the spot in front of the Deputy Commissioner . . . if you weren't my best detective, I'd, I'd . . ."

"What, Joe, what? Say it! Ship me out to Far Rockaway."

"You heard what the man said. You'd better prepare a statement. Keep it short—twenty-five words or less. You got—" he glanced at his watch "—one hour."

"You're hosting this thing, aren't you?"

"That's right."

"You know what you're going to say?"

"Some whack-a-ding-hoy is running around in black pajamas slicing off heads."

Sara pointed a finger at him. "That's good, Joe." She let herself out and headed toward her desk. Baltazar worked his eyebrows like he was transmitting a secret message and nodded toward the front desk.

"You got a visitor."

David Kopkind lounged, one leg up, on the wooden bench facing the bullpen.

Unexpected pleasure flushed Sara's system, along with a small rain of embarrassment. She'd only just met the guy. And she had work to do. She was under the gun. She was going on live TV in one hour. She walked over to the wooden rail separating the visitors' area from the bullpen.

"Mr. Kopkind. What brings you here?"

He grinned and stood, completely un-self-conscious. "Detective, I've been invited to a party at James Bratten's house."

"Bratten the retired NBA All-Star?"

"Yeah. He's a devotee of Eastern culture. Owns a lot of swords. I'm his polisher. A lot of big-time collectors will be there."

Sara was immediately hooked. "You're telling me *why?*"

"I thought maybe you'd like to go as my date. Give you an opportunity to see some of these players, and the type of sword we're talking about. Adrian Hecht will be there."

Hecht, a big-shot developer and owner of the New York Apples, for whom Bratten played, was putting together a major development near the former site of the Twin Towers. Cops rarely received invitations to such functions.

"When is it?"

"Tomorrow night. I'm sorry it's such short notice . . ."

"I'll go."

"Great. Great! Can I pick you up?"

"Where is it?"

"Bratten's got an estate in the Hamptons."

"You have a car?"

"Sort of. It'll get us there and back."

Sara did the math. She could ride her bike to the Village, hook up with Kopkind. It would work. "I live in Brooklyn. I'll meet you at your place. What time?"

"If you live in Brooklyn, I could pick you up."

"No, I'll come there. Say, about five?"

"Great! See you then."

She gave him the briefest of smiles. " 'Bye."

When she turned around, heads swiveled back to work, not quickly enough. Baltazar's desk was closest.

"James Bratten—that's the high-priced district, Pezzini. Better use the right fork."

"Thanks, Baltazar. Think you could show me?"

"Anytime."

"Not with egg on your tie."

Baltazar looked down, chagrined. There was, indeed, a fleck of breakfast still clinging to his lifeless, loose tie.

"Try that astronaut food. It's hard to spill."

Sara returned to her desk, thumbed on her computer and composed two short statements, one for her boss and one for herself. She was acutely mindful that she'd become something of a media darling. She wouldn't have gotten nearly as much attention if she'd looked like Janet Reno.

Next, she pulled Jorgé Candido's rap sheet. There

wasn't much: one arrest for assault as a juvie, plus a couple of parking violations.

She was relieved to learn he wasn't a serial killer.

The news conference was held in the media room of the courthouse next door. At 4:45, Sara and Siry went next door via the skywalk, down the marble steps to the first floor, where a tall black cop Sara had never seen was on duty at the door. The media had gathered, hanging out on the broad apron, sucking on cigarettes as if their lives depended on it. The new breed, who didn't smoke, had already staked out the best positions inside.

Sara went over Siry's notes with him in the hall. "You ready?" he asked.

She nodded.

"Let's go."

They entered the media room through the door near the dais. Klieg lights turned the room into an incandescent star chamber. There were about twenty reporters bunched toward one end of the long, rectangular room. Siry had long ago learned not to look into the lights, but to look into individual faces. Reporters immediately started asking questions.

"This have anything to do with Al Qaeda?"

"Is it true the victims were decapitated?"

Siry held his hand up and waited for silence. "Hello. I'm Captain Joe Siry, of the Eleventh Precinct. As far as we know, there have been two homicides: Thaddeus Bachman and Scott Chalmers. Both victims were beheaded. We have some significant leads which we are following, and will report to the public as soon as we have made progress."

"Is this Detective Pezzini's case?"

Siry turned the dais over to Sara. "The first murder occurred in my precinct and I was assigned the case purely on a random basis."

"Oh, come on!" screeched the reporter from the *Village Voice*, a belligerent leftie who was convinced the cops had nothing better to do than conspire to deprive minorities of their civil rights. "You've developed a reputation for weird cases, detective. What about the Orc killings? And the Cemetery Demon?"

"Well, Mr. Mathers, the press tends to amplify any lurid angle. Admit it. You love me, because weird sells papers."

The reporters laughed. Siry and Sara beat a hasty retreat. The tall black cop stopped the stampede of reporters after them as they made their way to the second floor and across the sky bridge.

"I thought that went rather well, don't you?" Siry asked.

"I don't know. We'll have to watch the news later and see."

The detective bullpen was in a lather, cops milling outside the interrogation room.

"What's going on?" Siry demanded.

"We got him," one of the detectives replied. "The samurai killer."

CHAPTER
FOUR

According to witnesses, the alleged perp, a native of Jamaica named Sh'mall Ibanez, had boarded a bus at 110th Street with a machete hidden under his jacket. Screaming "White man is devil!" he began hacking his way through the bus, severely mauling two people before he was overcome by other passengers, most of whom were black or Hispanic.

Sara joined a hepped-up Baltazar at the one-way to stare at this sad specimen of humanity as he twitched on a bench. His dreadlocks looked like hair clogs in a drain. He was emaciated, had a black eye and a split lip, and wore baggy Oshkosh B'gosh coveralls. Sara thought she could smell his foul odor and bad breath through the glass.

Baltazar was practically frothing at the mouth, licking an Italian ice and exulting over the apprehension. "There he is! Don't look like much does, he?"

"Oh come *on,* Roy!" Sara protested. "*Look* at that guy! Have you seen the video? That guy can't even tie his own shoes, let alone sneak into a penthouse on Park Avenue."

"Pezzini, he confessed! Case closed."

"I want to talk to him."

"No way."

"Come on. It's my case."

"We already got a confession, and somebody tipped off the Public Defender's office, so one of their birds is headed our way."

"Come on, Baltazar. You owe me that much."

"Owe you? How do I owe you?"

"For all the bull puckey practical jokes I put up with, for one thing."

Baltazar grinned snarkily. "Okay. But I'm going in with you, in case he tries to twist your head off."

Siry stood behind them. "Go ahead. I want to see this."

Sh'mall Ibanez smelled like a cage at the zoo. He stared at them with pin-prick eyes, ivory yellow whites showing all around, like an extra from *I Walked With A Zombie*.

"White devils!" he barked.

"Mr. Ibanez, I'm Detective Pezzini. Would you mind telling me what you told this other gentleman earlier?"

"'Bout what, white devil woman? Dat I and I kill de white devil antique man and de guy on de park? Dat is not in doubt. I already told you. Jah come to I and I in a vision—he were the Lion of Judah riding on a black horse—he command I and I to kill de white devil."

"How did you kill them, Mr. Ibanez?"

"I *stab* dem wit' Judah's mighty sword!"

"Where did you stab them, Mr. Ibanez?"

He touched himself on the forehead and in the heart. "Here. And here."

Sara put her hands on her hips and turned toward Baltazar, her mouth a slash.

"We have the murder weapon," Baltzar responded defiantly.

The door opened and the public defender hustled in, a stocky woman with a butch haircut. "Mr. Ibanez, I'm Lisa Thorgard, your public defender. Please don't say another word. Detectives, do you mind?"

Sara looked at Baltzar. He shrugged. They left the public defender to her client.

"Roy, once they match the so-called murder weapon with the striations on our two decaps, you'll realize you're barking up the wrong tree. I mean, use your noodle, for God's sake. How in the world could a dirtbag like that get into Bachman's shop in the middle of the night? Bachman would never let him in."

"You think Bachman knew his killer?"

Siry stood to one side, his unlit cigar tracking the conversation like a boom mike.

"Yeah, I do. In both cases, the killer took a rare sword. Does that guy look like a sword collector to you?"

Baltzar began to crumble. "Okay. Okay! But he did maim two people on the bus! We got a dozen witnesses."

"Good for you."

There was a shriek and a scuffle from the interrogation room. Baltzar opened the door to find Ibanez straddling Thorgard, who was down on the floor trying to defend herself against his blows. Baltzar immediately applied a headlock and dragged Ibanez off the terrified public defender, while cutting off his air.

"Don't kill him!" Sara warned, rushing to help Thorgard, who was sitting up and coughing.

"I, uh, I think Mr. Ibanez would really be more comfortable being represented by an attorney of color," she coughed. Sara helped her to her feet and out of the room. Baltazar emerged a minute later and shut the door.

"He'll be all right. We're gonna put him in lockup until you straighten out your attorney differences."

"He didn't scratch you or bite you, did he?"

"No, I'm all right."

"What about you, Thorgard?"

The public defender searched herself. Her jacket was scuffed, but she was otherwise all right.

"We lucked out," Sara said.

"No crap you lucked out," Siry said. "Baltazar, the next time some nut job confesses to a murder, try to get some independent corroboration. You know—evidence? Know what I mean?"

"Sorry, chief."

"If it were that easy, I'd have retired long ago."

Raj was at his desk when Sara returned to the bullpen. "What's happening with the video tape?" she asked.

"We have secured the cooperation of Ravensoft Graphic Imageworks. I sent the tape over to them. They will isolate the image and work up computer models of weight, height, and right or left-handedness."

"Who are they?"

"They are just as the name implies," Raj replied in his sing-song lilt. "A company that deals in graphic and computer imaging. They are most famous for the bloody popular video game, *Soldier Of Fortune.*"

"Do you mean 'bloody,' as in literally drenched in corpuscles, or 'bloody' in the British sense, as if to imply emphasis or feeling?"

"The latter," Raj replied without batting a lash.

Sara batted Raj on the shoulder. "Bloody good work. Keep me informed. Anybody wants me, I'll be home."

Lupé Guttierez lived in a first floor apartment at Waubeska Place, with her mother and younger sister in one of the units that had been taken over by Section Eight. Lupé didn't understand the law, but at some point the landlord had forfeited forty percent of his building. It had been a complicated decision, resulting in the first decent housing for the Guttierez family in memory.

Lupé was hell on wheels. Streetwise and sophisticated, she looked far older than her fifteen years, and had been busted twice, once for shoplifting and once for whacking another girl over the head with a garbage can in a dispute over a boy. Now she was with Jorgé and he was going to make her a star, the way Tommy Matolla made Mariah Carey. Jorgé was getting his act together to buy a recording studio, and he was going to feature Lupé as his first release.

Lupé's mother, Bella, thought Jorgé was bad news. She warned Lupé that Jorgé was just going to grease her descent into hell, but mothers had been telling their daughters that since the world began, and they still ended up with sons-in-law they didn't like.

Lupé lay on the bed she shared with her sister Syreeta, earphones connected to the boom box Jorgé had given her, listening to Christina Aguilar wail. The walls of her room were papered with posters: Destiny's Child, Jennifer Lopez, Jay-Z, Shakira, even Madonna, who was older than Lupé's mother.

Lupé knew the cop lady was a witch the moment she laid eyes on her. Lupé had always been gifted that way, even Bella had to agree. Once, when she was five, she woke screaming in the middle of the night, terrified of a fire. She roused the whole house, and her mother was quite angry at the time until the living room sofa, on which a visiting boyfriend had been smoking a joint, exploded into flame. Prescient. That's the word her homeroom teacher used in class when Lupé had raised her hand one day and asked if they were about to see a film on sexually-transmitted diseases.

Why yes, my dear, however did you know that the teacher asked. I just knew Lupé replied. She knew other things as well—that Mr. Mayer the shop teacher was having an affair with Mrs. Anderson, the librarian. That the corner crack dealer would be dead that night of gunfire. Back in the fall of 2001, Lupé refused to go to school one day, with a feeling of impending doom. That had been September 11th.

When the witch with a badge appeared, Lupé could tell instantly. So sweet. So cute. So butch in her Joe Rocket jacket. She had the boys twisted around her little finger without even trying. But she didn't fool Lupé. Not for one second.

She fooled Jorgé. He was mucho macho, but he couldn't keep his eyes off the ladies. Lupé had learned at an early age that men were fickle beasts, and would dump you in a New York second for someone prettier, sexier, or younger. What really galled Lupé was that the witch was older! She had to be in her thirties, at least! And Jorgé was making a fool of himself over her, as if she were a fine young fox like Lupé.

Okay. Lupé had to admit that the witch lady was a looker. Maybe even a stunner. But that could have been the magic. Strip away her protections, she was probably a hunchback. Further proof she was a witch: she kept a familiar in the form of a large gray cat, which Lupé had observed from the stairwell. Knowledge was power. Toward that end, the teenager had taken to following the witch, whenever possible. That's how she learned the witch usually entered and exited the building through the rear door on Prospect Place, across from the medical center. That's how she learned the witch rode a motorcycle that she kept in the medical center garage.

Further proof she was a witch: The ease with which she'd brought down Hector.

It was true that some girls could fight. Lupé could fight. But no girl, no matter how tough, could bring down someone like Hector, veteran of countless street brawls, and the harshest weapon in Los Romeros' arsenal. Not that Los Romeros were evil. They were gangsta wannabes. They bought their drugs retail from Los Tecolotes. Some of them even had jobs.

There was only one way to fight a witch: with witchcraft. Lupé decided to pay Estrella a visit.

Taking off her earphones, she turned the boom box off, got off the bed, and went to her secret place in the closet. She pried up the loose floorboard and dug around, brushing aside insect larvae, rat feces, and dustballs, until she found the crumpled Chivas Regal bag in which Jorgé had given her a heart-shaped locket. She reached inside the bag and closed her hand around the wad of bills she'd been accumulating, mostly by snatch-and-grab at the street fairs. Lupé was fleet of foot, and if she spied easy prey, mostly the elderly, waving their billfolds or purses, she would swoop down like a hawk, grab the booty and be gone so fast, they usually never got a good look at her. Sometimes they fell down. That was their problem. Incapable of empathy, Lupé never envisioned a day when she would be old and feeble.

Two hundred and twelve dollars—more than enough to convince Estrella to lay a terrible curse on the witch. Lupé examined her Citizen watch, another gift from Jorgé. It was 9:30. Her mother was stoned out of her skull on muscatel, watching videos in the bedroom with the jerk-de-jour. Syreeta was in the living room watching *Powerpuff Girls*. Not for Lupé—not tonight. She had to keep a clear head to deal with Estrella. Popping off the screen, she let herself out her bedroom window, hanging from the sill and dropping the three feet into the garden, lovingly maintained by the geezers, who were always complaining about her depredations. Big deal. It was just a stupid garden. She never looked at it, anyway.

Lupé caught the Atlantic Avenue bus to the Long Island Terminal, then switched to the Fourth Avenue Bus, which took her to the waterfront. She'd learned about Estrella from Jorgé, who let her accompany him once when he had to put a hex on Los Tecolotes, who'd jumped two Romeros the day before, putting one in the hospital. At least they didn't have guns. Jorgé didn't use a gun, either. He paid Estrella two hundred dollars to hex the Tecolotes, and a day later, two of them were shot dead in a drive-by by the Kingston Posse.

Lupé had always respected Los Tecolotes. In fact, Bobby Chacón, their Warlord, made no secret of his admiration for her the last time they'd met. Had she told Jorgé that Bobby Chacón told her she was a fine fox and wouldn't mind taking her out, it would have meant war. She held that in reserve, just in case.

Lupé got off the bus by the big red warehouse and walked toward the freight yard, which fronted the river.

Estrella lived inside the freight yard, in a switching box that hadn't been used in years. There were more ways into the switchyard than bulls to cover them. Lupé's favorite was through a hole in the hurricane fence, concealed behind a steel shed. She was barely able to squeeze through, scratching herself slightly in the process.

The switchyard covered about a square half mile, and used to belong to the New York and Pennsylvania Railroad, but had since been taken over by the city as a storage and repair facility. Old subway cars now occupied most of the rail space, and served as a canvas for the many area gangs. It was practically a daily show, with gangs sneaking into the yard nightly to spray their tags over their rivals' and establish their own. Sometimes, the tagging battles led to death. The railroad bulls didn't even have green cards, and mostly stuck to their shack playing poker and running out back to get high.

Estrella the Witch subscribed to a potent blend of Santéria and animism known as *Gounj'go*, which she'd brought from her native Santo Domingo. The switching box was located in an isolated part of the yard, on a gravel bed near the waterfront, next to a Con Ed transfer station that emitted a loud hum night and day. Estrella had lined the wall closest to the transfer station with aluminum foil to keep out harmful radiation. "Bad vibes," as she put it.

It was ten at night as Lupé picked her way across the plain of gravel, broken glass, and rusted rails in her black BKs, heading toward the transfer station and the little corrugated steel hut that was studded with odd objects designed to hold evil spirits at bay. She had dressed to impress in black Danskin leotards and pearl earrings, clutching her Nike backpack. Los Romeros didn't carry

67

purses. She made her way through an army of fifty-gallon drums oozing a yellowish green fluid that stung the eyes. When she was ten feet from the open steel door, a harsh voice emanated from within.

"Who go dere?"

"Estrella, it's me, Lupé, from the Waubeska Projects."

"I know you, girl. You come in here, tell Estrella what you want."

The door made a hideous creaking noise as Lupé forced it open to permit her entrance. Inside, the floor had been covered with wooden pallets; these, in turn, had been covered with a myriad of carpets and scatter rugs, some salvaged from the street, some purchased at St. Vincent de Paul, some given in trade, so that the net effect was that of a trampoline. This type of floor did not permit normal furniture, so Madame Estrella made do with a variety of cushions, mostly sofa bolsters swiped from furniture on the sidewalk waiting to be loaded into a truck.

Madame Estrella's pirated power line gave her light: several low lamps, and six candles provided illumination. Estrella reclined on a futon covered with bedspreads in one corner, smoking an American Spirit, using a hubcap as an ashtray. Nearby, a small cube refrigerator hummed. A color television crouched on a packing crate. Beneath it was a DVD player and a stack of DVDs including *Eyes Wide Shut* and *Bring It On*. Estrella's ferocious cat Duran crouched in one corner, yellowish eye regarding Lupé as she moved hesitantly on the spongy floor.

"Sit down. You got man trouble. See it in your face, girl."

Lupé slumped on the sofas. Was it that obvious? No.

Estrella was a witch! It wasn't as if she were parading around with a cuckold sign on her forehead. Besides. Girls couldn't be cuckolds, could they? No. Just chumps. And fools.

"My man Jorgé is seeing a witch from the police department!" she blurted.

Madame Estrella looked up, regarding her through turquoise catseye glasses. She'd made her mouth up like a Ferrari F-40, crimson lips revealing alloy teeth. "I know dat Jorgé. He got de wandering eye, girl, you know dat when you take up wit' him. What make you t'ink dis cop a witch?"

"I can see it! The way you taught me. Here." Lupé thrust forth the bag of personal belongings she had so patiently gathered by waiting in the basement garbage room, combing through countless loads of disgusting trash until she had identified her prey by the discarded promotional flyers with the witch's name on the label. "Here are some of her personal things. If you feel them, Estrella, you'll know, too."

Estrella took the clear plastic bag of discarded flyers, used cotton swabs, a discarded Lady Schick, with no change in expression. She held the bag beneath her nose and smelled the contents. She reached behind her and snagged a sterling silver platter with run-off grooves for the gravy. It was stained dark gray. She dumped the contents onto the platter with a muffled clunk. Duran got up from his cushion and padded forward. He must have weighed thirty-five pounds. One ear had been torn off in battle. He sniffed a cotton ball, batted at it with a paw, yowled and scrammed.

"You is right," Estrella replied. "She a witch, all right,

69

and she very powerful. Dat she be a cop, too, dat is furder evidence of her power. Normally, I would not touch dis witch. But I know you. I know Jorgé. I no like see him get sucked into her circle of evil. I help you cast a spell on dis witch. But you must go furder. I cannot do dis alone. Before I continue, I ask you, you got two hundred dollar for Estrella?"

Lupé reached into the backpack, dug around until she found her coin purse. She drew it out, snapped it open and took out two hundred dollars in tightly packed twenties. Three weeks of grab and runs at the Saturday markets. She could always make it back.

Estrella counted the money, folded it back up and stuck it down her bosom. It was safe there. No one but a crazy person would reach down there. "Okay. Dis what you got to do. I use dis material you bring me to cast a spell. You get your best man and plan an ambush. Dis woman not like udder witches. Not like udder cops, for dat matter. She very powerful. We must launch double attack. Me from here, your best man from dere."

Lupé's smooth forehead scrunched into a relief map of Afghanistan. "Where am I going to find a best man? I tol' you, my boyfriend is seein' her! That's why I came to you in the first place!" Her voice took on a whining, querulous quality.

"Ho, girl, you tink dis be easy? You tink a witch of dis magnitude just poof, go 'way? I take great risk helping you. You tink she not know when I begin to cast my spell? *Dat* is why you must distract her wit an all-out attack! Wit a man! Not some little girl. You unnerstan' what I'm saying, or am I talking to de wall?"

Lupé nodded sullenly. "I hear you." Frantically, she wracked her brain. Where was she going to get a man to

take on this lady cop? She couldn't go to Los Romeros--
they were loyal to Jorgé and would certainly tell him.

That left Los Tecolotes, Los Romeros' closest rivals,
and a force to be reckoned with in Upper Brooklyn. Head
Tecolote Bobby Chacón had the hots for her. And he
hated cops.

Afghanistan morphed into the Gobi Desert. A plan began to form.

$\mathbf{S}$ara arrived at the sword polisher's a half-hour early. She'd decided to take the bike, and stash it in his workshop. Earlier, she'd cased the alley and discovered that she could bring the bike in through a back door.

She left the bike at the head of his stairs, chained to the railing. That was only temporary. Left there, the bike would be picked clean, leaving nothing behind but one wheel, sans tire.

The door chimed pleasantly as she came in. Kopkind emerged from the hall, wearing canvas coveralls, face flushed. He beamed with pleasure as Sara shook her auburn hair free of helmet head.

"Hi! Sorry I'm early. I decided to bring my bike."

"You ride a bike? You mean a motorcycle?"

"Yup. Can I stash it in your workshop? It's not very big."

"Of course. Bring it around to the alley and I'll unlock the gate."

Sara left her helmet on the counter, went back outside, unchained her bike, pushed it over the curb and thumbed the engine. Passing a Harley guy going the other way she gave the Sign and he responded. She zipped halfway up the block, down the tight little alley made even tighter by the *de rigueur* illegally parked trucks until she came to the concrete wall directly behind Kopkind's shop. Kopkind stood with his back against the open steel door as she rolled the bike in without getting off. Inside was a common area serving the Feldstein Gallery and the apartments above. She wheeled the bike through another steel door propped open with a hard rubber wedge, then into the back of Kopkind's shop. It was a crowded area with racks of swords on the walls, a series of locked steel cabinets. In the center of the room was a peculiar installation resembling two miniature sawhorses fitted together to form a platform. It was made of sturdy redwood, and cross-braced, with its legs splayed outward for maximum support. A rectangular gray stone was clamped in place on a slanting board, facing a bucket of water. A balans chair, one of those Swedish devices on which you sat on your thighs and knees, faced the apparatus.

"It's a bit unconventional," David explained. "In fact, my old instructor nearly seized a piston when he saw it. 'You no can do this!' he said. 'Must use traditional todai mikura and shogi!' The traditional method is a bit more cramped. I tried it for a while, but it led to back problems. This is better."

"What do you do here?"

"I'll show you."

Kopkind waited until she had parked her bike in the corner and taken off her jacket. He knelt on the stool, picking up a long, curving piece of steel that lay on the table next to him. The piece of steel was sheathed in tightly wrapped newspaper. Unsheathing the blade, Kopkind reached into the bucket, doused the clamped stone with water, and began to run the blade back and forth over the wetted stone.

"This is a synthetic stone, made of aluminum oxide. It's okay for the coarse stuff, but when we get down to fine quality, only polishing stones from Japan will do." With an almost reverent expression, Kopkind ran the blade along the stone, creating an oddly soothing sound. *Swooosh. Swooosh.* Sara was mesmerized. For a while, both were lost in the sounds of the blade sliding over the stone.

The polisher shook himself as if coming out of a daze, and grinned. "Sorry. It's extremely therapeutic, once you get into it."

"Doesn't it kill your back?"

"Not too bad. And I have all sorts of ways to relax. One of which is to go to a party with a beautiful woman."

Sara grinned in spite of herself. Kopkind blushed, surprised by his own effrontery. "I'll just go out front and get my things," she said. "Have you got some place I can change?"

Leading her down a hall with doors to what she presumed were his private quarters, Kopkind showed her to a large combo bath/utility room with a mahogany hot tub mounted on a platform in the corner. There was a clothes washer and dryer, a large shower and a cabinet filled with fluffy towels. "Don't worry—I have a sink in the shop. Take your time."

Sara had brought The Little Black Dress by Dolce & Gabbana, and a pair of Black Satin low risers. Her cunning little beaded black purse barely contained her thirty-two Beretta and badge. Fashion demanded that she leave the .357 at home.

Kopkind was waiting in the foyer, lounging on the sofa in a pair of gray pleated Dockers, a loose-knit cotton sweater that reminded Sara of Shmendrick. The color. His eyes went saucer-wide as she emerged, and he whistled.

Sara smiled at him. "Don't get any ideas. This is strictly police work." She didn't believe it herself. Kopkind was refreshingly simple after the self-styled Romeos of the Eleventh, and the usual grade of overfed, oversexed egomaniacs who hit on her.

Yoshi came through the beaded curtain, snarling and yawning. Kopkind reached down and scratched the cat's neck. "Yoshi, guard the shop."

They left through the front door, which Kopkind locked with two different keys. "My car's in the Bleecker Street Garage, two blocks up. Wanna walk?"

"Sure." His hand naturally found hers as they walked up the street, taking in the show.

At the garage, Kopkind slipped the kid a fin and they waited on the street. "It must cost a fortune to store your car here," Sara said.

"Not so bad. I did a favor for the owner once, and he charges me a really low rate."

"What sort of favor?"

"Well, you may not believe this, but one night as I was delivering a sword, two punks tried to stick him up. I just sort of crept up on them by accident. I had no idea what was happening until I was like ten feet away. Then it all hit me at once. They were holding this guy up! And in one second they were going to see me. I didn't think, I didn't hesitate, I drew the sword and just happened to catch this guy's gun. It was like some kind of twenty-dollar special 'cause it hit the ground and fell apart. It was almost comical, these two guys standing there looking at the broken gun, so I figured what the hell. I brandished the sword like a berserker and started screaming in Japanese. They took off."

Sara regarded the sword polisher with new respect. "You speak Japanese?"

At that moment, his car arrived, an elderly steel gray Acura Legend in excellent condition. Kopkind held the door for her. The interior smelled of leather. It was only after Kopkind got behind the wheel and they took off that she became aware of his scent: a haunting, exotic musk. Sara approved. She couldn't abide men who slathered themselves with cologne like suntan lotion.

Kopkind took the Manhattan Bridge and worked his way toward the Brooklyn-Queens Expressway, then out to Long Island, Nancy Wilson singing on the stereo.

Ninety minutes later, Kopkind took the Bridgehampton Exit and headed toward the beach.

Bratten's place was a Bauhaus-inspired party palace lit from within like a Chinese lantern. It was a two-story white box with rectangular and round windows and aluminum decks, suggesting a cruise ship. Gray and crimson-jacketed valets moved in smooth precision to handle the influx of luxury automobiles. A valet held the door for Sara while another waited to slide into the driver's seat. The moment they were out, the Acura rocketed ahead and dove into a cubbyhole between an Audi TT and a Rolls Royce.

Nelly boomed from numerous speakers as Kopkind and Sara mounted the broad white marble steps to the front door, where a smiling personal assistant checked for invitations. Inside, the broad foyer gave way to an immense sunken living room, open to the deck and the sea in the distance. The living room was filled with brightly dressed party people, snagging champagne off circulating trays. The room was decorated with African and Japanese art, brooding mahogany masks and feather-light brush paintings, paintings of players and NBA greats. Several of the latter were in attendance, including Bratten himself, a handsome six-foot-nine-inch sun at the center of a swirling constellation of guests. Upon spotting Kopkind, he flashed his brilliant choppers.

"David. David." He came forward, hands extended, until he made contact. Sara paused two steps above the living room floor and still found herself looking up at Bratten.

"And who is this beautiful woman? Where you been hiding her? You been holding out on me?"

"This is Sara Pezzini, James. She's a New York City detective, so watch your step."

Bratten assumed a face of mock horror. "You're a cop?"

"Don't worry. I'm off-duty."

"Well, okay, then. Didn't know they made cops like you. Surprised there's any crime."

"You collect swords, Mr. Bratten?"

"Call me James. Yes I do. And like every other sword collector worth a damn, I get mine polished at Kopkind's."

"Would you show me your most valuable sword, James?"

Bratten's eyebrows made twin peaks. He held out his arm. "I'm gonna borrow your date, David."

Kopkind winked. "Okay, but don't try that NBA hustle on her. She's a cop. I see some friends of mine." He headed down the steps and across the crowded floor.

Sara accompanied Bratten past a free-standing pit fireplace, up some redwood stairs, and down a hall to a room Bratten unlocked by punching some buttons. Inside, a large room was illuminated by offset lighting and spotlights shining on specific exhibits. A number of swords were on display inside hinged glass cases. Sara noted the videocam hidden in a ceiling fixture.

Bratten led the way to the central glass case and indicated a katana, a full-length war sword, resting in a hand-cut teak base. "That's my Masumune. Paid two-point-five mil for that sucker, and it was a bargain."

"Masumune was a swordmaker?"

"One of the best. Lived in the thirteenth century."

"Have you heard of a swordmaker named Muramasa?"

"Of course. All serious collectors know about Muramasa. He was Masumune's rival. They held a competition to see who could craft the sharpest blade. Masumune stuck his sword in a stream and allowed a single maple leaf to drift against it. Cut the leaf in two. But Muramasa's blade was so keen, the water itself split and it was dry when he drew it out."

"Are Muramasa's blades valuable?"

"Does Oscar Robertson know basketball? Thing about Muramasa's blades, they got a reputation for evil, so many people died from them. Also, experts disagree on whether the first Muramasa—to my mind, the one and only—actually existed. So it's damn hard to find an authentic first generation."

"But that doesn't stop people from collecting them?"

"Hell, no. Some collectors even favor that sort of thing. Like my man Hecht. Hecht got me into this Japanese worship in the first place. Gimme a Masumune tanto to celebrate our first NBA championship."

"That would be Adrian Hecht, the Apples' owner?"

"He's here. I'll introduce you."

"I'll introduce myself," said a voice from behind.

Bratten and Sara turned toward the door, where Adrian Hecht had silently entered. He was a distinguished man with close-cropped silver hair, six feet, black silk jacket over black silk T, pleated black pants and sandals.

"You couldn't pull that ninja crap on me if I wasn't so tired," Bratten said.

Hecht came up to them, holding himself a little too carefully, aware he was a little drunk. "Adrian Hecht."

Sara took his slightly clammy hand. "Sara Pezzini."

"Watch out, Hecht. She da fuzz."

"You're a cop?"

"Homicide."

"Ahh. Terrible, what happened to Bachman. That your case?"

Sara nodded. "You knew Bachman?"

"Of course. All serious collectors knew Bachman. He was a gentleman, and extremely knowledgeable about Oriental art in general, and Japanese swords in particular."

"Do you own any Muramasas, Mr. Hecht?"

A funny look crossed the tycoon's face. Almost fear. So quick, if you blinked, you missed it. Then the old instincts took over, and he was the smiling confident captain of industry. "Nope. But I can dream, can't I?"

"So you don't believe in the Muramasa curse."

"I didn't say that. I don't know if James told you, but I'm a bit of a buff."

"He said you were the one who got him into collecting."

"Well, James was interested in all things Japanese before I met him. He already had his black belt in karate, and had been over there with the NBA All-Stars."

"What do you know of the Muramasa curse?"

"This guy just published a book in Japan, not available

over here. It's called *Way Of The Blade*, and it's a history of the great swordmakers. It's 756 pages long. I had it translated. Well, parts of it. The author has dug up all sorts of information that nobody ever knew about Muramasa, including how he died."

"Oh, honey," Bratten said, rolling his eyes. "Don't let him commence!"

"It's a long story."

"Maybe you can tell me later."

"I could do that." Hecht dipped two fingers inside his silk jacket and handed her an ivory-colored business card. "Call me. I am always happy to accommodate Manhattan's finest."

Bratten headed for the door. "You'd better get hip, Jack, before you step in it. I'm gonna head back, make sure my homies ain't pocketing the silverware. Close the door when you're done in here. And don't take anything—I know exactly what I got."

Bratten left. Hecht turned the full force of his considerable charm on Sara. "Love that bad boy. He's like a son to me. So what's happening with the Bachman case? Are you handling Chalmers, too?"

She nodded. "We have some leads. In both cases, a valuable Japanese sword was taken. Both Muramasas."

Hecht maintained his cool, but Sara could sense his unease through the Witchblade. "Let's head back to the party, Mr. Hecht. Or we'll end up on Page Six together."

Hecht grinned, held the door for her. "Please call me Adrian."

"Okay. Out here, you're Adrian. In the city, Mr. Hecht."

Most of the crowd had moved out onto the broad patio. A half-dozen sleek young men and women splashed

in the free-form pool while liveried bartenders dispensed
drinks from rolling bars. Sara spotted Kopkind talking to
an older guy with a pasteover, in a Ralph Lauren that was
too young for him. She walked up to them and took
David's hand.

"Oh, there you are. Sara, Bob Hotchkiss. Bob, Sara
Pezzini."

"Pleased to meet you," the businessman said, extending his hand.

"Likewise," Sara said. She shook his hand, recalling
Hotchkiss' name as one she'd found in Bachman's
Rolodex. A sword collector? What were the chances of
three of the city's top sword collectors all gathering at the
same spot, a day after two of their number had their
heads lopped off? Coincidence turned to dust beneath the
weight of circumstance.

"Mr. Hotchkiss, I'm investigating the Bachman homicide. You knew him, didn't you?"

Hotchkiss turned white. "I don't collect Oriental art."

"You *are* the Robert Hotchkiss whose name I found in
Bachman's Rolodex, aren't you?"

David looked ill at ease. She was embarrassing him.
Too bad. This was a break, and she intended to pursue it.

"Yes, well I, uh, my wife, my soon-to-be ex-wife, you
might as well know, was quite a collector. She has a black
belt in spending. She may have bought and sold some
things through Bachman."

"You *are* aware that he was killed two nights ago."

"I heard. A terrible tragedy."

Kopkind tugged at her hand. "Sara, this is a party."

She ignored him. "Someone phoned in an anonymous
tip that he'd been killed. You know anything about that?"

Hotchkiss turned red. If he could turn blue, he could rent himself out at patriotic events. "No, I do not. Now if you'll excuse me, I see someone I have to talk to."

He stalked off.

Kopkind glared at her. "Sara, I brought you here as my guest. You can't go around questioning these people as if this were a crime scene. For one thing, there are a half-dozen people here who could ruin your career with the snap of their fingers."

"Thanks for the advice, David. But I know what I'm doing. Didn't you invite me out here under the pretext of meeting the city's top collectors?"

Kopkind nodded ruefully. "Yeah, I did. I got no cause to complain."

Sara graced him with a smile. "That's what I want to hear! Come on, let's get some food before it's all gone."

Kopkind followed her inside to the buffet table. "It's never all gone."

Sara suddenly realized she was famished. She loaded a plate with bacon-wrapped scallops, Swedish meatballs, chilled shrimp, and carrot and celery sticks. She and David found an unoccupied table by the pool and dined in the warm night air while the sound system loudly pumped Jurassic 5. She was grateful for the respite. Not only Hotchkiss, but James Bratten and Adrian Hecht were among Bachman's customers. Who among them knew Bachman well enough to know when he acquired the sword? Sara made a mental note to dig into Bachman.

Later, they went for a walk, hand in hand, along the trail that skirted the upper level of the dunes. The wind sighed in the reeds, bringing with it the scent of sea. There were occasional pine bridges over rivulets, and they could see lights from the Jersey shore in the distance. It was ten-thirty by the time David asked for his car to be brought around.

They were on the expressway before Sara finally asked, "How do you know Hotchkiss?"

"I polished one of his swords a couple years ago. A Muramasa. I think it was stolen."

She shot him a glance. "David. Did it ever occur to you that that might be one of the missing swords?"

Kopkind paused for a second, his lips slightly parted. "Uh-oh," he said.

"I don't suppose you could identify it?"

"Of course I can. Each sword is unique. I made drawings."

"Drawings?"

"It's called *oshigata*. I draw all the swords I polish. It helps me to visualize and understand them, before I start polishing. I put the drawings up on my website, swordpolish.com. That was my one and only Muramasa. I was scared to death I was going to screw it up. They're virtually priceless. Fortunately, it's a very *togishi*-friendly blade. It wanted to be as sharp as possible."

"You talk as if the blade has a mind of its own."

"It does. It cut me."

Sara was about to say something else, but her arm tingled, ever so slightly.

She wrapped her hand around the Witchblade.

It was just past midnight when Kopkind unlocked the front door to his shop and invited Sara in.

"David, I've had a wonderful time. I'm going to get my bike and go."

"Guess I won't offer you a nightcap."

"Some other time. Really."

They entered his foyer. The little bell rang, and Yoshi advanced through the curtain, yawning and snarling.

"Really?"

"Yes, really. What is it with that cat?"

David stooped and scooped the basketball-sized mound of fur, causing Sara to involuntarily cringe as she envisioned the fur deposit on his shirt. "He's got some kind of sinus deviation that makes him do that. The vet says he's fine, and it would cost too much to correct."

Sara ducked into the washroom and quickly changed back into jeans, leather boots and jacket, neatly packing her party dress and accoutrements in the leather backpack. Her badge and gun went in the tank bag. As Kopkind held the alley door open for her, she leaned over and kissed him on the cheek.

"Call me."

She used the ride home to sort out her feelings. He was cute. And he was smart. And he had nothing to do with police work, an enormous plus. But she'd just met him, and she was in the middle of an investigation.

She sensed none of the brooding fury in Kopkind that she found in most cops. Even the best, like Joe Siry, nursed a secret kernel of rage that could explode at any time. Police work was not therapy. Even though it provided therapy, most cops refused to take advantage of the benefit. They just wouldn't admit they had a problem. Wouldn't be manly.

It was past one by the time she got home. Shmendrick scolded her as she let herself in her door.

"I'll tell you all about it in the morning," Sara promised, and headed for the bedroom.

CHAPTER
SIX

Sara woke with sun streaming in through the windows. She glanced at the bedside clock. Eleven-thirty. Sunday. No day of rest for her, but she'd promised herself a ride before she took another look at the evidence. Her father had had an old cop Harley and at least once a year, until he died, he'd take her up the Hudson to Brandywine.

Sara stretched, showered, spooned down a yogurt and a banana. She phoned the Fifty-second Precinct in the Bronx and connected with a desk sergeant named Bryan, whom she'd met when she first moved in.

"Danny Boy, it's Pezzini."

"Why aren't you at morning mass, darlin'?"

"Ha-ha. Listen. Do me a favor. Find out who owns my building, will you?" She gave him the address.

"Sure and I'll do that, darlin'. When you gonna buy the Sarge a cuppa?"

"Soon, Sarge, soon. And thanks."

Always, the debate: what to wear. It wasn't a matter of style, it was a matter of comfort versus safety. It was hot in the city. But leather was undeniably the best defense against road rash. In the end, she compromised, as she always did. Blue jeans, leather boots, jacket, and gloves. And of course the full-face Arai.

She rolled up the medical center garage ramp at 12:25 and headed south. It was Sunday, when even Manhattan's ferocious traffic rested. She zipped across the moderately crowded streets and soon reached the Henry Hudson Parkway. It was a sunny day in the high sixties. Sara was perfectly comfortable leaning into the pocket behind the Yamaha's miniscule cowl. When trucks passed her going the other way, she lay down on her tank bag, although no debris could penetrate the Arai. She was past Yonkers when she noticed the close-spaced twin gleam in her rearviews. Another bike.

Like dogs marking their territory, bikers were instantly aware of other bikes. She glanced down. She'd been cruising at eighty. She throttled back, waited for the other bike to catch up. She wanted to know what it was. The bike zipped around an amblin' Camry and pulled next to her. It was the beige and silver Hayabusa from the station.

Sara downshifted, opened the throttle and jerked back on the bars. The ferociously fast RZ-1 obediently reared up on its rear wheel as she wheelied away at one hundred per. The Hayabusa lagged a moment due more to the rider's surprise than any lack of ability. She dove into a cluster of slow-moving mini-vans, weaving from lane to lane, space to space, until she was convinced she'd buried the Hayabusa. Her pursuer emerged almost immediately behind her.

You want to play? Sara thought. *Fine. Let's play.*

She downshifted and accelerated to one hundred and forty miles an hour. At this speed, she had to concentrate far ahead on the four-lane expressway, looking for any potential obstacle. Fortunately, her reflexes were up to the task. Although she knew the Hayabusa could easily match her top speed, its rider had to outweigh her by approximately a hundred pounds, which would slow him down somewhat.

Wind whistling through the helmet sounded like a million police sirens in pursuit. The sound had never bothered her. Her father had taught her police sirens were the truest signs of civilization. Road signs and exits whisked by in a heartbeat. Trevor Mansion. Hastings-on-Hudson. They zipped through traffic like fireflies among armadillos, not slowing down until Sara crested a rise just past Dobbs Ferry and saw traffic stopped a half mile ahead, due to an accident.

The first exit led to Trevorton and St. Benedict's Retreat, A Cloistered Order of the Benedictine Brotherhood. Sara zipped off and took the left turn toward the river and the retreat. The Hayabusa was right behind her. The entrance to the retreat went through a wrought iron gate, open for Sunday, between brick pillars. The blacktop road wound between a hardwood forest until it came to the retreat, a three-story red brick Reformation structure with steeply-raked green copper roofs, a wide turn-around occupied by an old Cadillac and a heating/air-conditioning van, and a turn off into a walled alcove overlooking the Hudson.

Sara used the handicapped ramp to zip up onto the alcove. She kicked out her stand, and was taking off her helmet when the Hayabusa hove in beside her. The guy was big, all right. When he got off the bike, he towered over Sara. A moment later, he removed his full-face shield and it was the handsome black cop from the press conference. There was a slight Asian tilt to his eyes, as if there might be some Japanese in his family blood.

87

He stuck out his hand. "Hey, how are ya? Derek Sharpe. I'm the gang guy they hired from Hawaii."

Sara took his hand, looking up into warm brown eyes. "Pezzini, but you know that. You left Hawaii to take a job in New York? Why?"

"Man, I have always wanted to be in New York. This is the center of the world. If you can make it here, you can make it anywhere. Macadamia nuts and Don Ho get old after a while. How many reasons do you want?"

"Were you following me?"

Sharpe held his string-backed gloved hands up and waggled his fingers. "No, ma'am. But when I saw you zipping in and out of traffic up ahead, I thought I'd better take a look."

"As a copper? Or a biker?"

Sharpe grinned. "Both. Anyway, I've heard a lot about you. I'm glad it's you. How you coming with the samurai killings?"

Sara rolled her eyes. "I should have known. We're looking for a killer who's collecting rare swords."

Sharpe went over to the brick abutment and leaned on it, gazing down at the slowly trolling blue Hudson, a scattering of small pleasure craft, a barge working against the current, nudged along by a tug. The New Jersey Palisades were dense with growth, gleaming in the afternoon sun. It was a perfect day.

"Really? What kind? I know a little bit about swords."

The hair on the back of Sara's neck tingled. She didn't believe in coincidence.

"How is it you know a little bit about swords, Derek Sharpe?"

"I was midshipman on the U.S.S. *Ticonderoga*—an aircraft carrier in the Pacific during the nineties. We made some ports of call in Japan, where I was privileged to study kendo and iaido with some of the masters."

"Iaido?"

"The art of drawing the blade, striking the target, and returning the blade to the scabbard all in one smooth motion. Really, a perfectly useless skill."

Not quite, Sara thought, seeing jerky video image of the swordsman rising like a cobra to lop off Bachman's head. As she said, she didn't believe in coincidence. But this guy was a cop. Just because Sharpe was into swords didn't mean he was the samurai killer.

"And you have a Japanese bike," she said.

"Two, actually. Got a Shadow 1100 for cruising. My favorite movie is *The Seven Samurai*. I like sushi. I like sumo. What is sumo, anyway, but sushi with larger pieces of meat?"

Sara laughed. Sharpe flashed a Steinway smile.

"Too bad you couldn't have been with me last night. I had all the big-shot sword collectors in Manhattan, in one room."

"Really? Where was that?"

She told him about Bratten's party. Sharpe listened intently. He seemed even more interested when she mentioned Adrian Hecht.

"I'm investigating a series of vandalisms down at his new site, near Ground Zero."

"He wants to give me the grand tour. What kind of vandalisms?"

"The kind that verge on sabotage. Cables nearly cut in two. Sand in gas tanks. Some kind of jive-ass Third World up-against-the-wall motherporker all-purpose protest. You know. Down with capitalism, Hecht is an exploiter of the masses and a despoiler of the environment, etcetera, etcetera." Sharpe's voice had a performer's singsong quality. Sara was mesmerized.

"The Anti-Global Village Gang?"

"Exactly."

"Seems to me the public has less tolerance for this sort of thing in the wake of 9/11."

Sharpe sighed and rested his weight on his elbows as he leaned over the Hudson. Sara noticed his incredible biceps. He wore a sleeveless safari vest over a muscle shirt. "These people are True Believers. They are immune to reason, or public sentiment. Yeah, they do have a lot in common with the Taliban. On the other hand, Hecht has powerful enemies who would like to see him fail. It's possible one of them is using this bunch as a cover, to cause mischief."

"You got evidence, or is this a hunch?"

Sharpe peered into the distance, as if he'd spied a hawk above Jersey. "You know Bob Koske?"

"Amalgamated Truck Drivers of America. Twice indicted, never convicted. RICO's perennial runner-up of the year."

"Last year the Teamsters gave fifty grand to PETE: People for the Ethical Treatment of the Environment. Makes you wonder. So I'm down there at odd moments, looking for saboteurs."

Sara looked Sharpe up and down. Physically, he was the exact opposite of most New York gang members, who were small and feral. "Rotsa ruck. You said you know a little about swords. Have you heard of Muramasa?"

Sharpe's face darkened. "Of course. The so-called evil

blades. In Japanese mythology, restless demons haunt the earth. Muramasa's blades were legendary for being associated with them. These demons were cursed to wander forever until they had performed some task, by inhabiting the bodies of the living."

"Some form of possession?"

"Exactly."

A year ago, Sara would have dismissed Sharpe's comments as nutwork. Not now. She had seen too much.

Sharpe clapped his hands and whirled, abruptly giddy. "But we are in America, Detective! You're an educated woman. Surely you don't believe in such superstitious nonsense!"

"No, of course not."

They both laughed.

"Virtually every surviving Muramasa is accounted for. I think there are in the neighborhood of three dozen, including long and short swords, all from the later period, *not* the original Muramasa, the one who made the bloodthirsty blades. From time to time, rumors surface of a long-lost masterpiece, but there hasn't been an important discovery since '95, when the last Masamune was discovered."

A busload of tourists had disgorged behind them, and they found themselves surrounded by seasoned citizens with cameras, some of whom clucked at the bikes.

"One more thing," Sharpe said. "Ever think that the thefts may just be a dodge to cover up the murder? I'm thinking of Chalmers. Big shot like that has enemies. If the killer gets you wasting your time looking for some kind of samurai ghost, so much the better."

"Hmmm."

"Uh-huh."

"Change of subject. Do me a favor?"

"What?"

"See what you can find out about the Brooklyn Romeros, and their leader, Jorgé Candido."

Sharpe pulled out a small spiral pad and made some notes. "I'm on it."

"Come on," Sara said. "Let's get out of here before someone turns us into the monks for parking violations."

They rode into Reedsburg, found seats at a sidewalk café beneath a Bacardi awning at a round steel table, and ordered café lattes. Antique hounds from Long Island rummaged down the busy little Main Street, SUVs parked diagonally in orderly ranks.

"So, Sara, word is you're a freak magnet."

"I attracted you, didn't I?"

Sharpe displayed his teeth, like a flashing "SMILE!" sign. Sara liked having him around. He sent off no predatory vibes. He made her feel safe. "Touché," he said.

"How far does your fascination with the Japanese go, Sharpsie? Do you work out?"

"I have a few black belts."

"I'll bet you have. Maybe you'll take a look at the tape. I'd like to hear your opinion."

"What tape?"

Sara told him about the Bachman video.

"Sure," Sharpe said, glancing at his watch. A Seiko. "I'd be glad to. I have to head back. My partner's expecting me to make the salad."

"Who's your partner?"

"Just a guy I know works on Wall Street. He's still shaky in the morning."

Sara was impressed, with both Sharpe and the Powers

That Be. It was one thing to see a gay cop on some television drama. It was another to have an openly gay cop functioning in a real New York precinct. Of course they did cover the Village. And Sharpe was hardly a screaming queen. He would fool many women.

They split the tab and agreed not to race each other back into the city. They rode together into central Manhattan, where Sara finally peeled down Broadway, with a wave and a wiggle of the Yamaha's pert rear.

As Sara headed across Prospect, a 1979 Pontiac detached itself from the curb down the block and cruised slowly her way. The car was painted a metallic emerald green, with orange and yellow flames sweeping back from the front wheels.

When it drew close, Sara saw Jorgé at the wheel, do-rag around his head, grinning like Pepe LaPew. "Wait up, chiquita!" he waved through the open moon roof.

Sara paused. The car pulled up at the curb. It had gold spoked wheels. The interior was lushly appointed in rolled and pleated green and yellow naugahyde.

"What's this? Official ride of the Green Bay Packers?"

Jorgé grinned vacantly, trying to hide his ignorance. "This my sweet ride, *guapa*. Listen, siddown here with me for a sec. I been thinking 'bout what we talked about, you know, and I got my boys doin' good now."

Sara looked for a door handle. The door clicked open of its own accord, and she slid on to the faintly aromatic seats. Of *course* he spritzed his car. "How are they doing good?"

"You know, I got to thinkin' about the Guardian Angels an' I figure, what the hell, we can do that. So that's what I got my boys doin'. Just this block, but if things work out, who knows, maybe we'll spread out and do some more."

Sara regarded Jorgé dubiously. Gangbanger to neighborhood saint overnight? She didn't think so. On the other hand, she must never underestimate her own sex appeal. She'd learned that the hard way.

Jorgé pulled away from the curb and cruised down Prospect Place, the elaborate stereo softly playing Heavy Hittaz, a Houston-based rap group.

"If you're serious about this, we're going to have to have a meeting between you guys and the residents so you can introduce yourselves. And we need rules. Like, no boom-box playing in the common areas."

"I already put out the word on that."

"Really."

"Yeah, really. You don't believe me? You heard any loud rap music last couple of days?"

Sara avoided the common areas, but decided to take Jorgé at his word. It wouldn't hurt to get the whole gang together and photograph them. Brooklyn Gangs would thank her for it. On the other hand, she might alienate Los Romeros. The medical center had some unused meeting rooms. She was certain she could get permission, especially if she got Jorgé to extend his jurisdiction to the center, which had been plagued by petty thefts, vandalism, and assaults.

"Okay, that's good. Thank you. But listen. If you're doing this so you can get in my pants, fuggedaboudit. You're not my type."

"'Eyyy, pretty mama, I din't say nothin' about that. I already got an old lady."

"If you're talking about Lupé, that girl can't be older than seventeen. How old are *you*, Jorgé?"

"What year is this car?"

Sara looked around. "I don't know."

"It's a '79."

"That makes you an adult, and her a minor. I'm not going to bust you for statutory, but I do hope you're not just messing with her. She might get the idea you actually love her."

"I do love her," he grinned. "I love all my women." Proud to be a playa.

"Take me home, Jorgé. I need a bath."

"You smell just fine to me, pretty mama."

"Take me home."

As Jorgé pulled up to the main entrance, Lupé peered through Venetian blinds in her first floor apartment, knowing she could not put her plan into play soon enough.

SEVEN

Raj was waiting for her when she arrived at work the next morning. "We have analysis from Raven Software," he sang as agreeably as a robin. "Come and see!"

Sara squared her gear away and followed Raj into the audio/visual room, where the monitor had been pre-cued. Raj played the sequence from the antique store in slow-motion while he read from the report. "Assailant anywhere from five-nine to six-four, weight between one-fifty and two hundred and fifty, and can be in age from early twenties to early fifties."

"Oh, that's terrific. That's wonderful."

"All is not lost," Raj continued. "They have narrowed the possibility that it is a man to one in ten million. And he is right-handed."

"Oh, great. Thank you, Raj."

"I'm sorry it was not more helpful."

"You did your best. I appreciate your help."

Returning to her desk, Sara found a six-inch Freddie Krueger super-glued to her telephone, with the crudely lettered word balloon. "DON'T LET DETECTIVE PEZZINI GET ME! I

GIVE UP!" Fortunately, she returned before the glue had set and was able to twist it off. She held the doll up and confronted five detectives burying their noses in their work.

"This is very childish!" she declared, tossing Freddie in the bottom drawer with the Godzilla, a flying monkey, and a Medieval Spawn. She worked her way through the daily flurry of interdepartmental memos and Requests For Assistance, and dug out Adrian Hecht's business card. She was very interested in what the builder had to say about the mysterious Muramasa, and his crosstown rival Chalmers. Hecht took her call, invited her to his offices in the Griepp Building, on Forty-sixth Street and Park Avenue—a stone's throw from Grand Central Station.

There was a message from Bryan in Brooklyn. Esther Management owned Waubeska Place. The principal shareholder and Esther Chair was one Murray Rothstein, who lived in Upper Salem. She made a note in her pad.

At the Griepp Building, a bushy-browed security guard loomed. She showed him her badge and asked him for Hecht's office. He pointed her to an elevator.

The Griepp Building was an Art Deco masterpiece built in the twenties by the railroad tycoon, Marvin Griepp. Hecht had bought the property in '91, saving it from almost certain implosion, renovated it, and rented it out, except for the twenty-third floor, which he reserved for himself.

Sara got off the elevator into a hexagonal reception room with marble floor inlaid with Tuscan tiles. A marble fountain bubbled in the middle of the room, water trickling from a nymph-held vase. A smart young man led her through a maze of corridors to Hecht's corner office, overlooking the Met Life Building and points south. The broad, airy office held a cluster of sofas around a coffee table, a media wall with a fifty-two-inch screen, a free-form redwood desk, and a large display table atop which sat a model of Hecht Gardens, his business/retail/residential project three miles south on West Street.

Hecht was on the phone when she came in, tilted back in his Freedom Chair, snakeskin boots on the redwood slab. He waved at her, motioned toward the model. While he talked, she walked over to the table and looked at the development. In miniature, it had a Disney-esque quality—tiny automobiles unblemished by road salt or collision, streets spotless, soaring steel skyscrapers gleaming in the morning light. The plan incorporated a central courtyard with reflecting pool and gardens, and a performing arts center that resembled a nun's wimple with windows.

In one corner of the office stood a woodcarving of the ferocious Japanese demon Fudo The Immovable, rope in one hand, sword in the other. Nearby was a glass display case that held a two-sword display, the long *daito* and the shorter *wakizashi*. It also contained a number of wrought-iron discs with slots in the center, which Sara deduced were the guard part of the sword.

Hecht hung up the phone, plunked his boots on the beige carpet, and rose. "Those are my *tsubas*, or sword guards. I believe the one on the left to be a genuine thirteenth century Muramasa, but I have been unable to obtain verification. The others date from the fourteenth and fifteenth, and include a confirmed Masumune."

"They must be worth a lot."

"They are priceless, Detective. I don't mind telling you, these murders you're investigating have made me nervous."

"Do you have security?"

"You bet. But just knowing I'm in your jurisdiction makes me feel better."

Sara did not acknowledge the remark. "What kind of security?"

"Well, no one can get up here without a visual scan. I identified you myself. I figure anyone manages to disguise themselves to look like you, well, how bad can it be?"

Sara gave a tight little smile and thought of twelve different ways she could kill Adrian Hecht before he could take another step. "What about you?"

"I have security. It was with me the other night, you just didn't notice."

"What did you want to tell me about Muramasa?"

"As I said, I've arranged for a private translation of a book called *The Way of the Sword*, by Ryozo Nakamura." He returned to his desk and began sifting through a stack of papers. "Until recently, no one knew what happened to Muramasa. I'm talking about the *original* Muramasa, the one who lived in the thirteenth century, not the fifteenth century bunch."

"Of course."

"Ah. Listen to this:

"In the 5th month of the 7th year of Joji, the swordsman Udo, a hanshi of Ise province, approached Muramasa, the greatest swordsmith of the day, about forging a sword using iron from a meteorite. Udo was certain that the unearthly lump of brown iron was a harbinger of death, as it had fallen from the heavens on the very day that the previous Shogun, Yoshimitsu Ashikaga, had passed away, less than one year earlier. Udo swore the rock spoke to him, instructing him to fashion it into a weapon, to slay his enemies, and to aid him in achieving his ambitions.

"Udo was in love with a young woman of the Gozen family, but she had been betrothed to Udo's rival, Oji, in an arranged marriage. Udo knew that he could not defeat Oji in a fair duel, as Oji had mastered the Kenseito style of swordfighting. Udo believed if he defeated Oji in combat, the Lady Gozen would be his.

"Udo went to Muramasa and said, 'You are known as the greatest swordmaker in the land. I need you to forge me an exceptional weapon which will aid my victory. A blade that is guaranteed to cut down my enemies.'

"Muramasa said, 'I can do what you ask, but the cost will be great . . .'

" 'I will pay any price,' Udo replied.

"Muramasa set to work with the strange meteoric iron. He fasted and ritually purified himself with water. He prayed to Gozu and Mezu, the horse- and ox-headed demons of hell and damnation to empower the Kami of the sword he was forging. He collected eight turtles and eight cranes, symbols of long life, cut their throats and mixed the blood into the water in his quenching trough. He finished folding and forging the blade and quenched it in the tainted water. Satisfied with his work, he named the blade Kyutensai and made a final prayer in the name of Meifumado (Buddhist hell) that the blade would never rest until it had tasted the blood of its enemies. With a chisel, he signed and dated the blade, marking it finished and sealing in the evil Kami.

"Muramasa had asked Udo to return in thirty days. Instead, Udo spied on the master swordmaker, and just as Muramasa declared the sword finished, Udo appeared, seized the sword, and beheaded the swordmaker, lest word of his sword reach Oji before Udo. Udo then turned his *fury on the four apprentices and cut them down one by one as they tried to flee.*

"Thus armed, Udo confronted Oji as he rode with his young bride near the family estate. Udo stepped into their path and challenged Oji to a duel, convinced that once the Lady Gozen witnessed the depth of his love, and his great skill, she would join her heart to his. The two combatants drew their blades, assumed offensive stances. They stared for several minutes, attempting to perceive each other's possible weaknesses. Udo attacked with Shin Choku-giri, which Oji sought to parry with his sword. Udo's blade cut Oji's sword in two, and did not stop until it had cloven Oji himself in two.

"Lady Gozen, beside herself with grief and fury, drew her dagger and threw herself at Udo, who slew her as well. Bewildered by this turn of events, Udo's soul became sick with the need to kill. He went on to slay over a hundred innocent men, women, and children before he was finally killed.

"The sword Udo commissioned and Muramasa made is called Kyutensei, or 'Rooted In The Sky.' "

Hecht put the piece of paper on his desk and beamed like a child who had just completed a successful recitation. "Could this be the item you're looking for?"

Sara's mouth was a slash. "You mean, could this be the item the *killer* is looking for. But if you just had this translated, how would the killer even know about this sword?"

"I don't claim to be the only source of knowledge on the subject. Such a famous sword would be mentioned countless times in Japanese monographs, about which we would have no knowledge. Therefore, the killer has special knowledge."

"Therefore, the killer might be Japanese, or at least understand Japanese."

Hecht beamed wider. "Exactly."

"That's very helpful, Mr. Hecht. Who, among your circle of collectors, speaks Japanese?"

"Bratten speaks a little, but not enough to read. Besides, I've known that boy since he was in college. There's not a mean bone in his body. And with his money, he could buy the sword legitimately."

"Really? Even millionaires have limits."

"True. Maybe he couldn't buy the sword. But he's not your killer—that's just ridiculous. I understand why he's a suspect. Then again, you have to consider other possibilities."

"Excuse me?"

"The spirit of Udo, searching for his lost sword. Japan is rife with legends of restless warrior spirits. They say the spirit of a man could pass into his sword, and vice-versa, if he subscribed to Bushido."

"A reincarnated fourteenth century ronin who's looking for his lost sword? Thanks a lot, Mr. Hecht. I prefer to think the killer is a normal human being. But why's he even looking in New York? Why not Japan?"

"There are a lot of swords in Manhattan. Returning servicemen after WW II ran off with everything they could find. That's how most of them ended up over here in the first place. And, of course, Emperor Meiji decreed you could no longer wear them, which put most of the traditional swordmakers out of business. They're only now just beginning to come back."

"Okay, I see your point. And I appreciate you're sharing this with me."

Hecht came over and looked out the floor-to-ceiling

window with her. "I appreciate your not laughing in my face. I hope you're not just trying to be polite."

"No. One thing I've learned is not to discount anything. Not that I buy your reincarnation theory . . ."

"I thought you might be receptive. I know a little bit about you, Detective Pezzini. You attract bright lights and strange energies."

They stood side by side looking south. "I understand you've been having some vandalism at the site."

"Nothing we can't handle. We're working closely with the Nineteenth."

"How's it going?"

"We're on schedule for our grand opening next week. I hope you'll be my guest."

"That's very kind of you, Mr. Hecht."

"I wish you'd call me Adrian."

"Only at parties. May I borrow your Muramasa *tsuba*?"

"For what purpose? Do you know what it's worth?"

"Sir, I can't tell you just now, but it would aid greatly in my investigation. And, of course, I accept full responsibility."

Hecht laughed. "You couldn't pay for that *tsuba* with your entire stock portfolio, if you have one. What the hell. Anything to help our brave girls in blue, right?" He opened the hinged top of the display case, reached in with his handkerchief and picked up the finely wrought iron disc. "Don't touch it with your hands. The oil can permanently harm the design."

Sara accepted the disc in the handkerchief, wrapped it carefully, and deposited it in her jacket pocket. "Thank you. May I have a copy of your translation?"

Hecht handed her an envelope. "There's an invitation in there, too. *Puleeze*, R.S.V.P. My social secretary gets all bent out of shape if you don't. I may have some more news for you in a few days."

"What sort of news?"

"Can't say. My translators work slowly." He winked.

CHAPTER
EIGHT

When Lupé first floated her plan past Bobby Chacón, he stared at her like she was a two-headed goat.

"Whoa. What is this? What for you signing me up? Kill a cop? You crazy, girl. Not even for you. Why not get Jorgé do the job? He your man, not me."

"Bobby, didn't you hear what I said? She's a *witch*, aragon! She got Jorgé so hexed up, he don' know his ass from a hole in the ground. He don' listen to me." Her voice lowered to a conspiratorial whisper, even though they were seated in Bobby's tricked-out Celica across from Fort Greene Park, with no one around but pigeons.

"You kill her, you take her power. Think, Bobby! A witch who is also a cop! Think of the power you would have in her shield alone! Man, all you have to do is shine that shield at someone and *bam!*" Lupé snapped her fingers. "They disappear in a puff of smoke."

Bobby hunched down in his bucket seat, eyes gleaming with avarice. He was from Santo Domingo, and he believed in witches. He'd seen the lady cop, and she possessed an unearthly beauty that put crazy thoughts in his head, kept him up at night. But she was just a woman, and if he had a blessing from Estrella, it might even the odds a little. Nor did he see a need to involve *todos los Tecolotes*. He was the leader. He was equal to any two Romeros, including Jorgé.

He even knew the medical center parking garage, where she kept her bike. Before 9/11 and the tightened security, he'd regularly cruised the underground garage, looking to rip off car stereos, drugs, anything he could find. Just thinking about catching the lady witch/cop in the underground parking garage made him sweaty. And his reward, should he successfully remove her from this earth? Not only power, but this sweet young thing who had thus far resisted his advances. And it wasn't just because she was the girlfriend of Jorgé, his mortal enemy.

"Hold out your hand," Lupé commanded. Only fifteen, but already bossy and domineering. Bobby held out his hand. Lupé dropped in a hard little plastic figure. Bobby stared. A little troll doll. Pieces of colored thread, human hair wrapped around.

"What is this?"

"Madame Estrella tol' me give this to you. It give you the power you need to take her down."

Armed with such power, Bobby felt invincible. He would do the lady cop, then party with Jorgé's girl. Life was good. It was six o'clock, and the lady cop ought to be on her way home now. Lupé had been spying on her for a week. Sometimes she came home at the end of the day, sometimes not. When she came, she always stashed her bike in the medical center parking lot.

Bobby started his car and pulled out into traffic. His sub-bass made manhole covers jump, one more thudding burden on the cacophony that was the city. Ten minutes later, they pulled up at the med center's main entrance on Park Place. Lupé was driving. Bobby wore a clean white orderly's tunic and looked like any other med center employee as he got out of the car. The med center required all employees to wear picture identification, but security was spotty.

He casually followed a Datex-Ohmeda delivery vehicle into a docking area, appearing at the rear just as the driver was opening the rear door. "Lemme give you a hand, bro," he said.

He entered the medical center carrying a large cardboard box. The security guard down the hall assumed he was with the delivery truck. The delivery truck assumed he was with the clinic. Bobby just kept on walking with that box, past a nurse who smiled at him, down the utility corridor until he came to the stairwell leading to the underground parking garage.

Bobby knew from past forays that the lady cop locked her bike to a concrete post on Level 2, within sight of the elevators. He went down one level, let himself out on Two, and stripped off the orderly's uniform, leaving the dark of his skin and his black muscle shirt. Bobby was a hard-body, five-eleven. He pumped four days a week. An experienced street fighter, he feared no man, and hated cops, who'd been giving him grief all his life. He crept along the dim far wall until he came to the utility closet he'd scoped out earlier. Locked, but nothing he couldn't fix with a tire iron. An obliging Lincoln driver had left the doors unlocked, permitting Bobby entrance to the trunk. He popped the door on the utility closet, carefully laying the tire iron behind a pillar in the dark, in case he needed a weapon.

Like most gangbangers, Bobby wasn't good on stakeout. He muttered, he paced, he smoked two Basic cigarettes. He wasn't much of a planner, either. His plan was to wait until she got off the bike, grab her from behind, drag her into the utility closet and do 'er. Then he heard it.

The unmistakable whine of a high-compression, four-cylinder engine coming down the ramp. Bobby quickly fixed his do-rag back on his head and grinned fiercely to himself. This was going to be fun. He hid behind a pillar about twenty feet from the well-lit patch of yellow-striped concrete where she stashed her bike. There was already a BMW there, shackled to the wall like some mechanical beast.

With a roar, the lady cop hove into view on her white and blue bike, zoomed up to the striped patch and stopped the bike. She shut it off, set the kickstand, and got off, swinging one long leg over the bike as if it were an Olympic event. Bobby was practically salivating. He decided to wait until she took off the helmet. It would make her more vulnerable.

An instant later, she had the helmet off and swung her long brown hair around. She was some fine booty. She took off her backpack and set it on the ground. Bobby waited until she bent over to run the Kryptonite bike lock through her front wheel. He made his move.

He had his arm around the lady cop's neck and was pulling her backward before she had time to squawk. Bobby knew from experience you really had to mash your forearm against the windpipe to keep her under control, and from getting off a shout. The lady cop struggled ferociously as he dragged her inexorably back toward the utility closet, using her boot-clad legs to kick back at him with her heels, but Bobby kept his hip turned into her so as not to give her a target. She got her legs around one pillar and Bobby had to brace one foot against the pillar to pry her loose. She reversed direction and lunged for him, getting her feet on the front bumper of a Mercedes, kicking off, and suddenly she was airborne.

The abrupt reversal of position freed her from Bobby's grip as she somersaulted over one shoulder and landed on her feet with one arm spread out for stability, hair spilling in her face. No problem, Bobby thought. One hundred and five pounds of woman.

She sprang forward, catching him by surprise and planting the top of her head in his groin, driving him backward until he smashed into the grill of a Lexus. That hurt. Damn, woman! She was not cooperating. She was making noise. Next thing you know, some pain-in-the-ass Good Samaritan was going to shuffle up. He had to end this quickly.

Bobby slithered toward the pillar where he'd stashed the tire iron. She nearly got him with a kick. How could she get off a bike and kick that high without tearing her hamstrings, Bobby wondered. His hands closed around the tire iron and he came up swinging, trying to shatter her forearm.

The shock of hitting something harder than bone zapped back from the tire iron and resonated up his arm, making his teeth ring. Bobby looked in astonishment to see what he'd struck with the tire iron. The lady cop stood in a combat crouch four feet away, green eyes seething, one hand encased in some kind of metal gauntlet. Where had *that* come from? She wasn't wearing it when she got off the bike.

The gauntlet formed a fist and catapulted forward, striking Bobby full in the face and flattening his nose. He could hear the crunch resonating in his skull. Blood exploded in all directions. No lady cop was worth this. She was more witch than cop, any fool could see that.

Bobby put his head down and ran for daylight, trying to barrel past the lady cop. He got one foot on the Lexus' bumper and leaped onto the hood, over the greenhouse, and off the trunk, directly into the path of a Ford F-150 coming up from Level 3. The orderly at the wheel drove too fast. Collision of truck with Chacón left no doubt. It sounded like a train wreck.

By the time Sara reached the truck, the Witchblade had withdrawn into costume bracelet mode. One look at the crumpled husk, and she knew her attacker was dead. She didn't hesitate. She dashed around the truck, got up on the step and looked in at the driver, who was hunched over the wheel, breathing in high, thin gasps.

"Are you all right? Are you hurt?"

The guy squeaked a little, then moved hesitantly. "I never saw him! Jesus Christ, he came out of nowhere. He leaped out of thin air!"

"Okay, calm down. It's all right. I'm a police officer."

"Oh, God, am I under arrest?"

"No, sir. I doubt you'll be charged. That man assaulted me."

The driver turned his head. Big guy, honest, blank expression of a Canadian lumberjack, still wearing his orderly's greens and a laminated badge. Elmer Henderson.

"Mr. Henderson, why don't you get out of the vehicle and sit down with your head between your legs. Make sure nothing's broken."

Two more orderlies appeared. The brouhaha had attracted attention. Seeing Chacón's body, they immediately turned to get a stretcher. Sara held out her badge.

"Hey, you guys. I'm a cop. My name is Sara Pezzini. Let me make the call."

One of the orderlies, who'd seen her around, waved. Sara went back to the driver, got him out of the truck, made him sit with his back against the wall. Looking in the cab, she snagged an empty McDonald's bag from the busy floor, had the driver breath into the bag—an old trick to reduce shock.

She checked the crumpled body for identification. The man was no Einstein. His wallet was in his hip pocket, connected to his leather belt by a chain. He had no driver's license. He had two credit cards in names that couldn't possibly be his. A little plastic troll figure adorned with colored thread and beads. He had the business card of a bail bondsman, and a membership card for something called the Afta Owaz Club, to which he'd signed his name.

Bobby Chacón.

When Lupé heard the crunch, she knew it had something to do with Bobby. Guy could mess up an omelet. She stayed put, scrunched down in the Celica a block away from the medical center, parked in front of a Korean grocer. When the cop cars started showing up, she figured Bobby had blown it and it was time to split. Good thing Bobby taught her how to drive. Good thing the Celica had an automatic.

Driving too fast, sitting too low, Lupé made her way to the switching yard, parking the car in a cinder lot next to a rusting Erie and Lackawana pick-up truck. She was leery of leaving Bobby's fine ride unattended, but there was nothing to be done for it. The car was not visible from the street, and would hopefully still be there when she came back. Damn all thieves anyway, she thought.

The old woman was asleep when Lupé reached her shack, flat on her back on her makeshift bed, making a noise like a low pressure valve. Lupé knocked loudly on the rickety wood doorframe.

Estrella sputtered, opened her eyes, did a little jolt like she didn't know where she was, recovered and sat up. "What you want with Estrella, girl?"

"Lupé. My name is Lupé. Don't you remember? I was here yesterday. I paid you two hundred dollars to help me get rid of the lady cop."

Estrella reached for her cigarettes. "Dat right. How did it go?"

"Not good. Bobby never came out. I think he blew it."

Estrella lit her cigarette with a pungent Zippo, puffing like a locomotive building up a head of steam. She fumbled around among her cushions and produced a police scanner. She turned it on, adjusting the frequency. Snatches of conversations came and went.

". . . responding to automobile fatality in the parking garage of the Neame Medical Center, Prospect Place in Brooklyn. Looks like a gangbanger waiting to assault someone."

Madame Estrella turned off the scanner and buried it beneath the cushions. "So. You is right. You give him the charm?"

"I gave it to him."

"Hmm. Dis witch more powerful den I thought. My mistake. I tol' you I make it right, girl, an' I will. I see now dis Bobby a weak vessel in which we place our hopes. It be mistake to send just one man. You need five to take her down."

Lupé reeled. She knew Los Tecolotes, but they were

112

likely to be furious when they found out Bobby was dead. That could work to her advantage.

"Udderwise, you must do da deed yourself."

Lupé thought about it. She was not afraid of the lady cop. The only thing she feared was getting caught, spending the rest of her life behind bars.

"Tell me how to stop her with my homies."

The witch fluttered her fingers, palms up. "I need two hundred more dollar."

Lupé's mouth dropped open. "I already gave you two hundred dollars, and your stupid plan didn't work! All I know, the cops come looking for me next! Madame Estrella. You see that Zippo lighter by your knee?"

Madame Estrella's claw automatically closed around the lighter.

"That Zippo lighter carries a lifetime guarantee with no conditions. Once you pay for it, it works or the Zippo company replaces it free. And that lighter only cost five bucks! Madame, I'd like to tell the community good things 'bout you. But here you be, charging me twice for the same job . . ."

Estrella held up her hand. "I see your point, girl. Hokay. Dis what I do. I help you dis time, no more money, 'cause I should done right by you inna first place. It dis witch—she much more powerful den I first t'ink. Madame Estrella should have charge you five hundred. But what's done is done. You listen to Madame, an' if she work for you dis time, you don' forget come back and see your madame."

The Celica remained untouched where Lupé had left it. She let herself in, started the engine, and headed for home. Problem: Where could she leave Bobby's ride that it wouldn't get ripped off? Bobby had kept the car right in front of his crib on Duke Street, watched over by his homies and his pit bull Samson. But if Lupé showed up, they'd want to know what happened. Once they learned, they'd never let her keep it. Certainly Chango, Bobby's second-in-command, would demand the car for himself.

Lupé figured she had as much right to the car as anyone. Bobby owed her that much for screwing up the plan. The more she thought about it, the more Lupé figured Bobby owed her. He'd only succeeded in making her life more difficult. She thought about parking the car directly beneath her window, but the cops would notice and come with questions.

After driving around for a while, Lupé headed for the church. St. Patrick's in Brooklyn wasn't like St. Patrick's in Manhattan, but it was a substantial church made of good Vermont granite, with a small parking lot in back surrounded by a chain-link fence. More importantly, the parking lot was invisible to anyone on the street, and Los Tecolotes had nothing to do with the church.

Lupé bumped the Celica up over the high driveway sill, driving carefully between the charcoal granite wall of the church on the left, and the red brick wall of the apartment building on the right—red brick that bore many a scrape attesting to the narrowness of the alley. Lupé barely had six inches clearance on either side. She got the car back there without mishap and parked it next to an old Cadillac sedan.

She shut the engine off and breathed deeply. She hadn't realized what a strain driving was. She wasn't used to driving, and had tensed every muscle in her body, fearing a collision. It was a relief just to sit there surrounded by high walls with nobody giving her any crap. After a while, she leaned over and flipped open the glove compartment. May as well check her assets. Bingo. A loaded, 38 revolver. She slipped it into her B.U.M. Original Equipment backpack, which served as her purse.

The door to the church opened with a hideous screech. Father Donagin emerged on the concrete lip and stared down into the parking lot. "Excuse me," he said.

Lupé got out and smiled. "Hello, Father! It's me, Lupé Guttierez."

"Lupé?" The priest's face cracked in a smile as he came carefully down the iron steps, holding tightly to the rail. He had to be in his late seventies. He'd been there long before Lupé came to New York. Before Lupé was born. "Haven't seen you at church in a while. What are you doing back here? Is that your car?"

"Father, it's for my mother. It's a gift. We all pitched in together—all the kids and cousins and nieces and nephews. It's for her fortieth birthday."

"Why, that's wonderful, Lupé. I wasn't aware your mother drove."

"Oh, she always want to drive, but she say, 'What am I going to drive? I'll never have a car.' Don' worry. We not let her drive around 'til she get her license. But Father, it's a secret."

"I won't tell anyone."

"Can we keep it here for a few days? Until her birthday?"

"When's her birthday?"

Lupé did some fast mental calculation. She needed to buy as much time as possible without arousing the priest's suspicions. "Four days."

Everything should be settled by then.

CHAPTER
NINE

Better Bodies, the health club where Sara worked out, was located in the Shienbaum Building on MacDougall Street, downstairs from All Japan Martial Arts. Sara tried to work out at least three times a week. Better Bodies was not one of the newer health clubs, with row after row of gleaming stainless steel machines—John Heinz, the proprietor, didn't believe in gizmos. He barely believed in weights. If he had his way, everybody would train using jump ropes and the climbing wall.

Better Bodies stank of stale sweat and liniment. It had a creaky hardwood floor, numerous heavy bags, made of leather and patched with duct tape, and a raised boxing ring in one corner where Eric Morel and Roy Jones Jr. had trained, among others. Sara was one of a handful of women who worked out at Better Bodies. A lot of cops worked out there. The grizzled veterans hardly gave Sara a second glance. Working out was serous business. If they'd wanted to ogle young women, they would have joined one of the numerous upscale health clubs with whirlpools, daycare, and Tae Bo.

Late Tuesday morning found Sara in baggy sweat pants and shirt, wearing bag gloves and wailing on an eighty-pound bag. She'd earned her black belt in Tae Kwon Do while an undergraduate at Cornell, and had continued to work out with the Police Athletic League and at Better Bodies since joining the force.

A boom box in the corner broadcast Huey Lewis' "The Heart of Rock and Roll" as Sara alternated punches and kicks. Out of the corner of her eye she saw Heinz approaching. He was a well-developed, thirty-five-year-old who'd studied with Royce Gracie and taught Brazilian ju-jitsu.

"Hey, Sara," he said. "James Bratten and Derek Sharpe are about to go at it upstairs with kendo sticks."

Sara paused, panting. "Since when does Sharpe work out here?"

"Since he showed up last week," Heinz replied, heading for the stairs.

Sara grabbed a towel and followed. Up a long, narrow flight of stairs, the All Japan Martial Arts Academy occupied a four-thousand-square-foot studio with hardwood floors and a glass wall protected by a room-length barre overlooking MacDougal Street. When Sara arrived, the smallish visitor area was jammed with cops and honchos. Sara worked her way to the front, resting her arms on the four-foot banister separating the holding pen from the vast hardwood floor.

On the floor, four kendo students sat cross-legged in front of the floor-to-ceiling mirrors. In the center of the large room, facing each other, identically dressed in heavy black cotton uniforms, stood the combatants. Their faces were covered with bamboo masks, heads covered with heavy black cotton. They wore padded cotton gloves

118

and each held a shinai, a multi-sectioned wooden sword. It was easy to tell them apart. At six-four, Sharpe was the short man.

Sara had arrived just in time for the formal salute preceding combat. Baltazar, whom she'd spotted earlier doing sets, appeared at her elbow.

"This is gonna be good. Bratten was channeling Ali, bragging on how he was the baddest cat who ever played the game, and he could take any two guys in the joint. Sharpe made some crack that when the Apples did an exhibition game in Tokyo, two of 'em were picked up for shoplifting. Bratten called Sharpe a punk and here we are."

"Does Bratten know Sharpe is a cop?"

"I don't think so. I don't think they even know each other. It's a case of hate at first sight."

The instructor, a wiry little Japanese by the name of Ojima, held his hand up to signal the start of the contest. His hand fell. The combatants clashed in a blinding series of strikes, like two trees fighting each other. It was difficult to tell which was an attack and which was a defense, so quickly did the blows fall. Sara knew that in kendo, there were only seven blows and one thrust. The blows flowed one into another, from attack to defense and back again, as the combatants moved swiftly around the room, their feet tracing semi-circular patterns. Both men were big, but Bratten was extra-big. He towered over the tall cop by four inches. Even so, it was the shorter Sharpe who soon proved dominant, driving his larger opponent around the room like a reluctant bull.

Bratten was good. Sara could see the moves that had earned him NBA All-Star status five years in a row. But despite his superb athleticism, and his size advantage,

Bratten could do nothing with his smaller opponent. Sharpe seemed almost psychic in his ability to sense where Bratten's blows would fall. He effortlessly deflected Bratten's attacks, turning each defense into an offense until it became evident to everyone that the cop was playing with the basketball star. Just when it seemed Bratten was beginning to tire, Sharpe ended it with a spectacular rising blow that caught Bratten's grip, causing him to lose the shinai which soared through the air and thumped against the wall.

Sharpe instantly stopped, stood upright, and bowed deeply. Bratten had no choice but to respond. "Crap!" he muttered as he headed for the sidelines, stripping off his protective mask. Sharpe walked calmly to the side of the room and sat, cross-legged, before he removed his mask.

The crowd dissipated. Sara followed Baltazar down the stairs to Better Bodies and drifted toward the heavy bag, consumed by one overriding thought: Derek Sharpe was one of the finest swordsmen she'd ever witnessed.

Sara showered in the women's locker room at the station and returned to her desk to finish her report on the assault, for the Brooklyn Seventy-first Precinct. The image of Sharpe, effortlessly disarming Bratten, kept getting in the way. She tended to give all cops the benefit of the doubt. And she liked Sharpe. But she didn't believe in coincidence, and her curiosity about the new cop had been set free. She needed to obtain as much background information on Sharpe as she could, without alerting Internal Affairs. She wondered about contacting his life partner. All she knew about him was that he worked on Wall Street.

All street cops hated Internal Affairs, and vice versa.

DEMONS

The Eleventh had been saddled with a particularly odious internal affairs officer named Selzer. Another case of hate at first sight. Selzer had it in for Sara for the simple reason that she represented unobtainable beauty. No way was she going to sic Selzer on Sharpe, even if the latter *was* the samurai killer.

There. She said it.

She found herself staring at the jumble of words on her computer, until Raj rose and left the room. She leaped up and followed, catching up with the Hindu cop in the hall.

"Raj, hang on a minute." The slight cop paused at a landing next to a window protected by iron bars. Raj was her go-to guy in computers. "Can I trust you with something?"

"Most assuredly."

"Could you get me Derek Sharpe's service record, run a background check?"

"Sharpe—the new policeman from the Bay Area? I could do that. Will you tell me what it's about?"

A public defender banged into the stairwell at street level and headed up, toting an overstuffed briefcase and breathing heavily. They exchanged greetings and waited until he exited on the third floor.

"Sharpe is an expert swordsman. I need to know where he studied."

Raj's eyebrows rippled with understanding. "I will use my home computer."

"Thanks, Raj. I owe you."

"Nonsense. It is I who owe you, for the assistance you rendered in the case of the vanishing sardine truck."

Sara planted a quick kiss on Raj's cheek and headed back to her desk. Someone had crazy-glued another Spawn figurine to her desk, with the word balloon, "EEK!

DETECTIVE PEZZINI IS AFTER ME!" She broke Spawn loose with a pop and held it up like an Academy Award. "Thanks, guys. These are highly collectible." She tossed it in the bottom drawer with the others. One of these days she intended to take all her toys over to the Child Burn Unit at Sloan-Kettering.

A check on Bobby Chacón produced a rap sheet like a Chinese takeout menu. Head of the Brooklyn Tecolotes, Chacón had served four years at Ossining for assaulting a police officer. Los Tecolotes were active in the crack market. But the assault on Sara had a personal feel to it. The troll doll had been festooned like some kind of religious fetish. In addition to the colored thread and beads, Sara had discovered some long brown hairs that looked suspiciously like her own. She was familiar with some of the more arcane paths to power favored among New York's many immigrants: weird religions from the Caribbean and Southeast Asia, ritual sacrifice of hogs and chickens. Sometimes a child.

Sara phoned Nelda Garrulitis at the *New York Post*. Nelda wrote the Page Six gossip column.

"Garrulitis," she answered in a voice like crunching snow, the result of a three-pack-a-day habit.

"Nelda, it's Sara Pezzini."

"Do you have a zombie sighting for me?"

"Nelda, I need your help. What do you know about an investment banker named Robert Hotchkiss?"

"Consummate bore. Quite the whiz-kid in the nineties, but his career seems to have stalled, and his society wife, Janet, is giving him the heave-ho. Looks like a nasty divorce battle. Hotchkiss has retained Lawton & Cates. The former Miss Dolores Greenbaum has employed the flamboyant women's rights advocate, Mildred Squires."

"You think he's strapped for cash?"

"Men like Hotchkiss are always strapped for cash. The only reason I know about this insignificant little man at all is because he married the former Miss Dolores Greenbaum, of the Kensington Greenbaums. What's this about?"

"Murder investigation. Please don't mention this to anyone and you get the scoop."

"What's the scoop?"

"The samurai killer."

"Seriously?"

"Seriously."

"What are you looking for?"

Sara told the gossip columnist her theory that the samurai killer was collecting swords. "I need to know if either Hotchkiss or his wife has tried to peddle something through Bachman recently." She did not mention she thought Hotchkiss was their anonymous informant.

Sara accessed info.com, a for-fee investigative service that had access to credit reports, military records, rap sheets, your fourth-grade report card. Robert Hotchkiss had been born in 1950, the only son of Arthur and Anne Hotchkiss of North Salem. Arthur Hotchkiss had served with distinction in the Pacific during WW II. He'd been on Iwo Jima, that hellish two-mile patch of beach that cost the lives of twenty thousand Americans.

At four P.M., the phone rang.

"Pezzini, Homicide."

"Sara, it's Dave Kopkind."

Sara unconsciously relaxed her neck and shoulder muscles, surprised at her own relief. She hadn't realized she'd wanted him to call. "Hello, David. I want to thank you again for the other night. I had a lovely time."

"Yeah, well, I thought, you know, maybe we could do it again, or something. Like maybe dinner and some music. There's this little jazz club around the corner featuring the Ray Rideout Quartet—he's an absolutely ripping sax player . . . "

"I'd love to."

Pause. "Really?" Genuine shock.

"Yes, I'd love to. I can't Friday. But Thursday or Saturday . . ."

"Thursday? You want to come by my place? If that's a hassle, I could drive over to Brooklyn."

"No, no, no! Manhattan is the center of the universe. One should always head for the center. I'll come to your place. Around seven?"

"That would be great!"

"See you then."

Sara hung up. A minute later, Baltazar looked at her in annoyance. "What are you humming about?"

David Kopkind was walking on air. He'd only been in a handful of relationships in his life, and none of his prior girlfriends approached Pezzini in the looks or brains department. Amazing, the way she'd knocked on his door. Every red-blooded American male entertains daydreams of a beautiful woman coming to his house, but no one expects it to happen. So what if she was a cop, and there'd been a murder? Through some mysterious process he didn't understand, Kopkind had convinced her to go on another date with him.

Kopkind was from Syracuse, the third son of a career Air Force guy and stay-at-home mom. Both Kopkind's older brothers were in the Air Force. He himself had enlisted in the Navy, served a three-year hitch, decided he wanted a civilian life. The Navy posted him to Japan, where he first became interested in swords, and the rudiments of polishing. After his honorable discharge, he remained in Japan an additional six months, apprenticing to a master polisher named Ohara. By the time Kopkind left for the states, he and Ohara had celebrated St. Patrick's Day with green saki, and swore undying fealty to each other.

He went into the polishing studio, picked up the newspaper-wrapped long sword, knelt at his polishing table, the *todai-mikura*, and unsheathed the sword. It was a *Hisakuni* from the year 1199, the master's signature and the date chiseled into the tang. Kopkind had been working on the *shitajitogi*, or foundation. The sword was in sad shape, having been neglected for hundreds of years. Rust had gained tiny foxholes in the surface from which a spider web of decay expanded. But the steel was good, and Kopkind was confident he would be able to remove the blemishes. After a full day of polishing, he'd succeeded in smoothing out the two upper surfaces, or *shinogi-ji*. Once they were finished, he would tackle the lower surfaces, or *ji*, saving the *kissaki* (point) and *mune* (back edge) for last. All other parts of the sword had to be trued first, before making any adjustments to the cutting edge.

Dribbling water on the stone, Kopkind ran the blade back and forth over the block of *arato*, coarse polishing stone from the Ohomura Quarry in Shinano Province, the traditional source of good quarry stone throughout Japan. Kopkind was convinced that, somewhere in the vastness of the United States, good polishing stone existed. Possibly in the West. He intended to conduct a search someday, with the idea of opening a quarry in the

United States. Good polishing stones commanded anywhere from a couple hundred to a thousand dollars. Kopkind obtained his through Ohara.

He found the back and forth action of the blade soothing, a form of meditation. He lost himself in the vibration of the blade in his hands, the hum in his ears. And what appeared before his mind's eye but Detective Pezzini, wearing The Little Black Dress. He imagined her in his arms, the taste of her lips, the scent of her hair.

Ouch. Kopkind looked down. He'd sliced open his left index finger. Served him right for daydreaming on the job. At least, he thought, it wasn't one of the cursed Muramasa blades, like the one that had cut him last month. Kopkind was bleeding heavily, crimson droplets splattering the wet stone, running over the edges. He got up holding his hand, went to the large utility sink against the wall and ran cold water over the wound. He opened the first-aid box attached to the wall and fumbled with a Band-Aid. Yoshi came into the room, yawning and snarling.

"Don't just stand there. Do something!" Kopkind commanded, tearing open a Band-Aid with his teeth. At last he got the bandage around the cut and the bleeding stopped. His hands looked like leather that had been dragged over barbed wire, he'd cut himself so often. He'd gone two years without a cut, then the Masamura. Now it had been barely three weeks since the last cut.

Yoshi suddenly leaped onto the workbench, scrabbling for an instant at the ledge and knocking a mallet and a chisel to the floor, before gaining purchase and letting out a shriek. An instant later, the door chimes tinkled softly. Wiping his hands, Kopkind headed for the front.

Adrian Hecht stood in Kopkind's front office, wearing aviator shades and a black cashmere sweater, clutching a long, narrow package wrapped in brown paper and taped shut. It took Kopkind a minute to register. It was a little like finding Bill Gates in your foyer. They'd been introduced at Bratten's party, but what did the developer want with him?

"Mr. Hecht," Kopkind said. "What can I do for you?"

Hecht was examining the certificates and prints on the wall. "Bratten tells me you're the best sword polisher in New York."

"Well I don't know about that . . ."

"Bratten is not one to use hyperbole. As you know, I'm a collector."

"I've heard. I'd love to see your collection sometime."

"That can be arranged." He held up the package. "I'd like you to polish this."

"I appreciate that, but I'm booked through August 2005."

"I'm an impatient man, Kopkind, and I have a great deal of money. Name your fee."

Kopkind grimaced. He'd always thought of himself as a man of honor. Bushido was based on honor. But he was also a man with needs and aspirations. There was no shame in accepting a special commission for a windfall profit. "Mr. Hecht, I hardly know where to start. I make a good living . . ."

"I will pay you one hundred thousand dollars if you can turn this sword around in five days."

"Impossible." But was it? The hundred grand danced behind his eyes like children circling a maypole. If he worked twelve hours a day—a grueling prospect—it was possible. A hundred grand bought a lot of polishing stones. "What kind of sword is it?"

"I don't know."

"Excuse me?"

Hecht stifled a sneeze by pressing up on his nose. "I've taken a bit of a gamble and purchased a sword sight unseen from a dealer in Japan."

"How . . ."

"I've been dealing with this gentleman for many years. He's dying, and wants to leave something for his heirs. He is selling me something that has been in his family for generations, with his personal guarantee that it's what I'm looking for."

"What are you looking for?"

"I believe it to be a lost Muramasa."

Yoshi brushed aside the beads and entered, snarling and yawning. Hecht took a step back. "I'm allergic to cats."

"Sorry." Kopkind scooped the cat up and dumped it back on the other side of the curtain. "You don't know which one?"

"I was hoping you could identify and authenticate it for me. My agent tells me the signature was removed centuries ago."

"What's the rush?"

"I want to show it next week."

"Would you like a cup of tea?"

"I don't have time right now."

Kopkind blushed, but didn't bother to deny it. "Does this have anything to do with Bachman? He was a friend of mine."

An angry look came into the developer's cold blue

eyes, and for an instant, Kopkind was afraid Hecht was going to take a poke at him. He took a half step back to be ready, just in case. The look passed. "Don't be absurd. I've never dealt with Bachman. I knew him, of course. We'd show up at the same gallery shows. I had no business with him, and I had nothing to do with his death." Hecht dared Kopkind to argue with him.

Kopkind didn't take the dare. Men like Hecht, men who were accustomed to ruling empires and making split-second decisions affecting the lives of thousands, were seldom dissemblers. Kopkind considered himself an excellent judge of character. As far as he was concerned, Hecht was telling the truth.

"All right, Mr. Hecht. I believe you. Tell you what. Leave the sword and I'll get to work on it right away. I'm not sure I can deliver in five days, but I could do it in a week."

Hecht frowned. "I don't want to have to postpone my party. I was hoping to show the sword there."

Kopkind shrugged. "I tend to allow myself more time than I actually need."

"You'll do it?"

"I'll try my best, but I won't guarantee I can turn it around in five days. If I stay at the bench too long, I get tired. My concentration falters."

Hecht held up a hand. "I understand. I just don't want to show a blade that looks like a bad case of varicose veins. However, this deal is contingent on absolute discretion. No one must know you have this sword, understand?"

Kopkind nodded.

"No, you don't understand. I mean absolutely *no one*. Not your lover, not your mother. No one."

Kopkind took a step backward and bowed his head. "Wakarimasu," he said.

Hecht took the sword polisher's card and left. Yoshi came back into the room, curling between Kopkind's legs. He knelt and picked the cat up. What could possibly be so urgent about polishing an old sword?

"My, my. Adrian Hecht. Whoda thunk it?"

Carrying the cat and the sword, he went through his showroom into the backroom where he'd been polishing, unconsciously whistling the "Colonel Bogey March." He was excited about the prospect of the mystery sword. A collector as important as Hecht would want an important sword. If Kopkind could identify it, and verify the identification, it would send his stock, already high, through the roof.

One wall was covered floor to ceiling in oak bookcases he'd built himself. The shelves were filled with books, many of which he'd obtained in Japan. Standing on a stool, Kopkind reached for the top shelf, which badly needed dusting, and, using both hands, retrieved an ancient, leather-bound tome titled *Kuyamigusa*, published in Japan in 1890, and translated by a Christian missionary in China, who had obtained it in trade.

As an antiquarian, Kopkind was aware of the book's value. Strictly as a collector's item, it was priceless. The fact that he owned probably the only existing copy of an English translation didn't phase him. Recognizing the *oshigata*, he'd snatched it up at a bargain basement price. It had proven to be an invaluable tool for appraisals. The book contained detailed histories of most of the great swordmakers, beginning in the twelfth century. The book was 768 pages long and weighed forty-one pounds.

A cloud of dust rose like residue from an underground

130

nuclear test when Kopkind set the book on the workbench. He imagined the lonely missionary, one Rufus T.K.
Laughlin, by name, spending endless hours in the shade
of a gingko tree laboring at his translation. Ironic, that a
man of peace would devote his life to translating a book
of war. Laughlin had apparently been trained at Oxford
or Cambridge, because he had included an extensive bib-
liography and index. The project must have consumed
the bulk of his adult life. How utterly quixotic, Kopkind
thought. Living in China, translating Japanese, the Reverend Laughlin made himself a double-outcast.

Kopkind searched the index for Muramasa. The entries
covered half a page, and included not only the earlier,
shadowy, legendary Muramasa, but his descendants who
were active through the sixteenth century. Yoshi leaped
on the workbench, purring like a generator.

Burying his face in the cat's fur, Kopkind said, "Yoshi,
guard the book. I need tea."

After he had prepared a cup of tea for himself, Kopkind pulled up a stool and began to read. As a sword expert, he was aware of the Muramasas' reputation, and the
Tokugawa Ke's efforts to destroy them. He'd only read
portions of the book previously, because it was a chore to
decipher Reverend Laughlin's cramped, angular penmanship. Kopkind read slowly, running his finger under the
text.

Eventually, he came to the tale of Shigeyoshi the
Magistrate.

$\mathbf{S}$ara headed home at six P.M., unfazed by gridlock as she zipped down the dividing line between lanes, ignoring honks, curses, and the single finger salute. She stopped at a Delitalia on Murchison Street and picked up some pre-fab fettucini alfredo and a bottle of California Merlot, which she bungeed to the rear seat.

She arrived at the medical center without incident, locked her bike to the pole, waved to the newly visible security guard, and walked up out of the parking ramp, across Prospect Place, and into the rear entrance of her building. She made it all the way to her door without incident. She set down her backpack and box of food on the floor while she unlocked her door.

"It's a miracle!" Ben Weiskopf declared from behind her.

Inwardly, she cringed. All she wanted was to make it inside her apartment without incident, turn off the phones, soak in a hot bath, eat her dinner and watch *NYPD Blue* in peace. Bracing herself, she pasted on a happy face and turned. "What is, Ben?"

"The hoodlums! Whatever you did, it worked! An overnight transformation. The whole building is talking. Of course, I told them what happened, that our own fourth floor cop had a little talk with them, and you know what they said? You know what Mrs. Milman said? She said you couldn't possibly have had anything to do with it, because you're a tiny little woman, and who would listen to you? So I told her, 'Mrs. Milman, you don't know Sara very well, do you?' Anyhow, I made a bundt cake. I don't know if you like bundt cake . . ."

"Ben, that's awfully sweet of you. I wish I had time to chat, but you're going to have to give me a rain check. I'm still on the job."

Weiskopf's ears pricked up. "Some big case? Are you after the samurai killer?"

The power of the press. Her elderly Brooklyn neighbor knew about the samurai killer. "Something like that," she smiled. "I wish I could discuss it with you, but it's a matter of internal security."

"I understand, I understand. Well, at least let me give you some of this bundt cake." He retreated into his apartment leaving the door open. Sara got her own door open and shuttled her goods inside, returning in time to accept Weiskopf's small replaceable plastic container. "I want that container back when you're done."

"Of course." Smiling, she nodded to the old man, said good night, and entered her apartment.

At last she was alone, except for Shmendrick, who did not make demands. She began filling the old claw-legged tub while she put her things away and undressed. No phone messages. Thank God for small blessings. In the bathroom, she poured bath oil into the tub, stripped off her clothes, piled her hair up, clipped it in place, and lowered herself slowly, carefully, into the hot water. The tub was so full, any excited motion would cause water to slosh on the floor.

She relaxed, with only her head protruding from the bubbles, feeling the tension dissipate from her muscles.

She wondered how her partner, Jake McCarthy, was doing, relaxing on a Jamaican beach somewhere with the stewardess du jour. He'd sent her a post card of smiley-face black children thrusting flowers at the camera. *Jeez,* he wrote. *You can buy any freakin' thing you want on the beach at Negril! I mean anything. Good thing I'm not working. Love, Jake.*

She slipped deeper into the water, until only her head and the tips of her knees protruded. At her last physical, the doctor told her she was in perfect health. Since acquiring the Witchblade, she hadn't had a sick day. Last December the entire precinct came down with the flu, except for Sara. Detectives joked she'd made a deal with the devil, but it was not a laughing matter to her.

Most of the time she didn't know it was there. It only manifested during crisis, or sometimes gave a little surge for reasons Sara didn't understand. Like talking to Hecht. It had given a little surge then, just enough to remind her she was wired. Like a one degree warming of her nervous system. Like a ripple down her spine. Just enough to say, *I'm here. I sense something. Something's not quite right.*

Hecht and Bratten were both collectors. Both men of action, although Hecht had to be in his fifties. Did Hecht or Bratten want the sword enough to kill for it? Sara considered motive the least important aspect of police work. Motive was important to juries and defense lawyers, not to cops. Motive was the most slippery of aspects. Sara had encountered mothers who drowned their children because they heard voices from God, a man who bludgeoned his neighbor to death over a parking space dispute, murderers who took umbrage at the way people dressed, looked, or behaved.

Men would certainly kill for a sword, if not a thousand other reasons. Anything could become an obsession, even collecting. *Especially* collecting. Sara recalled one case in which one suburban hausfrau had stabbed another to death in a dispute over a Beanie Baby. Poopsie the Bear, in Jets livery. Her own father, Vincent Pezzini, collected jurisdiction patches that he mounted on red velvet and hung on the rec room wall.

That both Hecht and Bratten were prominent members of the community with no criminal records meant nothing. But Sara couldn't feature either one sneaking around in a ninja costume. Bratten, on the other hand, had demonstrable skills with the sword and was easily capable of beheading someone. Hecht she didn't know—but she intended to find out. In any case, she was convinced that as outlandish as the crimes were, they had natural, if not reasonable, explanations. There were rich collectors all over the world who would pay seven figures for a sword, and only look at it themselves.

She had to consider Sharpe's suggestion that the sword thefts and ritual beheading were just covers for the murder of Scott Chalmers. Or Bachman. But Chalmers struck her as a far more likely candidate for murder, with all those bitter ex-wives and business rivals.

As the water began to cool, she pulled the plug with her toe, reluctantly levered herself out, drying off in a hotel-sized white towel. Shmendrick stuck his nose in the bathroom, licked her leg and split. She put on panties, fleece-lined workout pants and a sweatshirt, and headed for the kitchenette where she uncorked the Merlot and popped the fettuccine in the microwave. The sounds of traffic from St. Marks Place washed against her walls like surf.

She turned on the little TV without sound in the kitchen and flipped through her mail. Two magazines: *American Rifleman* and *Real Simple*. Utility bills, three credit card offers, and a plain white envelope with her name written in block letters by an unsteady hand. It looked like the lettering on the anthrax letters to Tom Daschle and Pat Leahy.

Sara went cold. For an instant, she was seized with an irrational desire to pop the envelope in the microwave and nuke it. Then she remembered the Witchblade. It lay lightly on her wrist, something a girl would wear to a garden party. Dormant, inert, unconcerned. She trusted the Witchblade to protect her, and if it sensed no danger, she was in none. There was no scientific explanation. It had nothing to do with science. This was beyond science, in a world as complex and mysterious as the workings of a computer to an ant.

The microwave dinged. Sara jumped. Shmendrick jumped, too, onto the counter. Sara let out a whoosh of air and collapsed back onto the plastic chair. "Okay, let's everybody settle down."

Holding the envelope in her left hand, she opened it with a steak knife, then shook it out on top of her copy of *Real Simple*. A single small sheet of paper fell out, with a crude drawing of a lady cop, like something a bored kid would draw in math, with exaggerated boobs and a Gestapo hat and a badge, surrounded and attacked by three savage . . . wolves? There was a totemic quality to the drawing, the wolves widely spaced, forming a triangle. Sara could easily imagine coming across the drawing on the wall of a cave in the Southwest.

Sara had an enemy. Someone who knew where she lived. But what did it mean? Was the drawing a warning? And if so, what was it supposed to accomplish, other than putting Sara on her guard? She checked the postmark. Brooklyn Post Office 10029, within walking distance.

The microwave beeped again, a dull but reliable servant. Sara fetched her fettucini, pried off the lid, and picked at it with a pair of chopsticks. Adrian Hecht spoke earnestly, silently from the tiny TV in front of an architect's rendering of his project. The phone rang.

Damn, she thought. She was certain she'd turned the ringer off. She automatically answered. "Pezzini."

"Sara? It is Raj."

She was suddenly glad she answered. "What did you find?"

"Sharpe's a former Navy SEAL."

"What?!"

"Most assuredly. It was not easy for me to discover this, as his military records were sealed under executive order. One can only surmise he was involved in highly classified missions."

"How'd you find this out, Raj?"

"I rely upon this young chap I busted last year for hacking. He is most adept at these things. He hacked into the Defense Department computers. Again, I am assuring you not to worry, as he leaves no trace. Moreover, I am telling you that Sharpe was stationed in Yokohama for ten months, June 1994 to March 1995. While there, he participated in joint anti-terrorist operations with JDM Special Forces. The exact nature of these operations was beyond my capabilities, I'm afraid."

"Outstanding, Raj. Thank you. I owe you dinner at the cheap East Indian restaurant of your choice."

"You are owing me nothing, but if you are to treat me to dinner, I get to choose."

"That's what I just said."

"But I do not wish to dine Indian. I wish to dine French."

"Raj, you got it. French, Indian, whatever."

Sara hardly tasted the rest of her dinner. She was too buzzed. She didn't like the idea that a cop might be committing murder, but she couldn't ignore the evidence, even if it was circumstantial. Like many another doctoral candidate, Sara had suffered through an interminable semester on statistics which, if nothing else, taught her not to believe in coincidence. Sara's thesis, like her study of Latin, was on hold.

If Sharpe were the samurai killer, what was his goal? Collecting rare swords for a profit? Absurd. A Manhattan cop had plenty of opportunities to make easy money without resorting to ritual slaughter. Suppose it was a ritual? Suppose the killings had nothing to do with greed, but with some arcane philosophy as yet unrevealed? Motive remained a riddle wrapped in a mystery, inside an enigma.

Sharpe had sent off no warning bells. Quite the contrary. She found herself drawn to the tall, charismatic cop. It could be a devastating disguise. She hoped not.

One thing was certain: Her curiosity about the new cop was far from satisfied.

But it was not Sharpe's image that remained in her head as she finally faded away. It was David Kopkind's, accompanied by a low-voltage thrill of anticipation.

CHAPTER

ELEVEN

Wednesday rose bleak and wet. Sara left her bike, dressed in her gray London Fog and a wide-brimmed hat, and took the bus across the bridge to Manhattan, where she caught a subway to the Village. Police tape still sealed Bachman's front door, but the techs had done their work. The hardwood floor had been scrubbed clean, leaving a broad stain, slightly lighter than the rest of the floor. Techs had gone through the entire shop, performing inventory as well as looking for clues.

Sara bypassed the shop and pushed the button for the phone booth-sized elevator. She wanted a look at the private Bachman. She took the elevator to the fourth and top floor, and emerged in a cozy study/office, with a bathroom on the left and a bedroom on the right—obviously where the private Bachman spent most of his time. An English Renaissance desk looked out on Worth Street. The elegant oak desk had brass handles and a banker green blotter on top, a set of Waterford writing pens, and a journal.

She checked the bedroom. The bed had been neatly made. Four amber pill bottles sat next to the bed alongside a decanter of red wine, a glass of water, and a copy of *John Adams*, the new biography. Bachman's copious closet contained a selection of conservative, tailored, three-piece suits, dozens of long-sleeved white and pastel shirts, most with linked cuffs, and two dozen shining shoes arrayed in battle formation.

Returning to the den, Sara sat down and began to read. In precise script, the antiquarian listed his diet. On the morning of May 29th, he'd consumed a half pint of two percent skim milk, an onion bagel, and a shmear of low-fat cream cheese. Sara was grateful for the banker's diligence, but found little of interest. She skipped ahead.

Monday, June 7. Bob Hotchkiss phoned, anxious to unload the Muramasa his father brought back from Iwo Jima. I am reluctant. These things have a reputation, after all. And it has no papers.

"Excuse me," a querulous female voice rang out.

Sara turned. A woman had stepped out of the elevator freighted with two rope-handled shopping bags jammed with food. She was in her mid-thirties, stocky, dowdy, her short brunette hair pasted to her forehead by the damp, her designer glasses misting. She took them off and stared at Sara with small gray eyes.

"What are you doing here?"

Sara produced her badge. "Sara Pezzini, Eleventh Precinct. I'm investigating Mr. Bachman's death. And you are?"

The woman stepped forward, extending her hand. "Leesha Bachman. Thaddeus was my father. What's going on? The police won't tell me anything. The coroner said my father had his head cut off! Is that true?"

Sara mentally kicked herself. "Miss Bachman, I apologize for not contacting you sooner . . ."

Leesha held up her hands. "Oh, please. I'm glad you're taking the case seriously."

"Yes. Where do you live?"

"Newton, MA. I'm a schoolteacher. I had to hear my father had been killed on the evening news."

Sara hung her head in shame. "I'm so sorry. That should have been my first priority. I'm working the case alone . . ."

"Don't worry about it. Just tell me what you've found."

Sara briefly recounted developments and her theory. "When you arrived, I was looking at your father's journal. He'd just recorded the arrival of a Muramasa. I believe that's what the killer was after."

"But why did he have to kill my father? Why not just sneak in when there's nobody here and take it?"

"Maybe he couldn't get in by himself. Maybe he had to have your father admit him. Maybe it was someone who knew your father, and had made an appointment."

"I'm not much help, I'm afraid. I don't know about his business."

"Did he indicate anything peculiar to you recently? Anything out of the ordinary?"

"I'm sorry. There was nothing unusual."

"When did you last see him?"

Now it was the schoolteacher's turn to hang her head in shame. "About a year ago. I came down and he took me to a fancy society party at this place on Fifth Avenue. Very swank. One of his clients, I gather. He was trying to impress me. He was always trying to impress me, I don't know why. I loved my father. We just weren't very close, that's all."

"Do you remember who hosted the party?"

"It was Scott Chalmers, I believe."

This was new. Chalmers had not been in Bachman's Rolodex, but here at last was a connection tying them together. Both murdered men knew each other, connected by their interest in Japanese swords. There had to be a pattern, if only Sara could see it.

"Do you know the nature of your father's relationship with Chalmers?"

"Dad sold him some paintings, silk screens, wood prints, I believe."

"No swords?"

"None that I know of."

Sara recalled that Chalmers had bought his sword in an online auction. The boys at Lab had had Chalmers' computer for three days now. They ought to be able to provide her with copies of his e-mails, including the heated exchanges with the collector whom Chalmers had outbid.

"Did your father ever buy anything online?"

Leesha Bachman shook her head. "He didn't even own a computer. I tried to get him interested, but he was too set in his ways."

Sara gave the woman her card and asked her to phone, should she discover anything of interest. As Sara boarded the elevator, she looked back. Leesha Bachman was seated alone at her father's desk going forlornly through the drawers.

When Sara returned to her desk, there were three messages from Brandon Stern with the Mayor's office, one from the computer lab, and someone had glued a rubber

King Kong to her desk, with the word balloon, "HELP! DON'T LET HER GET ME!" Sara twisted it off and dumped it in the bottom drawer with the other monsters, then dialed Stern's number.

"Thanks for returning my call, Detective. I'll get right to the point. Scott Chalmers was a close friend of the mayor. We'd like to be personally appraised of your investigation as you proceed."

Great, Sara thought. *Just what I need—the mayor's office turning this murder investigation into a political football.* "No problem, Mr. Stern," she replied.

"Very good. And, ah, the mayor would like to meet you. He's long been a supporter of the police departments, and affirmative action in particular . . . "

Blah blah blah, Sara thought. "That's good to hear."

"Would it be possible for you to attend a small gathering at Gracie Mansion on the fourteenth, to commemorate the unveiling of a painting honoring the mayor's predecessor?"

"Huh?" *Excuse me. For a minute there I thought you were inviting me to meet the mayor.*

"His Honor would like you to attend a cocktail party the evening of the fourteenth, to unveil a painting of Mayor Guiliani. You may bring a date if you like, but please R.S.V.P. by Friday. Will you do that?"

"I certainly will."

Sara hung up, all abuzz. Suddenly she was in demand on the party circuit. After years of her social life consisting of *Ally McBeal* episodes and *Cooking Lite* video seminars, she had been cast into a fandango of social activity, rubbing shoulders with movers, shakers, and union breakers. It was exciting, and fun, and the thing that made it exciting and fun was she didn't have to go alone. She had a date. Someone she actually looked forward to seeing.

She felt like singing, "Sara's got a boyfriend! Sara's got a boyfriend!" And she hadn't even kissed him yet. Not really. Pecks on the cheek didn't count.

She phoned the computer center and learned that they had already sent over transcriptions of all Chalmers' e-mails for the past year. According to Mrs. Chalmers, he'd only purchased the sword five months ago. When Sara checked her mailbox, she found a three-inch-thick manila envelope with the e-mails. She returned to her desk and began to read. At least two dozen Nigerians had contacted Chalmers with schemes to smuggle twenty-three million dollars out of the country, if only Chalmers would give them his bank account numbers.

The sword first appeared in October of the previous year, as a bulletin to a user list from swordauction.com, specializing in Oriental swords. Chinese swords had their own history and tradition, but swordauction did the bulk of their business in rare Japanese swords. Sara understood that serious collectors seldom bought sight unseen. The sword had to be examined by experts to determine its authenticity. Unless the sword was so well known it came with a pedigree. Swords offered on eBay and other online auction houses were mostly junk. There were exceptions.

The swordauction bulletin said: FOR BID—AUTHENTIC MURAMASA WAKIZASHI, "*ISHI NO HANA*, STONE FLOWER," 1506, COMMISSIONED BY ISE SHINKURO, AUTHENTICATED BY THE HON'AMI FAMILY. TO VIEW THE SWORD IN DETAIL, GO TO XXXXXXXX. MINIMUM BID: $85,000. Sara went online and looked up the sword. It was beautiful, approximately two feet long, photographed in such a way that the light played on its flowing, wave-like accent line. There were links to numerous close-ups, details of the handle, the menuki, or hilt ornaments—in this case, a pair of gold tigers, as fine as anything she'd seen in a jewelry store or museum.

She instructed the computer to print out pictures of the swords. Minutes later, the printer, which Homicide shared with all the other departments, spewed out five sheets of indistinguishable gray sludge.

Think, Pezzini, think, she berated herself. Who had a high-quality computer and printer? Nelda immediately came to mind, but then the pictures would be plastered all over the *New York Post.* Brooklyn Yamaha was the answer. Like most serious bikers, she maintained close relations with her bike shop. Brooklyn Yamaha had state-of-the-art equipment. She phoned the shop and asked for the service manager, Clancy Imada.

"Clancy, I need a favor."

"For you, anything."

"I'm going to send you a file, and I want you to print it out for me, using whatever high-quality photographic program you have, okay? Just set it aside—don't show it to anyone. Can you do this?"

"Yeah, sure. I can do that. You gonna tell me what it's about?"

"I'll tell you later."

"Fine. Be that way."

Next she phoned Nelda at the *Post.*

"Garrulitis," the gravel-voiced columnist answered.

"Nelda, it's Pezzini. I need more dirt."

"What kinda dirt?"

"Scott Chalmers. I interviewed wife number three. What can you tell me about wives one and two?"

Nelda lowered her voice to a conspiratorial rumble. "I

146

try and light a cigarette in here, they unload with the firehose. This about the samurai murders?"

"Could be."

"Can you meet me?"

Sara agreed to meet her at four P.M. at the Java Jungle in the Pergament Building. She returned to the e-mails. The first threat appeared on December 7:

I know who you are. I know where you live. Stop bidding on the sword. Stone Flower is mine. Kagemusha.

How nice, she thought. *He even signed his name.* "Shadow Warrior." The e-mail was from a Hotmail account—anybody could start a Hotmail account in any name, and send it from anywhere. No help there.

The second threat appeared in mid-January, after Chalmers had purchased the sword.

I know who you are. I know where you live. I warned you. Kagemusha.

Sara accessed the database of daily complaints for that month, searching for something from Chalmers. Surely a good citizen like Chalmers, a friend of the mayor, would do the right thing and notify the police. Nada. If Chalmers read the threats, there was no evidence that he took them seriously. Perhaps he'd notified building security, or his internet provider.

Sara studied the e-mails for another hour, but there were no further revelations. At three-thirty, she packed up, grabbed her umbrella, and headed uptown toward the Pergament Building.

The Java Jungle was set on the mezzanine overlooking the lobby, a pert fern bar decorated with balsa parrots and palm trees, a real parrot in a cage behind the bar. "ARRR! *BITE* ME, MATIE!" it greeted Sara. She arrived early, grabbed a plush sofa in the back, and flipped through the *Times* until Garrulitis arrived, burdened like a bag lady.

The gossip columnist plumped down in the overstuffed chair opposite and hoisted her bulging briefcase on the table. It clanked. "Did you see that cunning little notions store on the ground floor? They have the apple coring machine I've been looking for."

"I'm so glad. What are you having?"

"I'll buy. I have an expense account."

"In that case, I'll have a double mocha latte."

Garrulitis rose and placed the orders. She was a broad-shouldered woman who alternated between lush and plump. She returned with two drinks, two forks, and a slice of raspberry cheesecake. "We'll split it," she said, sitting down.

A wild thrill rocked Sara's world. Cheesecake! She had to do it, for the sake of the job. Emitting great smacking noises and grunts of satisfaction, they ate the cheesecake.

"Okay," Garrulitis said, wiping her mouth with a napkin. "Chalmers' first wife was the former Miss Patricia Willoughby, society dame; father's Brian Willoughby of Abercrombie, Lusk, and Hanig—old Wall Street firm. They married in 1990—he was thirty, she was twenty-nine. Divorced in 1992, citing irreconcilable differences. Word is, he was playing around. He traveled a lot, had a girl in every port. There was no pre-nup, she got a very generous settlement, and today is working on husband number three, Otto Kruger."

"Not the type to bear a grudge?"

"No. But wait. Wife number two is more interesting. She is the former Miss Erika Madureira, a Brazilian model, whom he married on a junket to Rio in 1995. He was thirty-three, she was twenty-two. Apparently, Erika was the high-maintenance type, and something of a drama queen—altogether, a handful. She signed a pre-nup, then contested it. It was a bitter, ugly divorce. She used Albert Kammer. He used Sidney Mellon. The lawyers made out like bandits. Details of the settlement were undisclosed, but word is she got about five mil, and she still badmouths him every chance she gets."

Yeah, Sara thought. But she's unlikely to sneak into his penthouse at night and lop his head off. On the other hand, perhaps Kagemusha was her agent. On the other hand, perhaps Kagemusha was just an inconsequential Internet pest, and had nothing to do with the murder. "Where's Erika now?"

"Twenty blocks uptown, in her condo at the Wisconsin."

Sara raised her eyebrows in appreciation of the toney address, also home to several rock stars and minor British royalty. Perhaps a visit to Miss Madureira was in order.

"Guess who's invited to Gracie Mansion," Sara confided.

"Dish, girl. Dish."

Sara pointed at herself with all her fingers. "Moi."

Garrulitis' mouth formed a perfect "o." "What's the deal?"

Sara told her about the invite.

"That figures. Chalmers and Hizzoner were tight. Be careful, girl. Once you get their attention they can hurt you. So. You seeing anyone?"

A sly grin crept on to Sara's face. Garrulitis zeroed in

like an FBI sniper. "You are, aren't you? Dish, girl. Who is he? How did you meet him?"

"He's a professional sword polisher. I just met him last week."

"A what?"

Sara explained. Garrulitis expressed amazement that anyone made a living at such an arcane craft. Sara extracted a promise from Garrulitis not to spill the details of her social life on Page Six, while promising in return to give the gossip columnist an exclusive on some aspect of the investigation.

Sara took the bus to Brooklyn, switched twice to get to Brooklyn Yamaha. It was five-thirty when she arrived, and they were closing the doors. The manager recognized her and let her in. The new Warrior was on the showroom floor, and she paused to run her fingers over its sleek aluminum frame. No way. Not her style. She was strictly a toes down kind of girl.

Clancy Imada was in his office off the service bay. "Hi," he said. "Have a seat. Is this what you're looking for?"

He handed her a series of color computer printouts showing the sword. "I gotta say, you've piqued my interest. What's this about, the samurai killings?"

Sara slumped in her plastic chair. "What else? Do me a favor, willya? Don't tell anyone about this."

Imada put a finger to his lips. "I haven't told a soul. No one has seen those but me. And if someone did see them, they'd probably chalk it up to my crazy kamikaze nationalism."

"Long live the emperor and all that?"

Imada locked his hands behind his head and leaned

back in his executive lounger. "Not my style. I'm Brooklyn-born and bred. Ah'm an Amurican, gundamnit! When we gonna go for a ride?"

"Soon's I bust this case, Clancy. And thanks."

CHAPTER

TWELVE

Wednesday afternoon, surprisingly, beckoned dry and bright. Sara took the bike and arrived at the Wisconsin at 1:15. She chained the bike to the portico pillar, showed her badge to the doorman, and went inside. Erika Madureira lived on the twelfth floor of the historic Restoration wedding cake, next door to a reclusive British rock star who'd made his millions in the seventies. Sara had hoped to arrive unannounced, but the doorman must have phoned Madureira, because the door was open the limit of its chain when Sara stepped off the elevator. A pair of kohl-rimmed eyes looked out suspiciously.

Sara showed her badge. "Erika Madureira?"

"Yes?"

"Sara Pezzini, Eleventh Precinct. May I come in? It's about your former husband."

"What about him?"

"He was murdered. I'm in charge of the investigation."

"I know he was murdered. I had nothing to do with it."

"Miss Madureira, will you let me in? I only want to ask you some questions. You are not under suspicion."

"Do I need a lawyer?"

A seal-point Siamese darted out the door. "Willie!" the former model cried. Without thinking, Sara swooped down and scooped up the wayward tabby, handing it back to its owner through the narrow opening.

Madureira took the cat cooing and shut the door. A moment later, it opened. "All right. You may come in."

Madureira was unexpectedly tall, with a puffy, rumpled face that had been lifted at least once. Her curly dark brown hair hung in her eyes, telltale gray peeking out. She wore a quilted floor-length lavender housecoat and kept one hand at her throat, to close the collar, or to prevent anything from escaping. "Come. Come into the living room. I will make coffee. You drink coffee, yes?"

"Yes, please."

Madureira went into the small but complete kitchen adjacent to the living room while the Siamese twined between Sara's legs. The living room looked like it had been tossed and hurriedly thrown back together. There were copies of *Islands*, *Destinations*, *Vanity Fair*, *Cosmo*, and the *Crump Catalog* on the rosewood coffee table.

"I was very shocked to learn about Scott. Very shocked. We were not close, but still."

"You weren't still angry with your ex-husband?"

The ex-model barked. It was meant to be a laugh. "Life is too short to harbor grudges! I don't deny that we got along terribly, and that it was probably a mistake for me to marry him. I should have just slept with him and let him buy me a Mercedes. But, no. I had to let him make me a 'respectable woman.' He changed completely once

153

we were married. No more Mr. Nice Guy. He was very controlling, very jealous. At the same time, he was jetting all over the Western Hemisphere, sleeping with every stewardess in sight."

"Was he always that way?"

"Probably. We live as man and wife for two years, I hardly know him. He was so private, so peculiar. And he worshiped the ancient samurai. He wished he'd been born Japanese."

"Have you ever heard of someone called Kagemusha?"

"Who?"

"A man signing himself Kagemusha sent Mr. Chalmers threatening e-mails involving a Japanese sword both were bidding on. It was an online auction. Mr. Chalmers bought the sword, but it was stolen when he was murdered. It's quite possible that the thief was after the sword and had no interest in your ex, except that he got in the way."

"Scott was no hero, I can tell you that. He shrank at the prospect of physical confrontation. That's one of the things that soured me on him. In Brazil, we expect our men to fight!"

"Are you thinking of some particular incident?"

Madureira fished in the pocket of her housecoat, coming up with a red and gold package of Dunhill's. She shook one out, lit it with a gold turbo-lighter, puffed up a head of steam. "Several. But no one who would bear a grudge. The only one who would bear a grudge, in all those confrontations, was Scott. *He* would bear a grudge. But he would be too cowardly to act on it."

Sara considered Madureira too disorganized to plan so precise a crime, let alone carry it out. She gave the ex-model her card, and asked Madureira to call if she learned anything.

Sharpe's Hayabusa was in the motor pool when Sara arrived. Parking her bike next to his, she took the rear steps to the detective's bullpen on the second floor. Someone had glued a glow-in-the-dark Creature from the Black Lagoon to her desk with the word balloon, "DETECTIVE PEZZINI! YOU ARE INVITED TO THE MONSTERS' BALL! PLEASE RSVP INTERNAL AFFAIRS."

Gripping the Creature with both hands, she tore it loose, noting that her desktop was becoming pock-marked with glue craters. The bottom drawer was nearly filled. Time to cart the lot over to the Children's Burn Unit.

She turned to Chalmers' e-mails. They were alternately tedious and fascinating. Chalmers had carried on endless chitchat with a variety of pals all over the world. He traded online. Most of it was meaningless, but a number of exchanges had to do with the sword. The most notable were to a correspondent named Tadashi, in Indonesia:

Dear Tadashi: Eat your heart out! I just bought Stone Flower for one and a half mil. Be nice and I may show it to you when you come visit. Scott.

Dear Scott: The black flame of envy curls my heart. But I am happy for you, my old friend. I look forward to viewing this marvel. Tadashi.

There were numerous in that vein. She looked up. Sharpe appeared briefly in the doorframe to the stairwell as he headed down. On impulse, Sara sprang to her feet and went after him.

"Hey, Derek!" she called, as he was halfway to the street.

He paused, turned, his face breaking into a wide grin. "Oh, hi! How's the hunt for the samurai killer?"

She caught up with him, standing on a higher stair so she could look him in the eye. "I'm developing some leads. Say, I saw you kick Bratten to the curb yesterday. Man, where did you learn to fight like that?"

"In Japan. I feel a little bad about that. I probably went too far, but that pretty boy was shooting off his mouth. I remember when he came to Toyko for an exhibition game. That mack act doesn't go down well in Japan."

"What's up at Hecht Gardens?"

"Place has been real quiet, but we're coming up on a World Trade Organization meeting, and it's bound to get hit."

"Surely Hecht employs private security."

"Oh yeah, he's got Judson all over the place. Those guys make less than airport screeners, spend most of their time getting high or co-oping."

"What do you know about this soiree he's got planned for next week?"

Sharpe rolled his eyes. "That's going to be a real shanglally. He's holding it in the lobby of the Hecht Center for the Performing Arts. They're working 'round the clock to finish it up. It's going right down to the wire. I got myself assigned to security that night. You going to be there?"

Sara batted her eyelashes. "Why, yes I am. I feel better just knowing you'll be on duty, Officer Sharpe."

"Flattery will get you everywhere."

Sara crossed her arms and parked one hip against the wall. "Anything on the Romeros yet?"

"They don't seem to be involved in any major criminal activity. Brooklyn Gangs tell me it's more of a social group, and gave me a list of a dozen members, half of whom are either deceased or moved on into adulthood without incident. Candido's got no record to speak of, works as a gypsy carpenter for some Russkis, renovating old warehouses."

"Thanks, Derek."

"No problema. Let's go for a ride one of these days."

"I'd enjoy that. We'll talk at the party, if not before."

Sara returned to her desk, then stopped. She felt a chill, a surge of negative energy down her spine. Selzer, the Internal Affairs zombie, was staring at her from the far entrance. Seeing her looking at him, he turned and left.

Under the rules of conduct, if she had sufficient reason to suspect a fellow officer of a felony, she was supposed to file a report with Internal Affairs. In reality, such reports were few and far between, usually filed by sore losers on their way out. No cop would finger a fellow cop, even a crooked one, to Internal Affairs. No way was she going to put her suspicions before Selzer. The man had been sent by Central Casting. He was a cold fish with Coke-bottle lenses and a buzzcut. His cheap sports jacket had pills on the lapel.

Nope. If she wanted to know what was in Sharpe's place, she'd have to toss it herself.

Sharpe lived in a town house at 454 Huron Place on Staten Island. Checking the duty roster, Sara learned that

Sharpe was moonlighting as a security guard at Hecht Gardens. Nothing wrong with that, plenty of cops did it. It spoke to his enthusiasm—the guy was willing to spend his off-hours looking for perps. Might as well get paid for it. At five, she left her desk, donned her jacket, backpack, unlocked her bike, and put on her helmet. Sharpe's bike was already gone.

At five o'clock on a June afternoon, Manhattan resembled a giant puzzle, like one of those sliding checkerboards filled with letters, one missing. In other words, gridlock. Traffic moved in tiny increments, inching here, honking there, gesturing and threatening everywhere. Sara took full advantage of her bike, splitting lanes, cutting corners, fighting her way south to the tip of the island and the Staten Island Ferry. She walked her bike into the hold, setting the kickstand between two vinyl-wrapped pillars. She wished Yamaha would wise up and put center stands on all their sport bikes. The silly little kickstands almost seemed designed to fail. Sara decided to stay with her bike rather than mingle. Smelling of the sea, the hold conducted a discordant symphony of squeaks and groans. Faint odor of deep-fried clams trickled down from the concessionaires.

She needn't have worried. The ferry was steady as bedrock and her bike hardly shifted at all, not even when the ferry slugged the pier twenty minutes later. Sara put her helmet on before zipping between the cars to the front of the line. She was first off once the ramp was lowered. She was gone by the time the first car hit the pavement.

She'd already found the appropriate map of Staten Island, mounted it in the clear plastic pouch atop her tank bag with Sharpe's address circled. Fifteen minutes later, she found it: A new development on its own dead-end circle, neat little two-story townhouses, each with its own attached one-car garage. Although the houses were planted cheek-by-jowl, they were designed in such a way as to give the illusion of privacy. Sara tucked her bike right into Sharpe's alcove and locked the front wheel.

Although no one was watching, Sara went through the motions of knocking on the door and ringing the buzzer. She placed her right hand on the knob. Immediately above it was a dead bolt. Breathing deeply to relax, she channeled her energy into her right hand, into the Witchblade. She formed a mental image of the door swinging inward.

There was a tingling on her wrist and when she looked down, her hand was buried in a metal apparatus. It might have been a glove, but the index finger extended into the keyhole and the deadbolt. There was a click, and the door swung inward. Sara slipped inside, shut the door, and stood with her back to it trying to still the rush of blood in her ears.

She was breathing hard. She had just committed breaking and entering. Other cops, sad to say, could commit minor felonies without blinking an eyelash. There were tons of studies comparing the psychology of cops and criminals, finding them similar. Not Sara. For as long as she could remember, she had a burning need to right wrongs. Not that a mere technical felony put her in a fainting spell. But it was against a fellow cop, someone she liked and admired, and she wasn't used to breaking the law.

Gradually, her beating heart stilled and she listened.

She heard the compressor in the refrigerator, the whoosh of air through the ventilation system, the tick of an old clock in the living room. She looked down. She wore high-topped Adidas black sneakers. Safe enough. She wore a latex glove on her left hand. Except for the kitchenette, the first floor was carpeted and consisted of a high-ceiling living room looking out on a tiny, fence-enclosed back patio. There were two stone Japanese lanterns on plinths in the back yard, along with a tiny koi pond. Sara would have bet money there were fish in the pond.

The living room was sparely but elegantly decorated with Japanese brush paintings, an Hiroshige print, and a couple of black-and-white Ansel Adams prints of the Grand Canyon. And, of course, the swords. There they were, mounted on a credenza, without so much as a plexiglass case or man-eating tiger to protect them. A wakizashi and a tanto. Sara could tell they were valuable just by looking at them. The hilt was wrapped in ray skin, and finished in leather wrapping. The silver menuki depicted a fish.

She stepped closer, but didn't touch them. "Well, either these aren't the murder weapons, or he's incredibly stupid for hanging them in plain sight."

The voices of the Witchblade chuckled ominously in her head.

The downstairs bathroom was tidy and held no surprises. Nor did the kitchen. Sara used only the gloved left hand in opening drawers and cupboards. Sharpe had a couple bottles of saki socked away, otherwise appeared to be a teetotaler.

She crept carefully up the stairs to the second floor.

There were two bedrooms and a bath. Sharpe used one of the bedrooms for his office.

It was here Sara found the safe. It was a full-size Sheffield, tucked into the closet, and it was locked. Sara scanned the office first. A desk, with a computer. How she would have loved to boot it up and try to get in. But that would have left a record, one a clever cop could easily discover.

Photo of a man taped to the shelf—stylin' dude with California hair, tennis whites, grinning like a box of Wheaties. Carefully, using her gloved hand, Sara removed it and turned it over. TO THE SAMURAI, FROM SURFER DUDE. No signature.

There was a leather address book on the desk. Sara went methodically through it. Most of the entrants were old, and lived in California. One was circled three times: Ralph Munster. Ralph at work, Justine and Associates, old-line Wall Street investments. Sharpe's banker pal. She found his card lying on the desk and took it. She put the photo back.

She leafed through the stack of papers on the desk. Mostly police work, plus some correspondence with pals, none of it of much interest. Copies of *The New Yorker* and *Law Enforcement Monthly*. Burning with impatience, she forced herself to go methodically through the contents of the desk. There was nothing that would connect the tall cop to the samurai killings other than his Asian tastes. She even checked the titles on his bookshelf, pulling out each volume to look for hidden compartments.

Finally, she turned her attention to the safe. It was six feet tall and made of reinforced, carbonized steel, dark green with the Sheffield logo painted in old-fashioned gold leaf script on the front. Planting her feet at shoulder width, Sara willed herself to relax and extended her right hand. Her palm immediately began to tingle, as if she'd slapped it hard against a flat surface. Her hand flew to the dial of its own volition, abruptly encased in shiny metal. Whatever was in the safe, it beckoned to the Witchblade and vice versa. She turned the tumblers like a kid playing table hockey.

Click, click, click, the thing unlocked. She pulled the heavy door toward her on silent, well-oiled hinges. Her eyes settled first on the guns. The black nylon stock of the AR-15, the bulldog body of the Heckler & Koch MP5A3, the pistol-stocked Ithaca pump-action twelve gauge. Either Sharpe was a serious collector or he was planning an insurrection. Sara knew a lot of cops were gun nuts, but Sharpe hadn't seemed the type. For some reason, she felt a vague disappointment.

Next to the guns, held vertically in place by a series of cotton sashes, were six long narrow bundles wrapped in cotton rags. Sara knew what she would find even before she unwrapped the first bundle. A spasm of apprehension had settled in her neck, but her hand was alive with a mind of its own. She had to restrain it from unwrapping the bundle too fast.

She set the bundle flat on the floor of the office and unwrapped it carefully. And there it was. A long sword, a daito, housed in a black-lacquered wood scabbard, with mountings through two rings. There were four bundles in the safe, counting the one on the floor. A string of obscenities bubbled from her lips. Not Sharpe.

It was all circumstantial, unless she could match one of Sharpe's blades to one of the missing swords, or somehow match striations produced by one of his blades to the neck wounds of the victims. Carefully, she grabbed the sword by the handle and the scabbard and drew it part way out. Even in the pale evening light, the blade gleamed and shimmered like a thing alive. Unfortunately, she knew from David that the blade's creator had signed his name on the tang, beneath the wrappings. The sword's peg seemed to be buried beneath the ancient silk handle wrapping, and she didn't want to risk damaging the several hundred-year-old handle to take a look. She doubted her ability to render the Japanese characters accurately. The best she could do would be to make detailed notes of the blades' appearances, and see if they matched descriptions of the stolen swords. She kicked herself for not bringing a camera.

Then what? How could she introduce evidence and get a search warrant? Sharpe was completely above suspicion. He was a cop. She was committing a felony by tossing his apartment. Working swiftly, she unwrapped each blade and made a series of detailed descriptions in her notepad, including sketches of the handles and the points. None were Stone Flower. She drew with her right hand, which again behaved as if it had a mind of its own. Her drawings were uncannily neat and accurate.

She knew points were all-important in determining a blade's origin. She was extremely careful not to touch any part of the blade itself, and not to let the blade touch the ground. She pointed the tip of the blade toward the light and peered at it from the pommel, as David had taught her. She balanced the blades carefully on a book to lift them off the floor while she sketched. Finally, she returned all the blades to where they had been, in the proper order.

There was a safe within the safe, a recessed wall cabinet. She opened the door and found a Glock .45 inside with a barrel-mounted laser—typical macho toy—and a series of manila envelopes. She took out a manila envelope, opened the unsealed end, and shook out a series of eight by ten black and white glossies. A man clad in S&M leather, studded dog collar, zippered mask, more belts and straps than a gladiator, chained spread-eagled to a bed. Sara felt a lurch, as if her plane had hit a vacuum, a sickening feeling in the pit of her stomach. She looked at the rest. They were similar. Some were worse.

She told herself it could be crime evidence. She told herself some men had harmless fantasies. But she could not tell herself that the man chained and shackled in one of the photographs wasn't Sharpe. And if that was him, someone else was taking the picture.

CHAPTER

THIRTEEN

Thursday promised to be one of those "hot town, summer in the city" days of which the Lovin' Spoonful sang. Sara could feel it lying in bed at six-thirty in the morning. Her apartment was old, and the only air conditioning came from what she could cram in the window. Her own unit was currently in storage in the basement because it took up too much space when it wasn't running. She'd have to haul it up and put it in. She'd have to do it before she left for work if she didn't want to return to an oven.

Sighing, she got up, washed her face, put on some old jeans and a sweatshirt, her beat-up hiking shoes, grabbed a pair of canvas gloves and descended five flights to the basement, where she had a storage space among many others, protected by a Master padlock. The basement was dark and filthy. She got the lock open and wrestled the air conditioner close to the door, but no way would she be able to cart it up single-handed. It wasn't the weight. She could handle the weight. It was just too awkward. She needed another set of hands. Where would she find one in this zoo? There was Matt, the janitor, but he was

165

likely still sleeping it off, and he looked as if he'd keel over from a thrombo any day.

Frustrated, Sara ascended to ground level, forcing open the creaking service door at the back of the corridor and stalking out into the foyer in search of muscle. And there, parked by the curb in his '79 Chevy, was Jorgé. When she got to the car she saw that Jorgé was sleeping, his seatback reclined, legs up on the dash, wearing Ray-bans and a raspberry beret. The windows were open. She reached in and shook his leg.

He came awake with a start. "Huh? Whassup?"

"Jorgé. What are you doing here?"

He looked at her, took off the shades, rubbed his eyes with a fist, put the shades back on. He lay back for a minute until juice reached the sparkplugs. "Officer Pezzini. Jes' doin' what we discussed, lookin' out for the folks."

"You've been sleeping out here all night?"

He glanced at his fake Rolex. "Since about four—that's when I called it quits. I figure the people know my ride, nobody's gonna try anything with me out front."

The only people who ever tried anything were Los Romeros, Sara thought. But she smiled. "You're just the man I want to see. Help me carry my air conditioner up from the basement and I'll buy you an Egg McMuffin."

"Sure, okay. Jes' give me a minute to get my stuff together."

"I'm in the basement."

Sara returned to the basement, eyeing a box full of vinyl records that had belonged to her father. Might be worth something on eBay, she thought. Moments later, Jorgé appeared at the end of the dusty corridor.

"Yo, mamacita! Where you at?"

"Down here."

Together, they carried the air conditioner out of the storage locker. Jorgé held it while Sara set the lock, insisted on carrying it solo to the freight elevator at the back of the building. She let him show off. It was too hot to argue. He mounted the thing in her bedroom window, accepted a cold Diet Pepsi.

"What's that on your arm?" she asked.

Jorgé looked down. "Which arm?"

"The right one."

He stared at his biceps. "Our Lord and Saviour Jesus Christ."

"What's on your stomach?"

He peered at her, half-smiling through his bandito mustache. "You really want to see?"

"Sure. Don't be bashful."

Jorgé peeled off his muscle shirt. He had the hard, lean body of a greyhound, ribs you could climb like a ladder, six-pack like rolled naugahyde. A heavy crucifix was tattooed on his abdomen, its base in his groin.

"The Lord's cross. I got a skull on my right arm." He turned.

Sara made a little spinning motion with her finger. "Forget the skull. Are you a Christian?"

"I'm Catholic. Most us Boricua are Catholic. Aintchoo? I mean, you bein' Italian and all."

"Yeah, I am, although it's been a long time since I've been to confession."

"Me too, chiquita!"

"You're a gangbanger."

Jorgé started to protest, but Sara held her hand up and

continued. "I'm a cop. I appreciate this turnaround you've pulled off, but I'm not sure what's behind it. I don't believe in miracles. Now anything you've done in the past, I don't want to know, unless it becomes a police issue. I guess what I'm saying is, I'm suspicious. I've been a cop a while, and in my experience, hardened street criminals very seldom change direction. You know what I mean?"

Jorgé listened with an open face that reminded Sara of a dog. "I ain't no hardened street criminal."

"You look like one. The way you wear those pants, drooping down to your butt, that's prison-style. You can understand where loud music and hanging out on the stoop would scare some of the residents."

"Oh sure, that's what I'm tellin' you, chiquita, I'm down with what you're sayin'. I know there ain't no future in hangin' out, dealin' a little dope from time to time—not to say I done it! I mean, I know people who do, but I don't consider them hardcore street criminals."

"See, then we got a problem. I catch anybody selling, doing, or holding dope on these premises, and I personally will make sure they go away for a long time."

Jorgé stared at her for a minute with large liquid eyes. "Okay."

"Okay?"

"Yeah, okay. I mean, what the hell? I'm twenty-six. I got to think of my future."

"That's right. Thought what you're going to do?"

"I don't know. I'm a pretty good carpenter, but man, trying to get into the union . . . "

"I hear you. Maybe I can help. In the meantime, I want you to do something for me."

"What's that, pretty lady?"

"Think about what you want to do for a living that's

legal. I have to kick you out now while I get ready for work." She was glad she didn't say *Think about what you want to be when you grow up.*

"Happy to oblige. Say. How's about you and me checkin' out this salsa band over at La Hacienda Saturday night?"

She smiled, placed a hand on his gleaming bicep. "I'm sorry. I'm seeing someone."

Brave smile. "Tha's okay. You get bored with him sooner or later." She watched him swagger down the hall toward the elevator.

Lupé watched in disbelief and fury from her bedroom window as the witch roused her man from his car. Twenty-five minutes later, her fury metastasized into murderous intent. She'd been holding off, out of fear of acting too soon. Too soon after the last debacle. Not this time.

This time the witch would die, and her faithless lover, too.

Sara arrived at her desk by nine. There was a message from Brandon Stern: HIS HONOR IS VERY KEEN TO HEAR OF THE LATEST DEVELOPMENTS IN THE CHALMERS INVESTIGATION. PLEASE CONTACT SOONEST. DON'T FORGET TO R.S.V.P.

Sighing, Sara RSVP'd before turning on her word processor and preparing a report for the mayor. As if she didn't have anything better to do. She said that she had interviewed Chalmers' wife and at least one of his ex-wives, and ruled them out as potentials, but that Chalmers had been receiving harassing e-mails regarding the sword. She was checking these out.

There was nothing in the report about Sharpe.

It was time to beard the lion in his den. Specifically, it was time to call on Robert Hotchkiss. It was Sara's experience that persons of social standing would often cooperate rather than embarrass themselves in front of their colleagues.

Hotchkiss worked for the Dynasty Group, with offices in Hecht's Twelve South Plaza. Sara left her bike at the station and caught a ride uptown with a Cheetah Express driver. He dropped her off right in front. Sara carried a leather Haverhill briefcase as camouflage. In taupe Armani slacks, olive ribbed cotton short-sleeved pullover, and khaki jacket, she was indistinguishable from hordes of other bright young things on the make. The Dynasty Group was on the twelfth floor. The receptionist stared at Sara's badge as if it were the Hope diamond.

"Point me to Mr. Hotchkiss, please, and don't say anything. I will be discreet."

The receptionist pointed. Hotchkiss was on the phone when Sara appeared in his office doorway, to his astonishment. First he was pleased, then flummoxed, finally distressed when he recognized her.

"Phil, I'll have to call you back." He hung up. "Come in and shut the door, please. What can I do for you?"

"Mr. Hotchkiss, I'm aware that you're involved in divorce proceedings, and I understand your need for discretion. But this is a homicide investigation. I believe you phoned in the tip about Bachman's death. I believe you went there that morning to discuss with him the sale of a sword your father brought back from Iwo Jima."

Hotchkiss stared at her for a minute, then leaned his elbows on his desk and buried his face in his hands. "You have no idea the strain I've been under."

"Tell me what happened," Sara said softly.

"You're right. Bachman was handling a sword for me. My father brought it back from the war. He was a Marine sergeant. I never told Janet about it. Janet. That's my soon-to-be bitch of an ex-wife. I'm leveraged to my eyeballs. She finds out, or her attorney, they'll go after it. I got two kids in college. I got a nut you wouldn't believe."

"I feel for you, Mr. Hotchkiss. I'll try and keep your name out of it, but it would be helpful if you told me what happened when you discovered the body. Everything you can remember. There's a murderer running around."

"I know. All right. Hang on." He picked up his phone and instructed the secretary they were not to be disturbed. "My father found the sword in a cave on Mt. Surabachi. Technically, they weren't supposed to bring this stuff back but everyone was doing it. He used to bring it out and show it at parties. He stopped showing it in the early seventies; he knew it was worth something. He died in 1989. I had the sword in the basement, never thought about it until recently. I took it in to Bachman to be appraised."

"It's my understanding that sword appraisers are few and far between."

"That's right. Bachman couldn't issue a certificate, but he knew enough to recognize what it was. He said he could find a buyer."

"What was it?"

"The swordsmith was Muramasa. Apparently, there are two distinct lines of Muramasas. This was the later one, who was active in the fifteenth century. I'd been keeping the sword in a safety deposit box here at Dynasty since my father's death. I took it in to Bachman two weeks ago. Last week, I'd made an appointment to discuss the terms of the sale. Bachman was nervous, because technically, the sword is considered a cultural treasure of Japan, and they have successfully sued to get them back. There's a huge black market for the things."

"Did he have a buyer in mind?"

"Yes, but he wouldn't tell me over the phone. I got there around ten o'clock and the place seemed closed. Nobody answered the bell, but the gate was unlocked when I tried it. So I went in. I didn't notice the blood until I fell on my ass. I nearly fainted. It's the most shocking thing I've ever witnessed. It's the worst thing that's ever happened to me."

If that's the worst thing that's ever happened to you, Sara thought, *you are one lucky bastard.* "Tell me exactly what happened."

Hotchkiss walked her through his grisly discovery. He ran a hand through his thinning hair. "And there on the counter was the head, planted on the receipts spindle."

"Do you know Scott Chalmers?"

"I've met him a couple times. I wouldn't say we were close friends."

"How do you know James Bratten?"

"Dynasty maintains a skybox at Apple Stadium. Bratten came to us for a loan. I'm his loan officer, and I've always been a huge Apples fan. And the Jets. And the Yankees."

"What about the Giants and the Mets?"

Hotchkiss shrugged. "Screw 'em. I can't be all things to all people."

Sara smiled in spite of herself. "You did place the nine-one-one."

Hotchkiss nodded. "Pay phone in the Café Belladonna.

I don't suppose . . . if you find my sword, there's any chance you could return it to me?"

"After the disposition of the case, you can petition to have it returned from the police evidence lab. However, that's open to the public, so your wife might find out."

" 'Might.' There's no might about it."

"Who's her lawyer?"

"Elron Dubuis."

"You have my sympathies. I would appreciate copies of any documentation you have concerning the sword. I'd also like pictures, drawings, descriptions, anything like that."

Hotchkiss leaned forward, opened the bottom right drawer of his desk and began to rummage. Sara looked around. Pictures of his two kids, smiling, fresh-faced boy and girl. Pictures of the treacherous wife had been removed. Pictures of Hotchkiss and some pals on a golf course. Certificates of achievement and appreciation. A crystal ball. *Be nice if it worked,* she thought. *We could have avoided this mess.*

Hotchkiss handed her a legal envelope with Bachman's old-fashioned script. "There's the description he gave me last week."

"I don't understand. If he had the sword, and you had the description, why did you go visit him?"

"He said he had a buyer, but he didn't feel comfortable discussing it over the phone."

"Why not?"

"He was a peculiar man. For example, do you know he had a bagel and cream cheese, a grapefruit, and a vanilla yogurt for breakfast every morning?"

"I don't see what's so strange about that."

"Every morning of his life, for thirty-five years, without exception?"

"It's odd. I grant you. But I don't see why he was afraid to mention the buyer's name to you over the phone."

"I don't know. Maybe he thought his phones were bugged."

Sara's eyes opened imperceptibly. "Thank you, Mr. Hotchkiss."

At the precinct, Sara phoned Bachman's. No one answered. Leesha had probably arranged for the body to be shipped to Newton for burial. Sara left work at four o'clock, overnight kit bungeed to the back of the bike and crammed into her tank bag, and headed toward the Village. Yellow police tape still sealed the entrance to Bachman's shop, but the place was no longer guarded. Sara had requisitioned the key from evidence. Pulling onto the curb, she tucked the bike in close to the building, removed her helmet and locked it to the frame. She locked her bike, went up the steps, and unlocked the front gate. A different key unlocked the hand-carved double doors.

The place smelled faintly of antiseptic and dried blood. Sara switched on the lights in the shop and stood in the doorway for a minute. The place seemed to have been left untouched since the technicians left, the antiques all still in place. At some point, someone would have to take inventory, if only for dispersal of the estate. The phone was behind the counter, next to where the killer had planted Bachman's head. It was a Radio Shack voice recorder. The lab had already analyzed the tape. Nothing helpful. Sara pushed the announce button.

"Greetings," said a dry voice with a touch of Europe. "You have reached Thaddeus Bachman, specializing in Oriental antiquities. I regret no one is present to take your call right now, but if you leave a message, someone will get back to you. Our office hours are from nine A.M. to five-thirty P.M., Monday through Friday. Special hours by appointment. Thank you."

She turned the phone over and, using a tiny screwdriver attached to her keychain, unscrewed the base. She examined the phone closely, but found nothing resembling a bug. Next, she traced the line back to the wall, went out into the hall to the elevator. Bound to be a transfer box in the basement. If a crook had access, he could put the bug there. The elevator opened at her touch. She stepped into the tiny booth, pushed the button for the basement, and waited for the nictitating door to close.

The elevator descended groaning, like an old janitor complaining about his arthritis. The basement was surprisingly well lit with fluorescent fixtures, and consisted of row after row of storage locker jammed with cardboard boxes, rolled rugs, coddled paintings, a lifetime of collecting. Sara found the exchange box. There was only one line into the house, with a phone on each floor. There was no bug.

Sara went to the second floor, which housed a library and what appeared to be a guestroom, where Leesha had spent the night. The soap in the guest bath was still damp. Sara went through the whole house but could find no evidence of a bug. She looked behind the pictures. She looked beneath the tables, chairs, and desks. Nada.

Finally, conceding defeat, she called it quits. Going methodically through the house, making sure she left everything as she found it, she let herself out the front door, locked it, closed the gate and locked that. She turned and gazed across the street, at the little sword polisher sign beneath The Feldstein Gallery. She looked up. A tailor advertised in the second floor windows. The third floor appeared to be residential, blinds open, except for one window, open perhaps one third, on a darkened room.

You could bug someone without even entering the house by shining a laser on a window. The window acts as a speaker membrane—much like the eardrum—vibrating with whatever sound is produced inside. The bounced laser beam comes back, faithfully recording every sound. Apprehension mixed with excitement, Sara crossed the street. Instead of going down into the tiny alcove that serviced Kopkind, she went up the broad granite stair to the arched Roman entrance, into the elegant little foyer, the door to the Feldstein Gallery open, garrulous customers inside. Behind a glass, the building's occupants were listed in white plastic letters. Kopkind. Feldstein. Art the Tailor. Grossman the Accountant. The third floor contained two private apartments: Bloomberg and Andersen. The building was managed by the Chalmers Group, Scott Chalmers' management company.

Head swirling, Sara stepped out into the late afternoon sunshine. She was certain that the apartment with the slightly open window was vacant. She didn't believe in coincidence. Chalmers had been gaga for swords. Perhaps he had been Hotchkiss' mystery buyer. But why the subterfuge?

She glanced at her watch. She was actually fifteen minutes late for her date with David. She'd warned him she was coming over early to shower and get ready. She descended to the basement shop and entered through the tingling door. Yoshi appeared, followed a moment later by a smiling David, slightly disheveled.

"Hi! Make yourself at home." He glanced at her closely. "You look like you're either on the verge of a great discovery, or you've lost your mind."

"The former, I hope. I'll tell you about it."

"Good. Because I have a story for you, too. Take your time. I've got three hundred strokes to go."

"David, can I stash my bike in your workroom?"

"Sure. I'll go open the door."

She went outside, brought the bike around, threaded through the gate and door and parked it in a corner of his workroom. She looked for the sword on which he was working, but couldn't see it. Unclipping her leather overnighter, she disappeared into the bathroom.

Sara showered, toweled off, and changed. They were going to a jazz club, not a party, so she'd brought a pair of jeans and matching jacket, and wore an emerald-colored silk T. Finally, the make-up, a minimalist operation, thank her lucky stars. A touch of blush, a flash of Cover Girl goglam! Gem, a smear of Neutrogena, hey, presto! She was transformed from gorgeous to spectacular. The Armani Ella was last to go on, in Certain Strategic Spots.

She turned off the fan and opened the door. "In here," David called from the living room. She entered. Kopkind, who'd been standing at his entertainment console loading CDs, took one look, slapped his forehead, and leaped off his feet like Dagwood Bumstead confronted with a conundrum. He landed on his back in a perfect judo roll, slapping the carpet, but maintaining his cartoon characterization.

"Whoo! Whoo!" he barked, like the wolf in a Betty Boop cartoon.

Sara was pleased, couldn't help blushing. "Okay, come on, get up. You've seen me all dolled up before."

Kopkind got to his feet, a goofy grin on his face. He wore khakis and an olive green coarse weave cotton shirt, neatly tucked and held in place with a leather belt. "I thought we'd have a glass of wine before heading over. It's only a couple blocks away, if you don't mind walking."

"I love to walk."

David pushed a button, and Charlie Haden's Quartet West began to cast its film noir spell through the speakers. He opened a lacquered cabinet and poured two glasses of pinot noir. Sara sat on a fold-up futon sofa. One wall was covered floor to ceiling with oak shelves, supported by designer cinder blocks. The shelves were crammed with books, DVDs, CDs, and the entertainment system, a large-screen television with all the perks: VCR, DVD, and a sound system. One wall was exposed brick, decorated with several paintings and a Japanese wood cut of a priest traveling toward Mt. Fuji. The hardwood floor was mostly covered with a thick, Southwest Indian style rug. Aside from the futon sofa, there was a leather chair and a series of cushions, a low, free-style walnut coffee table, and in the corner, what appeared to be Shinto shrine.

Kopkind handed her a drink, toasted. "Cheers."

They sipped.

"David, do you know your upstairs neighbors?"

"Who, Feldstein? Sure."

"No, I mean those two private apartments on the third

floor. Do you rent from the Chalmers Management Group?"

"Yeah."

"You know, Chalmers was the samurai killer's second victim."

The polisher's face twisted in consternation. *That* Chalmers? I had no idea."

"What about Bloomberg and Andersen? Those are the two names on the mailboxes for the third floor. Do you know them?"

"No, I've never met either one. I've been here for two years, too. It's funny."

"Do you think it's possible there's no one in those apartments? At least one of them?"

"Where are we going with this?"

"I want to take a look at that one apartment with the open window facing Bachman's shop. I'm wondering how the killer knew Bachman had what he wanted. One answer is, he may have bugged the shop, and one way you can bug a place without actually going inside is to bounce a laser beam off the windows."

Kopkind frowned, impressed. "Jeez. I don't know. I suppose we could go up there and knock on the door."

Sara smiled and set her glass down. "Let's."

They went out the front door, up the stairs to street level, up the stairs to Feldstein's entry, and into the building. Access to the second and third floors was both by stair and elevator. The elevator opened on the third floor vestibule, single window looking out on Worth Street, apartments to either side. Neither apartment looked lived-in. There were no homey touches, no welcoming mat or door sign. The apartment with the open window facing Bachman's belonged to Bloomberg. Sara knocked.

Nada.

Kopkind knocked on Andersen's door. No answer there. "Well. Curiouser and curiouser."

"Do me a favor. Keep an eye out while I fiddle with this lock."

"Hey, officer, I don't mean to tell you your business, but isn't that illegal?"

She turned her peepers on him. "Let's just call it extra-legal, okay?"

Kopkind shrugged, grinned. "Not like I'm a perfect citizen."

Bloomberg's apartment was sealed with a Masterlock deadbolt, very difficult to pick. Shielding the Witchblade from Kopkind with her body, Sara confronted the lock; an instant later, the tumblers gave. She turned the knob and the door swung inward.

Silently, she stepped into the apartment, holding up a hand to keep Kopkind back. She listened. She smelled. She tasted the air. The apartment was empty. Not only was it empty, it was unfurnished, save for the living room facing Bachman's. Set three feet inside the window mounted on a black tripod was a tube-like device that resembled a telescope, with a parabolic boom mounted directly below, also facing out.

"What's that?" Kopkind whispered, having caught the caution bug.

"It's a laser listening device." She looked at it closely without touching. It was plugged into a wall outlet. There was some kind of black transfer box with a cord going to the phone jack. Sara bet that when she checked the lease, Bloomberg would turn out to be a front for Chalmers himself. As Kopkind said, curioser and curioser. One victim of the samurai killer had been spying on another. Over a sword, she bet.

She took David's hand. "Come on. Let's get out of here."

They returned to David's living room, where he poured them each another glass of wine. "What does it mean?"

"I don't know. But I intend to find out. You said you had something to tell me."

"Do I ever! I don't know how much stock you place in ghost stories, but you know that book Hecht showed you? *Kuyamigusa*? Well, I have an English translation."

Without taking her eyes off him, Sara sipped her wine. "You do. Hecht told me he was paying someone beacoup bucks to translate. How did you come by a copy?"

"I bought it at a yard sale in California several years ago." He got up, stood on the stool and reached for his copy. A cloud of dust rose when he set it on the coffee table.

"Holy smokes. What does that thing weigh?"

"About forty pounds. Anyhow, you told me you believed these killings are about Muramasa's swords."

"Yeah. The killer's after a sword or swords."

"Well I've read the whole thing, believe it or not, and that struck a chord. So I began reading, and, sure enough, I uncovered this character who collected Muramasas. Let me just read it to you:

"*This incident concerns the lord of Funai, Bungo province, Takenaka Unemenosho Shigeyoshi, as well as his son, Genzaburo. At the time of the incident (1632), Shigeyoshi had taken up the important position of Nagasaki magistrate. While in office, there were some other*

*irregularities, and the shogunate in Edo initiated legal
proceedings. Shigeyoshi was convicted of his crimes, and,
as a consequence of his punishment, his property was
confiscated. As it happened, there were some Muramasa
blades among his possessions. In fact, the number was
said of have totaled twenty-four blades.*

"*Because of that crime, his sentence was banishment
to a distant island. However, the sentence was increased
in severity, and together with his son their seppuku was
to be presided over by the Grand Superintendent Mizuno
Kawachi no Kami Morinobu. Just the fact that Shigeyoshi
possessed a large number of Muramasa blades indicated
that he believed their price would increase after the col-
lapse of the Tokugawa shogunate. The fact that the
shogunate strongly despised these swords was the reason
that Shigeyoshi was ordered to commit seppuku.*

"*In the days leading up to his death, Shigeyoshi
handed out his swords one by one to his loyal retainers
until there was only one left, the sword Skyroot, which
had been commissioned by the demon swordsman Udo.
Finally, he gave Skyroot to his most loyal retainer. However, after Shigeyoshi's death, the retainer is said to have
traded the sword to a Dutch sea captain for a pair of
match-locked pistols. Thus, it is said Shigeyoshi's spirit
is doomed to walk the land forever, searching for his lost
Muramasa.*

"Your killer may be the reincarnated spirit of
Shigeyoshi," he concluded.

"Let me see that." Sara got off the sofa and knelt next
to Kopkind, who sat cross-legged on a cushion in front of
the coffee table. The old book had been entirely hand-
written in elegant penmanship that reminded Sara of the
style booklets she studied as a grade school student. It

must have taken forever—a true labor of love. Her fingers traced the ancient script, the sword polisher breathing over her shoulder.

It was her dream. She'd dreamed she was Shigeyoshi. Had she heard the story before, or had the spirit sought her out? Because of the Witchblade? But in her dream, Shigeyoshi did not succumb to the shogun's order. He had struck back, slaying his appointed executioner.

She was aware of David's fragrance, masculine with a touch of lime, followed by the touch of his hand on her arm. She turned toward him. "Umm . . . so, where are we going for dinner?"

"City Club, around the corner. Sort of a Spanish/French sorta place. Plus the music. This guy Ray Rideout is straight out of Bird, by way of Phil Woods."

"Who?"

"He's a terrific sax player. You'll like him."

It was seven by the time they descended the Mayan steps to the subterranean City Club. Many restaurants had occupied the space at 223 Houston Street. The basement reminded Sara of old Italian restaurants, with its exposed brick Roman arches dividing the rooms, white linen tablecloths, and paintings of the Pyrenees. They must have had that lovers' glow, because the waiters treated them like royalty, hovering, solicitous, eager to please.

It was a magical evening. David blushed charmingly when the waiter handed him the wine list, was grateful when Sara held out her hand. "Let me see. All children of Italian/Americans know something of the grape." After determining they were going to order fish and poultry, Sara ordered a California Chardonnay.

"You can order the French stuff. I'm not exactly poor."

She balanced her chin on her bridged fingers and batted her lashes. "I refuse to patronize the French, for a laundry list of grievances about which I shall not bore you at this time."

"Perhaps later?" he asked hopefully.

"Perhaps."

The band, sax, drums, piano, and bass, filed in and began to play "Fool On The Hill." They ate slowly, lingered through the long set, returned to David's just before midnight, and made love on the futon while Yoshi snarled and yawned around the base of the bed.

Sara lay in David's sleeping arms, wide awake. She was pleasantly exhausted, but her mind would not shut down. Was this the man who would make an "honest woman" of her? Would Vince have liked him? Possibly, but it'd be best to take it slow. She'd had her heart broken once too often in her life; the scars were still tender.

Did she believe in reincarnation? Since acquiring the Witchblade, there were few things in which she didn't believe. And in her experience, it was more than likely Shigeyoshi could live again to claim his precious sword.

Skyroot. The root of all evil. It was, after all, priceless, the desire of powerful men. Would the killings stop when the killer finally possessed the sword? Would the sword ever surface? What criteria would a ghost samurai use for choosing a host? Certainly, Shigeyoshi would want someone physically capable. Sharpe was capable. He also had the knowledge. And the swords.

The swords! She'd completely forgotten the detailed drawings she'd made of the swords she discovered in Staten Island.

David stirred, one hand falling to her hip. "What?"

"What, what?"

"I don't know. All of a sudden I felt you get all tense and it woke me up."

"I'm sorry. Go back to sleep."

David stretched languorously. "Mmm. What time is it?"

Sara glanced at the bedside digital. "Five o'clock."

David sat up, swung his legs to the floor. "Time to feed the livestock."

Sara watched him head for the bathroom, admiring his muscular backside and, oh, yeah, his butt. He was in and out of the shower in five minutes, dressed in jeans and a white T, and started rattling things in the kitchen.

Sara emerged from the bathroom a half-hour later. She'd pinned her hair up for the shower, and dressed in her sensible Gap khakis and a beige shirt. Fetching her notes from the previous night, she joined David in the kitchen, where he was whipping up scrambled eggs and cheese. He removed a bottle of grapefruit juice from the refrigerator.

"My old polishing instructor, Mas, told me to always drink grapefruit juice with eggs. It breaks down the cholesterol."

"I didn't know they had grapefruit in Japan."

David laughed. "Mas got that out of *Parade* magazine."

"David, I wonder if you could look at some drawings I made of some swords, and help me identify them."

"I can try."

She laid out her notes and drawings. David pondered them in silence. "I see a long sword with *chiri*, or grooves, on both sides. The groove tips extend past the *yokote*. This is a *hisaki-agari*, which makes it middle period. You've done a remarkable job. You even got the tempered line—a flame, or *kaen*. All I can tell you is that it appears to be a traditional long sword. I'd have to see the signature, or look at the blade in person. Where did you get this?"

"I can't say."

David went through the drawings. "I don't recognize any of these swords. Did you do these drawings? These are good."

"Can you tell if any of them are Muramasas?"

"No, I can't. But I can say, there's such diversity of styles, they represent the work of at least three different swordsmiths. Not much help, huh?"

"Nope." She kissed him on the cheek. "I like you, anyway. I have to go to work. Unlock your garage for me."

"When can I see you again? Is tonight too soon?"

"Yes!" Sara laughed. "I'm busy tonight. However, Saturday I have to go to the mayor's house for a cocktail party . . ."

"As in Gracie Mansion? As in the Mayor of New York?"

"Yes, and don't get excited. It's politics. Would you like to be my date?"

"I think I can make it."

Sara had repacked everything in her overnight bag and the detachable tank bag. David helped her carry them to the workshop, where she reattached everything to the bike, put on her jacket and helmet, straddled the bike and walked it out the door. David tried to kiss her through the helmet, but her lips remained tantalizingly beyond reach.

"Story of my life," she said, thumbing the starter. The Yamaha thrummed to life. David held the gate for her as she let out the clutch and slid into the alley. A United

DEMONS

Waste Management truck completely occluded the alley, like a rhinoceros in a chute, snorting, stinking, bellowing to frighten lesser creatures. With a sigh, Sara turned and headed the wrong way down the one-way alley until she exited on Second Avenue, turned, and headed uptown.

FOURTEEN

Sara was at her desk by 6:30, surprising even the jaded denizens of the night shift who were agonizingly pecking out their final reports of the day before wandering off to fall into bed. The telltale tang of forbidden cigarette smoke hovered in the air. Her desk was monster free.

The immediate problem was to either prove or eliminate Sharpe as a suspect. She awaited Siry's arrival with a mixture of dread and anticipation. It was the type of dilemma every supervisor hated: investigating one of their own. She needed to share her problem, but she didn't envy Siry his responsibilities. The worst part was, she *liked* Sharpe. Her private knowledge notwithstanding, everything about him indicated he was an outstanding cop. His Navy discharge had been honorable, and, of course, there was a reasonable explanation why he hadn't said he was in the SEALS—they were still considered covert ops.

In the meantime, she prepared a detailed memo covering everything she'd discovered in Sharpe's apartment, including the pictures. She did it in longhand, in a notepad, and put it in her locker. Shortly after eight, Siry arrived, looking as if he'd gone home the night before and fallen asleep fully clothed, then rose this morning without looking in the mirror. A heavy stubble covered his chin, and his normally dark and sunken eyes were even more so. He spotted Sara's anxious expression at once and motioned her into his office with a nod.

Once inside, she pulled the blinds. Siry sat at his desk and began to rummage through the drawers, retrieving a bottle of Alka Seltzer and a tube of Tums. "What? I can just tell by that look on your face. What is it?"

"Joe, is there any chance this office is bugged?"

Siry looked around, as if trying to spot a mosquito. "Bugged? By whom?"

"By Internal Affairs."

"That's illegal. I'd have whoever did it up before the police commission. Is it that bad?"

"Maybe we ought to take a walk."

Detectives and secretaries leaped at them like midway creature features. Chief, you gotta look at this. Chief, you gotta look at that. Siry waved them off with an unlit cigar. "Be right back! Keep your shirt on. Back in five. It'll keep."

Sara slapped a black Red Sox hat on top of her pinned-up hair. They went out the back, through the motor pool. No Hayabusa. Exiting the cage, they walked down Church Street, toward Ground Zero.

"Well?"

"I searched Sharpe's apartment yesterday. I found six swords concealed in a standing safe."

"What were you doing in Sharpe's apartment?" He

paused. "Wait a minute. You think a *cop* might be the perp?"

"I'm . . . not sure. He collects old swords. He's a master swordsman. I saw him pulverize James Bratten last week in kendo." There was more. But she couldn't bring herself to share it. Not yet. What if she were wrong?

"Hizzoner's on my ass. Where do we stand with all this? Don't tell me Sharpe's your only suspect."

"Hecht and Bratten are both collectors. Bratten, I can't see. He doesn't strike me as the obsessive type. But Hecht is. You don't get to be the biggest developer in Manhattan without a certain degree of ruthlessness."

"Sweet Mother of Christ. You're telling me your only two suspects are Sharpe and Hecht?! I can't tell the mayor that! He's a friend of Hecht's, too. And Sharpe—Christ, he's a vet. Have you seen his discharge papers?"

"Joe, trust me. I have other reasons I can't go into."

"So what do I do? Tip Internal Affairs?"

"Absolutely not. They'll only make things worse."

"You mean beyond the fact you did a B&E on another cop's house without a warrant, which means you ain't got squat for evidence?" He sighed. "Whaddaya want from me?"

"Your support, as usual."

He grunted. "Why do you always have to make these cases so damned complicated?"

Back at her desk, Sara went online and used Google.com to research possession in Japanese mythology. Of all the cops in New York City, she was least likely to dismiss such a notion. Motive? The killer was driven by ambition and blood lust from beyond the grave to recover his lost Muramasas. New problem: What if the host was innocent? How did she separate Shigeyoshi, if it were he, from the host body? One link spoke of an *oni yurai* ceremony to drive out demons.

A gust of Armani Pour Homme tickled her nose.

"Go away, Baltazar," she said without turning.

He hovered over her left shoulder. "Hey, fellas!" he shouted. "Pezzini's researching possession! She's got a hot one!"

Sara immediately minimized her screen but the damage had been done. There was a howl of laughter that echoed loudly in the room—then fell ominously silent.

Selzer had appeared at the entrance to the detectives' bullpen. He made his way silently toward Siry's office, radiating chill. Faces turned away.

Fifteen minutes later, he emerged, once again plunging the bullpen into silence.

Sara waited until he was five minutes gone before approaching the boss. Siry was poring over a report. "What?" he said without looking up.

"Joe, what did Selzer want?"

"None o' your freakin' business. It had nothing to do with you, okay?"

"Did it have anything to do with Sharpe?"

Siry looked up, touch of panic in his brown eyes. "No," he stage whispered. "Shut the door."

She shut the door, even though no one could hear what they were saying. "Selzer don't know nothin' about Sharpe, and let's keep it that way. I just found out Sharpe's moonlighting for Adrian Hecht. Did you know about this?"

Fear licked at her spine. Had she messed up? "Yeah, but lots of cops moonlight."

"Those two got a lot in common. They're both Nipponophiles. They're both nuts for those swords." He paused. "So . . . okay. Maybe there is a connection, like you figured." He fell silent.

"Okay," she said. "Sorry to bother you."

"Close the door when you leave. I gotta get some work done."

Sara returned to her desk and Google.com. There was more material on Hecht than she had time to read: a profile in *Fortune*, lengthy attacks on anti-capitalist websites lurid with conspiracy, and, of course, photos of Hecht and his women.

Her cell phone thrummed in her leather bag. She took it out. "Pezzini."

"Sara, it's Derek Sharpe."

Goosebumps marched up her neck. How could he know? He couldn't know. It was synchronicity, another piece of the puzzle slipping reluctantly into place. Trouble was, she was too close to the board to see the patterns. "What's up, Derek?"

"I think I may have stumbled on the break you've been looking for. I'm not comfortable discussing it over the phone. Could you meet me?"

"Where?"

"Hecht Gardens, say around eight P.M. You can find me in the trailer, inside the gate."

"Why not now?"

"I'm on duty now. I'm watching a bunch of Flying Tigers. They're watching a discount electronics store. Something's going down. Later." He hung up.

Flying Tigers was a Vietnamese gang, and Hecht was on the gang task force. With a supreme effort, Sara turned her attention back to her report.

Hours dragged by like injured soldiers. Sara was no

master spy. As careful as she'd been, she couldn't be certain she hadn't left behind a clue when she'd tossed Sharpe's place. A real paranoid would have left telltales, such as eyelashes pasted over doorjambs, little pieces of thread tied between cupboard and wall.

If he knew, if he were crazy, if he were a killer, maybe he was luring her downtown for other reasons.

No. Not another cop. But she knew from bitter experience that cops went wrong. She actually preferred a supernatural explanation. If the killer *was* a ghost, maybe they could contact him via séance. Yeah. And do what? Interview him? She had to look into this *oni yurai* business.

At half-past four, a delivery person appeared at the landing with a bundle of flowers asking for Pezzini. A cop pointed at Sara.

It was a dozen roses. Not even Baltazar's wolf whistle could knock her off her high as she reached for the little white card.

> *The winter sky breaks*
> *Dissolves into rose petals*
> *No match for your eyes*

It was unsigned. Sara shut her eyes, and smiled. Tonight was Sharpe. Tomorrow was the mayor's reception.

She couldn't wait for tomorrow.

She sought connections in the Chalmers/Hecht/Bachman triangle. Was it significant that Hecht and Chalmers had been rivals? As far as she knew, there had never been any personal animosity between them. What was new was the fact that both men turned out to be serious

Japanese sword collectors. Small world, indeed. If the eavesdropper above David's apartment *did* report to Chalmers, he would have known when the antiquarian acquired the latest sword. The missing sword. Was it Skyroot? Was that what this was all about? The ghost of a disgraced samurai, forced to commit seppuku, struggling to recover all his swords? It made as much sense as anything else, and Sara had seen weirder.

Or was it something more subtle? A dodge to conceal the real motive and target? Who would go to so much trouble?

She ran the serial number of the listening device through the manufacturer, Hagira, in Milford, Connecticutt. Hagira was owned and operated by an ex-policeman who'd turned to private investigating. It was a small specialty shop, turning out electronic eavesdropping devices to order. They were able to tell Sara that the laser listener on Worth Street had been purchased by Panther Security. Panther Security worked for Chalmers Property Management.

Sara phoned Panther. A secretary answered. Sara identified herself and asked to speak to Norm Hansen.

"I'm sorry, Norm has gone home for the day. May I take a message?"

"May I have his cell phone number, please?"

"I don't think I can do that."

"Ma'am, this is a homicide investigation, and I need that number *now*. May I have your name, please?"

There was a pause. "Mr. Hansen's cell phone number is 555-6895."

"Thank you."

It never failed. Ask someone for their name during an

investigation, they crawl under the nearest rock. She dialed Hansen's number. It rang and rang. No help there.

At four, Rubinstein's kid Amelia made the rounds selling Girl Scout cookies. Sara ordered two boxes of the caramel fudge. At five, she saved her reports, shut down her machine, and packed up.

It was a relief to confront the bike, which forced her to concentrate. She bungeed her leather bag to the back seat, jammed more gear in the tank bag, zipped her jacket, and put on the half-face helmet. Half-face was better, because you were right out there in the open, with no intervening sheet of plexiglass. You could smell the city. Sometimes a good thing, sometimes not.

Fighting traffic with all the resources at her disposal, she clawed her way to The Chinese Connection, a quaint little restaurant on the Lower East Side, near the Manhattan Bridge. For two hours, she relaxed and chatted with the owners about martial arts movies while she picked at an assortment of dishes, unaware that she was being observed through the misty window from across the street, where a tricked-out Celica was snug to the curb.

Tonight, the *bruja* was going down.

Lupé slunk low in the Celica's bucket seat, although she was invisible to the outside world through the tinted windows. She had the window open an inch to vent smoke from cigarettes. She was not alone. Two Tecolotes crouched in the car with her. Three more jammed in Tito's cat-puke yellow Cavalier behind them. The past few days had been an exercise in patience, never Lupé's strong suit. She had surprised herself with her dedication. Getting rid of the *bruja* had come to dominate her life, even as she was repeatedly haunted with dreams of flashing swords and gouting blood. She would never be able to move ahead, never reclaim her man until the witch was dead.

Nor was it as easy as pulling a trigger. If it had been that easy, Bobby would have done it. Lupé had a gun, Bobby's nine, tucked beneath her seat. Estrella had told her that ordinary bullets would be useless against the witch, who had magical protection, and Lupé believed her. But on this night of the full moon, if the witch could be isolated among iron, she could be taken down by a determined pack.

Lupé had the full moon, the iron, and the pack. Anywhere on Manhattan you were surrounded by iron. You couldn't get away from it. And she had the pack, at last. Five of the toughest Tecolotes with hard-ons for the lady cop. Lupé probably could have got them all just by showing them the witch's picture, and promising they could play with her before they killed her, but having a little insurance was always a plus. Jorgé, damn him, had taught her that. So Lupé had told them how the witch had killed Bobby. Los Tecolotes were hungry for revenge.

"How we gon' get the bitch?" Benito rumbled from the back seat, cradling a MAC-10 in his lap like a puppy.

"Jes' wait. After she leave the restaurant, we'll run her off the road, grab her, take her to the warehouse. Then you boys gon' have some fun."

Chango, who'd been Bobby's second-in-command and sat in the shotgun seat, put his hand on Lupé's thigh. "Like to have some fun wi'choo, chiquita."

Lupé casually shoved her cigarette into the back of Chango's hand as if it were an ashtray.

"Hey!" he howled, snatching his hand back and sticking it in his mouth.

Lupé didn't even look at him. "Hesh up, Chango. Don' make me put a curse on you."

Chango's eyes went wide, and he bit down on his anger. Lupé smiled inwardly. Maybe she could get Estrella to teach her a few things. In the back seat, the crack pipe sounded like a bowl of Rice Crispies. That's right, *hijos*, Lupé thought. Crack it up. Get in a real sharp mood for the lady cop. It was the only way she had of ensuring they'd hang around for the task at hand. Los Tecolotes did not have long attention spans. In the rearview mirror, she saw the telltale glow of a turbo lighter. She phoned Tito on her cell phone. She could hear his cell phone beeping through the cracked window.

"Yeah?"

"Don't smoke it all up. You got to make it last."

"Don't worry, Lupé. We're makin' it last."

"I ain't gonna take time go cop for you, you run out."

"Don't worry!"

Lupé hung up. At 8:25, the witch rolled her motorcycle out the front door. Lupé could not deny a certain admiration for the witch—so young, so beautiful, a policewoman, and she rode a motorcycle. A veritable litany of forbidden role models.

That, in itself, should have set the alarms off in Lupé's head long before the witch fixed her sites on Lupé's man. No woman could have all those things without paying a terrible price.

Lupé dialed Tito.

"I see her," he answered.

"Okay. Let's go. I'm gonna wait for a chance, try and knock her off the bike. You guys be waitin' to grab her."

"Don't hurt her," Tito cautioned. "That's our job."

By the time Lupé had whipped into traffic, the lady cop was four car-lengths ahead, not toward Brooklyn, but toward Ground Zero. Didn't matter. This was New York. You could still knock a bitch off a motorcycle and bundle her into a car without intervention. That was one of the things that made New York great. Freedom!

"Step on it! Step on it!" Chango chanted.

"You're losing her!" Benito said.

Lupé pulled the automatic transmission down a gear and stood on the gas. The tricked-out Celica shot forward with a chirp of its front tires, cutting off a cab driver, who leaned on his horn. They got hung up at Civic Center by the usual four fire truck progression, sirens blaring, lights flashing.

It was no use. No matter how fast Lupé drove, she was no match for a motorcycle in Manhattan traffic. She could have been driving a Viper, same difference. There simply wasn't room to maneuver. She refused to admit defeat. The witch cop would not escape.

Lupé finally turned off Vessey toward Ground Zero, chained, roped, and stanchioned off due to massive construction. Hecht Gardens was being built two blocks north. Lupé couldn't believe her luck as she drove by the massive chain link fence of the Hecht site and spotted the blue-and-white motorcycle inside the gate, parked next to a house trailer that had been trucked in to serve as HQ. The construction site was surrounded by an eight-foot-high hurricane fence topped with concertina wire.

Lupé got on the phone to Tito. "Don't go near the

fence. Meet us round the corner at Maiden Lane. The bitch is here."

They rendezvoused in the lee of another construction site, parking on the curb next to a vast hole in the ground while traffic swirled past on one side. A big white wooden sign said FUTURE HOME OF PACE-HONG KONG BANK/MARK ZINGG ARCHITECT/CHALMERS CONSTRUCTION COMPANY. The worn curb was fenced off at both ends with plywood construction, but the wall had been torn down for some reason, allowing the cars to snug in. They gathered in the narrow strip between the illegally parked cars and the plywood wall with cutouts to look at the hole. Chango wore black trousers, a black muscle shirt, hair net pinning back his obsidian curls. His shoes were the color of pure Peruvian flake. Tito and Benito wore baggy trousers and muscle shirts, without Chango's panache. Sammy and Li'l Mack looked like a pair of dwarves who'd been dipped in horse glue and dragged through a rag factory.

Lupé fingered Chango, Tito, Sammy and Benito. "You guys gon' do the job. You my wolf pack, *malditos*. You gon' mess that witch bitch up for me. Who got the bolt cutters?"

Sammy hefted the big clippers.

"You be sure you got them gloves on when you cut the cable, or you gonna turn into a Chicken McNugget."

"Hey!" Li'l Mack squawked. "What do I do?" The fourteen-year-old gangbanger was eager to get in on the action.

"You and me gon' drive the cars," Lupé said. "Can't leave 'em here. Don't use guns unless you got to. We don't need the fraggin' cops."

Chango led his Tecolotes toward the construction site.

He was six feet and two hundred and thirty pounds, and carried an Uzi submachine gun with a twenty-round magazine. He carried another magazine in the baggy pockets of his baggy jeans, in case he found himself pinned down by a division of Marines. The rest of Los Tecolotes were jealous of the Uzi, which Chango had taken off a drunk Paddy Boy on St. Patrick's Day.

Benito had his MAC-10. Sammy and Tito had a pair of cheap revolvers.

Lupé watched until they rounded the corner, then turned on Li'l Mack. "Whatchoo waitin' for—a sign from the Virgin Mary? Get in that piece of crap and drive."

FIFTEEN

When Sara arrived, the front gate was open just wide enough to admit the bike. Figuring Sharpe had left it that way, she pulled into the lot, got off the bike, and shut the gate behind her without latching it. She wheeled the bike up to the house trailer, a big job, propped up on heavy metal braces and connected like an astronaut to a series of external tanks and outbuildings. Fat cables trundled across the lot in bundles. Stacks of treated lumber formed orderly ranks perpendicular to an enormous, multi-leveled excavation that was beginning to sprout steel support struts.

Sara went up the two planks on cinderblock steps to the trailer door and rang the buzzer. No response. "Sharpe!" she barked, trying the knob. It was open.

She stepped inside—it was an orderly office with banks of monitors: twelve screens covering various aspects of the site. Blueprints were taped to a drafting table, others rolled into tight cylinders and shoved in cubbyholes. A large bulletin board covered one wall; on it had been fixed work rosters, security rosters, and an architect's rendering of the finished Gardens. The drawing reminded Sara of an optimist-hued spread from *Popular Mechanics*, circa 1980, describing a city of the future.

And then the lights went out, the screens went blank.

Sara reached for the phone on the desk, but that, too, was dead. She looked out through one begrimed window at Manhattan, its lights still aglows. Only power to the construction site had been cut.

Sara moved instinctively away from the door and un-clipped her stainless steel short nose .357 mag, Smith & Wessen K-frame round butt. The boys had been trying to talk her into a Glock .9 for years, but it didn't have a round butt.

Moving fast and low, Sara pushed the door open with a T-square. The area immediately in front of the trailer appeared empty. She wasted no time, slipping low out the door and over the side of the steps before anyone had a chance to draw a bead. It looked nice and dark under the trailer, so she rolled beneath its mass, retreated to the darkest corner, and turned her attention to the yard. At first there was no sign. She blinked rapidly, willing her eyesight to adjust to the dark. Within a second, it was so. Her night vision had increased uncannily since acquiring the Witchblade.

She wished she knew where the transfer box was, so she could gauge where they were coming from. A pair of legs ending in blindingly white cross-trainers padded lightly into the yard from the direction of the front gate. That's it—just the shoes, like some kind of mime act. She saw the rest of them trailing tentatively behind, like a rat pack in the jungle.

Some kind of gang. Were these the ones responsible for the vandalism? Where was Sharpe? One of them passed through a beam of light, and she saw the gun. As far as Sara knew, eco-terrorists didn't carry weapons. Guns were not healthy for children and other living things. These guys didn't look like greenies, either. They looked like a street gang, far from their turf.

She counted three. She couldn't see if they were all armed, but she had to assume they were. Where was Sharpe? She had no intention of drawing down on three armed gangbangers. She slithered out the back of the trailer and stood in a narrow corridor formed by the trailer and a seven-foot stack of steel girders. If she could get atop the girders, she'd be in a good position to see without being seen. She could hear them spreading out now, despite their clumsy attempts at concealment. She had to get some altitude now, before they separated too far from each other.

Spying an empty five-gallon laminex container, she jammed her gun in its holster, turned the pail upside-down, and used it as a stool to get a leg up. As she reached for the top girder, the Witchblade overwhelmed her right hand with a faint, crystalline ping.

"Whazzat?" said an adenoidal voice behind her.

Sara instinctively lashed out with her left foot, cocking it high and jamming it back into the neck of a fourth gangbanger who had somehow managed to get the drop on her. Her adrenaline-fueled kick slammed the punk so hard up against the trailer, his head bounced like a speed bag. A piece of heavy metal fell and clattered under the trailer. The punk fell to his knees, choking.

Tough crap, Sara thought, pulling out a pair of handcuffs. Before she had a chance to handcuff the punk to the trailer, gangbangers appeared at both ends of the narrow corridor.

"There she is!"

"Rush her!"

Sara dropped and rolled, leaving the one she'd struck retching on his knees. She rolled under the trailer, scrambled out, and took off toward the vast pit that dominated the construction site. Adjacent to the pit, a Manitex Crane rose hundreds of feet into the sky like some huge steel gallows. A series of steel barriers surrounded the crane's broad stance, hydraulic pistons resting on cracked concrete. The top of the crane hovered over the huge pit, from which the construction scaffolding had already begun to sprout.

A series of flashes opened up to her right, from atop the very pile of girders she'd set out to climb. A bullet whizzed by her ear. Several struck the ground. New York surged and pumped around them, drowning the sound of individual gunfire. Sara had no choice but to run for the protection of the triangulated steel protecting the tower's spine and ladder. She began to climb, the Witchblade gripping each rung with a clang, fingers folding into an iron grip.

Where was Sharpe?

They were closing in now from three directions, squeezing off shots at her. It had been a mistake to gain altitude—now they could shoot at her without risk of hitting each other. She thought of going back down, but that would only bring her within their range. They were closing in too fast.

The Witchblade yanked her hand around in a tight

little arc into a stunning collision with a bullet. No. She would not get hit. The Witchblade would not permit it. But could even the Witchblade protect her from three different shooters coming from three different directions? She looked up. The supports seemed to stretch into infinity. Someone let loose with a short burst of automatic weapons fire, and the Witchblade absorbed the blast with a bone-jarring clatter that traveled up her arm and left her shoulder momentarily numb. The gauntleted hand reached of its own accord for the next rung. She had no choice but to climb.

She saw the one with the auto now, it was Twinkle Toes, in his pure white sneakers. If he got directly beneath her, all he had to do was stick the gun into the shaft and fire straight up. Of course all she had to do was fire straight down. Bracing herself on the ladder with one foot and an elbow, she drew her Magnum, and fired a round straight down. Give 'em something to think about. She thought about pulling her cell, but now they stood in a tight little cluster around the base of the crane, discussing what to do.

" 'Ey, chiquita," one of them said. "You want to parrrrrty? We gon' have a little picnic witchoo."

"Up there or down here," another cooed softly. "Don't matter to us."

The three began to climb, outside the triangulated central support. Smart. Made them tough to spot, hard to shoot, if they didn't lose their nerve. Sara climbed, barely staying ahead of them. No one spoke. She could hear them breathing heavily as they worked, the occasional clang of metal against metal. At one point they stopped. Looking down, Sara saw the flare of a turbo lighter, heard the faint tinkle of burning crack. The pause that refreshes. They were at least a hundred and fifty feet up now, twenty feet beneath the gondola, which hung to one side and just beneath the horizontal crossmember, stretching far out over the pit.

Where was Sharpe? Had this group somehow managed to kill him? Inconceivable. They were just a bunch of low-life gangbangers! But they had the drop on her. They must have been following her. But why? She flashed on Jorgé, but her instincts told her he was okay. What about Lupé, then? Had Sara been negligent in not taking the girl more seriously?

Could be, she decided. She climbed the twenty feet to the base of the gondola, up onto the tiny steel platform. The door was locked. Locked! Who would lock such a place, two hundred feet in the air? Sara had no choice but to scramble up into the tiny crow's nest clinging to the back of the control gondola. From here, she could see down one side of the pillar, but she couldn't see her pursuers. She heard voices directly beneath her feet—they were clinging to the underside of the gondola.

Crouching, she drew her pistol. "Boys," she said clearly. "I'm a New York City police officer, and I'm armed. You have two choices. You can turn around and head down, or you can stick your snouts up over the rim and have me blow them off."

"Tough talk from the lady witch," a basso profundo rumbled from directly beneath. "We get done witchoo, won't be nothin' left but your badge."

Activity from the other side of the gondola. While Deep Voice distracted her, he'd sent one of his wolves up to take her by surprise. She was in a pickle. They were just waiting for her to commit to one of her attackers before another swarmed her from behind. Evidently they were so high on crack they no longer cared whether they soared, got shot, or did the dirty deed.

The kid was coming over the top. He'd scrambled up past the gondola and stepped out onto the steel roof, slithering on his belly, thrusting his gun in front of him. Must have picked up his ninja technique from a Michael Dudikoff movie, Sara thought, listening to his inept scraping. She waited until he thrust the gun over the roof, grabbed it in both hands, her left thumb on the cool blue metal of the gauntlet, braced a leg against the wall, and heaved.

The kid sailed out over the pit like a Frisbee. He screamed all the way down, struck with the sound of an ax hitting a melon. She'd only meant to throw him to the floor of the platform, but the Witchblade had had other ideas.

"Jesus!" a voice exclaimed from below. "She killed Tito!"

"Damn you!" she hissed at the gauntlet.

A hand reached for her pistol. Twisting, she punched the gangbanger flush in the face with her gauntleted right hand. His nose dissolved in a mist of red, but reeling back, he'd managed to snag the Magnum and flip it over his head so that it sailed out over the pit.

Next to losing your badge, losing your gun is the worst that can happen. Thus spake Vincent. *No, Pop,* she thought. *There's worse.* There were three of them now swarming the tiny platform, holding her down.

"Get her!" said Twinkle Toes, reaching for her throat, a coyote grin on his face. One grabbed her left leg. Another grabbed her right. The Witchblade went to work, snapping into the short one's crotch. His mouth made a per-

fect oval beneath a hairline mustache as he reeled back to
the limits of the platform, gasping for air. She shot out
her left leg, catching another in the thigh, sending him
skidding back. Now she was wrestling with Twinkle Toes,
who'd moved to straddle her. Saliva dripped from his
pronounced canines. Sara bucked with all her might and
threw him off. She scrambled free, sinking the Witchblade into Hairline Mustache's thigh like a tiger claw.
Metal flanges hooked deeply into his flesh as she literally
clawed her way over him to the gondola's roof.

From here, she could either retreat to the counter-
weight, a distance of some thirty feet, or head out over
the pit, where the crane did its lifting. The massive horizontal girder was triangulated with the flat plane on top.
The Witchblade wanted to stay and fight. It pulled
against her, trying to drag her back toward the cupola,
where the three survivors were checking their actions and
plotting. She could hear them discussing her clearly.

"She's a freakin' witch, Chango. Choo see what she did
to Tito?"

"She got lucky."

"I'm bleedin', you guys. What was that?"

"Put a rag on it. Me and Benito'll drag her back here."

"You go on and run, chiquita! You runnin' out of
room!"

The strange thing was, they didn't scare her. Not in the
slightest. Height scared her. Looking down, the bottom of
the pit was lost in shadow, far beneath ground level. It
was probably a three-hundred-foot drop. She crouched
inside the triangulated girder thirty feet out, another fifty
to the end.

Could Sharpe have set her up? Could he have somehow learned that she'd burgled him, that she was on to

him, and lured her down here to get snuffed? If so, why not do it himself? Sharpe was a hands-on guy. Could this wolf pack have taken him down? That didn't make sense, either. If they'd taken care of Sharpe, they would have already been at the site when she got there. But they weren't. They'd followed her in.

The telltale glow of a lighter flared on the far side of the gondola. *That's right, boys. Crank yourselves up.* A moment later, a silhouette entered the triangulated section of the beam, followed shortly by another.

"Benito, get up on top. We'll catch her between us."

"What we gon' do with our guns?" one of them asked softly.

"Leave 'em. She ain't got one, either."

At least they were down to two. They had no fear. They would have made great high iron workers. The lesser of the two boosted himself up to crouch precariously atop the giant horizontal girder while the leader, Twinkle Toes, slowly advanced, wolf grin dripping.

"I thought crack made you paranoid," Sara said conversationally.

"Nah, we used to it. Getchoo high, if you like."

"No thanks. I'm high enough." She took out her cell phone, the size of hotel soap, and flipped it open. It was dead. She faked it.

"Dispatch, this is Detective Pezzini, on the crane at Hecht Gardens. I need backup, and lots of it. Seem to be a bunch of gangbangers . . . just a minute." Holding the dead phone to one side she called out to her pursuers, watching with an uneasy mix of humor and apprehension. "Boys, what gang are you with?"

"We the Brooklyn Tecolotes, *guapa*," the kid on top sang with pride. Show-and-tell time.

Sara spoke into the phone. "You hear that? Yeah. Thank you." She folded the plastic clam and slipped it in her pocket. "They're on the way. You got maybe five minutes to get out of here."

The two looked at each other, grinning like mongrels at roadkill. Twinkle Toes began crab-walking her way. "Cops don't use cell phones, *guapa*."

"Everybody uses cell phones, Pancho. Bet you got one."

"Why you call me Pancho? My name is Chango."

Now the one on top had begun to creep forward. Sara glanced back. She was about forty feet from the tip of the crane, directly above the rolling lift unit or skyhook. She couldn't fly. She didn't know what the Witchblade could do if she took a dive. She'd never tested it that way. She had a feeling it wasn't designed for high-altitude bailouts.

They were so close now she could smell Chango's fruity cologne and the skinny one's rank body odor. "Benito, see if choo can grab her hair. I'll get her around the waist, we'll drag her back to that platform where we can lay 'er out."

Benito inched forward on all fours, like a dog crossing a frozen pond. "Cool."

Sara was limited. She had only a single rail on which to stand, maintaining her balance by gripping the side supports that ran the length of the crane. She wished she hadn't stopped carrying mace. The Witchblade played for keeps, and would probably kill these creeps if it went into action.

Benito paused about six feet away. "What's that on her hand?"

"Whatchoo got on your hand, *guapa*?"

"Just a glove, boys, like Michael Jackson. For shaking hands. Who wants to be first?"

"I do," Chango grunted, lunging forward, head down,

reaching for her waist. Her right hand lashed out in a ridge strike, catching him on his cheekbone and slamming his head to one side. Chango reeled back from the blow, gripping a rail with one hand and touching his bruised face with the other. He spit out a tooth.

"That's all right, *guapa*." Blood trickled from his mouth. "You just make me harder."

The one on top got down on his belly and reached for her hair. The Witchblade shot up, index finger poking through the kid's thorax like a leather punch, hooked around a floating rib, and yanked it loose like a car door handle. The kid gave a little sigh and slumped. Blood poured from the hole in his torso as from a faucet.

Chango got his head in her stomach and his arms around her waist and bulled her down on the single horizontal beam. The Witchblade dug for his eye with a thumb. Chango sprang back, shoving her violently, and she slipped off the edge of the beam. And as she flew toward the ground, her last thought was, *Why doesn't the Witchblade do something?*

The change was instantaneous. One moment, she was plunging through the air, seeing faint stars against city glare, the next, the Witchblade had expanded to enclose her entire body in a multi-faceted carapace with a series of extensions, like dogwood petals, facing the earth. It flowed over her skin. Her $160 Prada jeans ripped. Her leather jacket shredded. Sara instinctively twisted, watching the great void rush to her face. The dogwood petals swung around and covered her front, extending, extending . . .

The petals collapsed. She struck with a sense of rapid deceleration, followed by an elastic rebound. She bounced, spinning gracefully through the air, the petals sprouting again and dancing around her body so that they always faced the earth. The second arc ended on a pile of steel girders that would have cruelly broken an unprotected body. The series of petals formed a heavy cilia that absorbed the collision and pushed away, not so spectacularly this time. She tucked into a roll and landed lightly on her feet, breathing hard.

"Thank you!" she blurted. She was standing in the basin of the excavation, some thirty feet below street level, surrounded by steel and concrete infrastructure, warm breeze chilling her newly exposed body. The Witchblade had done a sushi chef on her clothes. She now wore her Reeboks, panties, a thin strand of denim around her waist, her leather belt with badge, and a sports bra which she had had the good sense to don earlier, expecting action. The corners of the huge excavation receded into blackness. Looking up, she saw the outline of the crane stark against the city lights. Blood dribbled at her feet. Something grew out of the sky, a mote expanding to fill her vision. She jerked back just in time to avoid being struck by a falling body.

The wiry one, Benito, with the hole in his ribs. A shudder rippled through her as she recalled the feeling of her finger poking through his side.

"Look out!" someone shouted from atop the crane. Her right hand jerked out, grabbed the ridge of a steel beam, and yanked her out from under a heavy piece of meat as it whipped by, grazing her cheek with blood. She stared down. The head and one shoulder of her primary assailant. She stared, trying to make sense of what she saw. Twinkle Toes had been cleaved in two, as neatly as a piece of prime porterhouse at the hands of a butcher. As she stared in horror at the cross-section of anatomy, dark organs oozing black, the other half dropped, one leg bouncing. The two parts of Chango lay together like the aftermath of a train wreck.

Sara looked up. Something glinted in the city light. A sword. A tiny figure held on to the girder with one hand and looked down.

"Sara! Oh, my God."

Sharpe. Where had he come from? He could not possibly have seen what happened to her, and had to assume she was dead. The construction site stank of set-up. If Sharpe had been there all along, why hadn't he come to her aid before this? Unless he wanted her dead. For whose benefit was he pretending remorse?

She could have said something. She could have called out to him, told him she was all right. She held her tongue, wanting to see how he'd react to her amazing disappearing body. Where had he come from? Where had that sword come from? What was he doing, moonlighting as a security officer, carrying a samurai sword? Was he nuts? Was he a psycho killer? She could hear him on his cell phone calling for an ambulance.

As Sharpe turned and headed for the vertical strut, a vehicle squealed its tires.

Sara stared at the neatly severed corpse and shuddered. That certainly answered one question. Was Sharpe capable of cleaving a man in two? He'd just done it. Not even the isthmus of the neck. Straight across the continent, Portland to Miami. She could hear him descending the ladder with an occasional clank as his hardware hit the steel. She burrowed back into an alcove formed by the juxtaposition of the steel beams and an immense spool of wire.

Sharpe appeared at the edge of the excavation, looking for a way down. He spotted a series of ladders descending in three stages, with scaffolding at the intervals, and came quickly down, something long, dark, and narrow strapped to his back. When he reached the bottom, he turned on a flashlight and strode swiftly, lightly to where the severed corpse lay. He shined the flashlight all around, unconcerned with his handiwork. The beam touched briefly on a third body, the one the Witchblade had hurtled to the ground.

No. Not the Witchblade. Sara and the Witchblade.

"Sara?" he said tentatively.

"Behind you."

He whirled, keeping the light low until it found her feet. "Thank God! I'm so sorry . . . this is all my fault. I saw you fall . . ."

"I need clothes."

The flashlight lingered a second, then switched off. "Right. Wait here a minute."

Sharpe scrambled up the scaffolding like a lemur, returning minutes later with a soft cotton sweatshirt and sweatpants, intended for a bigger person. Sara put them on and emerged resembling a moving pile of laundry.

"Where were you while those ebolas were chasing me up the crane?"

"I was in the control booth."

"Then why in heaven's name didn't you do something?"

"I wasn't conscious."

"You weren't conscious?"

"I know how that must sound. Listen, it's a long story. I called you down here because I learned something that may be pertinent to your investigation. I am so sorry about what happened . . . Listen, I have a problem. I had a blackout. I've been suffering from blackouts off and on, for about a year now."

"Excuse me?"

"Periods of time I can't account for. It doesn't happen often. I should probably see a doctor or something, but I don't want to get stuck at a desk."

"Stuck at a desk? Man, you're lucky you're not in Bellevue! How did you ever get by the screening board?"

"I have impressive credentials. My problem has never before interfered with my job. This is the first time, and I'm so sorry."

"Derek, you've got a lot of explaining to do. You cut that kid in half like a breakfast sausage. You think that doesn't make you a suspect? What are you doing with that thing, anyway?"

They could hear the sirens rising in the distance. When you didn't hear sirens, that was a rarity.

"I'll tell you. What are you going to say happened?"

"Exactly what happened."

Sharpe gestured to her hand. "Including that?"

Sara looked down and was surprised to see her right hand still enclosed in the gauntlet. *Go away*, she willed. It obediently morphed into the bracelet with the big stone. Sharpe stared.

"I didn't see that."

"No, you didn't."

"You going to tell me how you survived that fall?"

"Maybe."

"Okay, mutual defense pact." He pointed up. "You see that guy wire, running between the steel frame and the edge of the pit? That's how the gangbanger got cut in two. And as to how you survived the fall, you see that pile of dirt?"

Sara nodded tersely.

The ambulance arrived, accompanied by a squad car. Sharpe shined his flashlight up at them and waved. "Down here!"

Five minutes later, two EMTs with a folding stretcher reached the bottom, followed by two uniformed cops from the Nineteenth. When they reached Sharpe, he no longer had the sword. One cop took Sharpe aside. The other questioned Sara. She'd seen him before—his name was O'Malley, and he was nearing the end of his twenty-year stretch. Sara told her story, omitting the Witchblade.

"I lost my grip. Fortunately, I landed on that pile of freshly excavated dirt, and it broke my fall."

O'Malley looked from Sara to the pile of dirt and back. "Uh-huh."

"Just lucky."

"And how'd this one get cleaved in two like a piece of pork loin?"

"He fell on a guy wire."

O'Malley followed her finger, shone a light on the taut cable. "Ain't this one for the books."

It would never stand up to solid police work. A good cop would haul the wire down and try to match DNA samples. But there were no DNA samples on the cable, because Chango had never touched it. Fortunately, the cable was close enough to where the kid had landed as to be plausible. Given a choice, New York cops did not want to believe in Godzilla, the Tooth Fairy, or leprechauns. Okay, maybe leprechauns. By providing a plausible scenario, Sharpe had done their work for them. They weren't going to push themselves out of shape to prove the

deaths of a handful of miserable gangbangers was anything but divine justice.

Benito was easily explained. He'd landed on a rebar
mounted in the concrete foundation.

More cops and techs began to arrive. Four of them
climbed the crane tower with a portable stretcher, into
which they strapped the hapless Tito, who was babbling
for crack. As a witness, he was in no position to contra-
dict anything Sara or Sharpe had said. He'd spent the
fight writhing on the floor of the platform.

Lupé watched, dumbfounded, as the witch made mince-
meat of her Tecolotes. Confident that this time, between
Estrella's efforts and her own hard work revving up the
troops, she'd pulled up in front of the gates and parked.
She'd seen her Tecolotes get the drop on the bitch, close
in on her and then—what was that? Suddenly the witch
was climbing the crane. Her boys followed, but a funny
thing happened once they reached the crossbar. One by
one, the bitch picked them off, until only Chango and
Benito were left.

Then, just as Chango and Benito were about to sink
their meat hooks into the bitch, something happened, too
far away to see. The witch fell, turned into a Christmas
tree ornament, and bounced. She summoned her familiar,
an eight-foot demon who pitched Benito off and cut
Chango in two with a glittering blur.

As the demon descended the crane, Lupé floored it,
leaving a four-foot streak of rubber and a fairly reliable
tire track and car signature for the cops. She was fearful
and furious. Fearful that the bitch would somehow divine
her identity, if she hadn't already done so, and come after

her. Furious at her failure to put the bitch away, after so much effort. Furious with Estrella for her impotency. Furious with her Tecolotes. Furious with Jorgé for putting her in this situation in the first place.

It was like she didn't know him any more. The witch had him under her spell. He was obsessed with good deeds, reading up on his karma, practically manhandling little old ladies across the street. Quoting Jesus, Martin Luther, and Martin Luther King, Jr. It was enough to make Lupé sick.

But if they thought Mrs. Guttierez's little girl Lupé was going to fold her wings and crawl back into the nest, they were mistaken. There was more than one way to skin a cat. By now, it had become not so much a matter of jealousy as a matter of honor. Jorgé was ruined for Lupé, anyway. Last night she'd practically begged him to go after the chain around the neck of a woman coming out of a green grocer's on West 175th, and he'd just laughed.

"Jorgé don't play that game no more."

And she'd said, "You dumb greaser. You think this gon' get you in that lady cop's pants?"

She'd half-hoped he'd slap her. He just looked at her funny and walked away.

To hell with Jorgé. If he wasn't going to love her anymore, she may as well get rid of two birds with one stone. Jorgé *and* the lady cop.

She drove erratically across the Brooklyn Bridge, pulling over once at Cadman Plaza to toke up from her crack pipe. When she arrived at St. Patrick's, vespers were still going on, and she had to thread her way through a pile of vehicles to make it back into the church's tiny, crowded lot, where there was just room to park the Celica. She sat in the car lot for a minute, shielded by a van belonging to the Archdiocese of New York, and toked up again. She examined her crack stash—enough to get her through the night, if she didn't want to come down.

And she didn't. She nurtured her rage from a tiny spark into a devouring blaze. She reached beneath the seat and seized the pistol Bobby had left her, tucked it in her Powerpuff Girls' backpack, and headed for home.

Finally, they were done. It was half past ten. Leaving her motorcycle locked to the command trailer's butane tank, Sara accompanied Sharpe across the street to a Chock Full 'O' Nuts, where they got coffee and sat opposite each other in the church pew booth.

Sara regarded the tall cop opposite. He had to sit sideways to get his legs under the table. He looked like a fashion model. He suffered from blackouts. As if his body were being borrowed by an outside spirit.

"Where's your sword?"

"How'd you survive that fall?"

Sara smacked her fist on the table. Sharpe looked down at the gaudy bracelet. Sara tapped it with her left index finger. "See this? You hear funny stories about me when you got here? That I'm a freak magnet? It's because of this thing."

"What is it?"

"Some kind of sentient biotech parasite that's attached itself to me. No, parasite isn't the right word. Symbiote. It's called the Witchblade."

Sharpe stared at the bracelet. Gently, he extended a finger and touched it, leaving a faint moist outline that disappeared as they watched. "Why is it called the Witchblade?"

"That's what it calls itself."

Their eyes met. Sara noticed that Sharpe's were an unusual hazel. "It speaks to you?"

"Sometimes."

"How did you get it?"

"You remember Kenneth Irons—the auction he tried to
hold a couple years ago at the Rialto?"

"I was in Yokohama at the time, but I think I read
something about it. Big gangland slaying . . ."

"Yup. I was there, undercover. Irons was auctioning
off this artifact that allegedly conferred invulnerability
on the wearer, but he didn't know the damned thing had
a mind of its own. It chose *me*."

"Lucky you."

"You always moonlight with a sword?"

"Security is mostly long stretches of inactivity. I like to
work out on my own. I practice kendo and iaido, you
know."

"I saw you do a number on Bratten the other night."

"You were there?"

"Why'd you call me down here, Derek?"

"Do you know anything about swords?"

Do you? She refrained from blinking. "A little."

"I've always been fascinated with them. You know
Adrian Hecht has been searching for a particular sword."

"A Muramasa."

Sharpe's eyebrows did a complex pas de deux. "This is
a huge deal in the world of collectors. Most famous sword
makers in history, most experts think the Muramasa of
the 1300s never existed. They think he was a mistake
made by early sword book writers in the 1500s, since
there are none of his blades existent today. For sword
people, proving he existed by finding his greatest sword
would be like a UFO nut finding the Roswell spaceship in

a government warehouse somewhere. It would be about as big a deal as you could have, short of aliens landing on the White House lawn."

"Both Bachman and Chalmers claimed to have documented Muramasas in their collections."

"Those are later Muramasas. The thief can't tell the difference until he has the sword in his hands. The sword Hecht seeks is called Skyroot, and was made for a rogue samurai named Udo."

"I'm familiar with Udo."

Sharpe regarded her with hooded eyes. "You *have* done your homework."

"It's my case."

"I took this after-hours gig because I think Hecht's the samurai killer."

"I thought of that myself, but come on. The guy's a bazillionaire. Why would he get his own hands dirty? He could snap his fingers and have a dozen hit men at his beck and call."

"Hecht's not a gangster! He doesn't know those people. But he *is* ruthless, and totally obsessed with acquiring Skyroot. Well, guess what? The reason I asked you to meet me was to tell you that he's got it. It arrived two nights ago and he's showing it at his party next week."

"How do you know this?"

"I got a snitch working Newark International. Thursday morning, around two A.M., Hecht's private 747 touched down. They had to clear the sword through Customs. It was appraised by the Hon'amis, and valued at $3.6 million. Of course that is a very conservative estimate. It is the first Muramasa from that period the Hon'amis have recognized. This is a huge event in the world of swords and collectors, and hasn't officially been

221

announced. That's what the party's all about. There will be people from the Smithsonian and *Vanity Fair*. Hecht likes to see his photo in the society rags."

Sharpe talked about the sword with a religious fervor. His eyes blazed. He was a Believer. Did he want the sword for himself, or was he merely excited at the magnitude of the find? She wanted to trust him. But she had seen too much.

"Is that all you're going to say? You've got a snitch?"

He nodded grimly.

"Derek, may I ask you a question?"

"Shoot."

"Do you collect swords?"

He gave her a funny look, like he'd just stepped on an egg. "I have a few swords. Got 'em in Japan. You knew I was a Nipponophile. Why?"

"The legend surrounding Skyroot."

Sharpe's brown furrowed into a map of Mississippi delta. "Yeah?"

"Some say Udo's restless spirit haunts the earth, searching for his lost sword."

Sharpe stared at her for a minute. "So?"

"So you've been having blackouts. Periods where you can't account for time. Aside from the threat this poses to your work, don't you think this might indicate a deeper, personal crisis?"

They stared intently at each other in long silence.

"Brain tumor?"

She didn't reply.

"Possession?" Sharpe whispered.

Sara shrugged. "I've seen a lot of weird stuff. I've learned not to discount the so-called supernatural."

"You think the reason I blackout is because I'm being possessed by a ghost samurai?"

"For a while, I thought the killer was trying to hide the real target: Chalmers. But now I'm not so sure. Chalmers received several threatening e-mails from someone calling himself Kagemusha, because Chalmers beat him out in an online auction."

"Shadow warrior."

"What did you think when you cut that punk in two? *Were* you thinking?"

Sharpe rubbed his forehead with his knuckles. "When I came to in the control booth, you were already out at the end of the crane, those two scumbags reaching for you. I remember running out on the crane . . ."

Sara recalled the fight they'd had on the gondola. Would have been difficult for an ordinary man to sleep through that. But nothing about Sharpe was ordinary.

"Derek, if you killed those men under some outside influence, we need to find out. *You* need to find out. If you're a man, you'll turn yourself in and ask for a complete psychological evaluation."

"I can't believe we're having this conversation."

"I just hope you'll remember."

"I'll remember."

"Why did you conceal the fact you're a former SEAL?"

"That's classified."

"Come on, Derek."

"Seriously. I know how this must look, but I'm trying to lead a normal life. I was involved in some highly classified missions in the East, and one of the conditions of my release was that I not talk about my years in the military."

"I can check that easily enough. You need to take a leave of absence."

Beat. "You're right. I will, as soon as Hecht shows the sword."

"You need to take a leave of absence now."

"I can't do that."

"Why not?"

He gritted his teeth. "Because I have to see the sword."

"Is this Derek talking, or Udo?"

A look of immense confusion came over his face. A yellow gleam of fear crept into his eyes like a distant sun. "I don't know."

"It's okay to admit it."

"I don't know what's happening to me. I've always been in control."

"I know how scary that can feel. You need to see a shrink."

"I know."

"Promise you'll get help."

"I promise. Listen. I swear to you, I didn't murder Bachman or Chalmers! Just let me stay on the job through the Grand Opening."

"Derek, I'll have to think about it. But I promise you I won't do anything before telling you first."

"Fair enough."

It was almost one by the time Sara arrived home. She parked the bike, strolled across the busy avenue, and let herself into her apartment. Shmendrick scolded her until she picked him up and took him to bed with her, purring loudly. She needed a séance, with or without Sharpe's co-operation. Sara knew of numerous psychics in and around the city—mostly humbugs, a few not. In the morning, she'd see about contacting someone.

She slept until eleven, rolled out of bed and showered. Big day. The mayor's reception was that evening. She pushed it out of her mind. Derek Sharpe was a ticking time bomb. She phoned Siry at his home in Queens.

"Joe, it's Sara. Can I come over? I need to talk to you."

"What the hell, hey. It's a zoo here anyway. My brother and his family are here. Come on around back."

Siry's house in Rego Park was a white clapboard two-story job with Amityville windows. Fifty feet of crabgrass with picket fence girdled round. A place for little Joe to play, a port for Siry's Chevrolet. It was just past one when Sara arrived. She left her bike in the driveway between a Chevy Suburban and a Subaru with Connecticut plates. In the backyard, four adults were seated around a picnic table while four kids raced pell-mell, pausing to douse each other with Super-Soakers. Joe's kids were grown up. These had to be his nieces and nephews.

Siry's wife Dalia noticed Sara first, rose to greet her with a smile. "Hello, Sara. Would you like a beer?"

"Okay."

Siry introduced her to his brother Dave, and Dave's wife Ruth. Sara accepted a beer, and she and Siry walked around the side of the house, through the hinged gate, to the front yard, where they sat on the stoop, watching kids swoop up and down 243rd Street on their skateboards, in-lines, and Razors. One quaint candidate for the Society For Creative Anachronism even rode a bicycle.

"I heard about your set-to last night at Hecht Gardens. What the heck was that all about?"

She told him, omitting her knowledge of the sword's ancient history. Siry had little use for the supernatural, despite, or perhaps because of, Sara's previous cases.

"You think Sharpe is the samurai killer? Thanks for letting me know. What happens if I reach out to him? Is he gonna cooperate? Or is he gonna go nuts and chop down my guys?"

"I don't know."

"All right. I'm putting Sharpe on administrative leave."

"You do that, he'll know I talked. Internal Affairs will get involved."

"Well Sara, I don't see where you've left me much choice. You come to me with loads of circumstantial evidence, then last night Sharpe asks you to meet him, he doesn't show, four gangbangers do, and you're nearly killed. When he does show, he acts like some kind of nut instead of a cop. Any rookie can put the lie to your story about how a guy wire cut that kid in two. Something doesn't add up here. Something you're not telling me."

Sara experienced a sinking sensation, her heart being sucked toward the center of the earth like a pneumatically propelled drive-up bank capsule. She liked Sharpe. He would know instantly that the reason he was being placed on administrative leave was because Sara had talked.

A mad M80 went off in her skull, aimed at Sharpe for putting her in this situation. He was a cop! He knew what the job entailed. It was he who'd placed her in this untenable situation through his bizarre behavior.

"Say something. You're scaring me." Siry's voice seemed to come from far away.

Sara blinked. "What?"

"You got that look on your face."

"Joe. If Sharpe has mental problems, this could push him over the edge."

"Yeah, so I have to detail two plainclothes to follow him, and I ain't got 'em. I'm going to have to put in a special request to One Police Plaza, they're gonna want to know why . . ."

"Joe. Tell them you're closing in on Chalmers' killer. That'll give you the cover you need."

An expression of enlightenment slowly settled onto Siry's heavy features. "That's right! Now my only problem is keeping this away from the press. That's all the department needs. 'Samurai killer exposed as cop.' "

"I'd say that's the least of your worries."

"That's because you're not chief. You going to this thing at Gracie Mansion tonight?"

"Yeah."

"I'd tell you how to behave, except I think you know more about it than me. Have a good time and don't piss on or piss off the mayor."

"One more thing."

Siry slapped a hand over his face and dragged. "What?"

"Maybe we should alert Hecht he could be in danger."

"I'll take care of it."

"Thanks, Joe."

Two teen-age boys watched with a mixture of awe and admiration as she strapped on her beanie helmet and took off. She ran the tach up to nine, dropped the clutch, and did a wheelie.

Something to remember for the rest of their lives.

SIXTEEN

Sara needed a psychic. With all its powers, she wondered why the Witchblade wouldn't pitch in. There were limits to its powers. It didn't do readings, or contact spirits from the netherworld. Sara phoned Brooklyn Vice, spoke to a bunco expert named Palmer, and it was Palmer who told her about the witch lady Estrella who lived down by the tracks.

After leaving Joe's house, Sara headed for the switching yard that cut Brooklyn off from the waterfront at Map Street, using her badge to get by security at the freight-loading gate. A squat black security guard in a khaki Blane's uniform with "Hawkins" on the ID tag accosted her as she chained her bike to the hurricane fence surrounding a switching station.

"What do you think you're doing?"

She flashed the badge. "I'm looking for Estrella."

"You want the witch? She's down a quarter-mile, in an old switching shack surrounded by hex signs, next to the Con Ed box. She's hard to miss. What do you want with her? We always figured she was the bunk, but we let her stay 'cause she discourages taggers. Scares 'em spitless."

Sara set off through the freight yard, walking sometimes on the dull nickel-colored rails, sometimes on cinders, sometimes on ties, in and around boxcars on sidings, occasionally losing sight of the skyline. The switching yard was a maze. Most of the sidelined boxcars were covered with graffiti, Estrella notwithstanding. Sara recognized a dozen different gang monikers, including Los Romeros and Los Tecolotes.

Eventually, she emerged from the thicket onto a dusty plain, at one end of which sat the corrugated steel shack, roof draped with fishnets into which the owner had inserted various fetishistic objects, including Barbie and GI Joe dolls, green Rolling Rock bottles, faded Lotto tickets, and cracked CDs. There was no graffiti on the switching station.

A big old tomcat was sunning itself on a concrete block as Sara approached. It watched her with baleful yellow eyes and twitching tail, and when she drew abreast, let out a yowl that cut through the hum of the transfer station like a shotgun blast through fog. The cat leaped up and headed directly away from the hut as fast as it scabbed legs could scrabble.

The front door was open. Enya drifted from within. The door faced north east, so Sara cast no shadow when she finally stood in the entrance, took off her sunglasses, and let her eyes adjust to the gloom. The witch Estrella lay sprawled on mismatched cushions, one hand clutching a bottle of muscatel. The interior of the cabin smelled of cheap wine, body odor, sandalwood, and spice. Estrella was a dumpy woman, hard to tell her age, with a brown

face and black hair streaked with gray. She might have
been beautiful once, but age and hard living had left her
ravaged as a gravel road.

"Excuse me," Sara said. "Estrella?"

The old woman stirred, moaned. "Wha—? Who want
Estrella?"

"Detective Pezzini, Eleventh Precinct."

The old woman's eyes popped open. She sat up, lips
parted like an old purse left in the rain. An expression of
terror descended like the night.

"No," the witch croaked, working her legs as if to
scrabble backward. "Witch!" she shrieked. "You de
witch!"

"No," Sara said forcefully. *"You're* the witch. *I'm* the
cop. What's the problem? Have you been reading the
tabloids? Do you know me?"

Estrella had backed herself up against an old wooden
packing crate she used as a table, breathing hard, her
mouth a slit. Sara came into the room. Her eyes adjusted
to the gloom, a couple of candles the only light. Like a
filthy little Bedouins' den.

She crouched in front of the witch, and held up the
little plastic troll figure she'd taken from Bobby Chacón.
"Do you recognize this?"

The witch's eyes grew wider, until yellowish whites
showed all the way around. She reached frantically under
some covers. Sara dropped the troll and went for her revolver, had it up and the hammer back when Estrella held
up an ornate old cross draped with cheap plastic beads,
colored pipecleaners, and other ornaments. For an instant
they faced each other, the two witches, each holding their
shamanistic totem. Sara lowered hers first.

"You shouldn't make sudden moves like that in front of a cop. I might have shot you."

"What for you use de gun anyway? I know 'bout you. I know you very powerful witch. I make no excuses. The girl come to me wit' a job. You would have done de same."

Connections started sliding into place. Bobby Chacón's troll doll. The peculiar way in which the gangbangers had pursued her. The ugly little drawing she'd received in the mail. "Someone hired you to put a hex on me."

Estrella nodded, still grasping the crucifix. "You would have done de same."

"Uh, no. But that's not why I'm here. What you just told me suggests you had prior knowledge of an assault and did nothing. You also admit to helping the perpetrators. You're guilty of prior knowledge, being an accessory to assault on a police officer. I could arrest you."

The yellow eyes contracted. "Go 'head an' 'rest me, den."

"No. That's not why I'm here. I need someone to help me conduct a séance."

Estrella looked confused. Unconsciously, she reached for the muscatel. "Huh?"

"I need someone to help me contact a ghost, a spirit. Someone who's been dead a long time. Your name came up. That's why I'm here. I came to ask for your help in conducting a séance. While you're at it, you can tell me who set me up."

A look of low cunning stole over the woman's ferret-like features. She was as transparent as glass. Sara wondered how she'd managed to fool so many people. "I do not contact de spirit world. I know someone who does.

And dat de same person who set me after you. Lupé Guttierez."

It was 4:30 by the time Sara returned to Waubeska Place. She left her helmet with the bike, cut straight through the building to the front lobby and out the front door. Hector sat on the concrete abutment framing the stairs, wearing a pair of pleated Dockers, white T, and a set of headphones through which Sara could hear Malo faintly blasting. He puffed out his cheeks and blew up on his mustache when he saw her, took the headphones off.

" 'Ey, *guapa*. How you doin'? Man, that was some hurt you laid on me the other day."

They did a complex soul clasp. "No hard feelings?"

" 'Ell, no. Din't hurt my stock with the ladies to learn you laid me out, specially 'cause I so humble about it." He flashed a disarming grin, displaying a gold tooth with a small ruby.

"Nice tooth. Where can I find Lupé Guttierez?"

"You live here and you askin' me? She in the ground floor apartment on the right with the picture of Selena on the door. I tell that girl she ought to switch to Thalia, but she don't listen."

"What are you doing out here?"

"Guardin' the place. Watchin' out. Helpin' little old ladies with they groceries. That's what Jorgé told me to do, and that's what I'm doin'."

"Hector, you surprise me. You turn out to be very intelligent and well-spoken. You keep on like this, and there's no limit to how far you can go."

Hector balanced his forearms on his thighs and regarded the street with equanimity. "Jes' doin' a job."

Sara went inside. The inner security door was locked,

at least. She let herself into the apartment proper and followed the hall around to the right on faded rose carpeting. Life boomed faintly through the walls: a snatch of Snoop Dogg, a few bars of Tony Bennett, an argument in Spanish. The halls were fragrant with cumin, curry, a wild mix of spices. The Guttierez apartment was number 124. There was a poster of the late Latin singer Selena taped to the wall, along with some humorous postcards and phrases in Spanish.

Sara knocked. A moment later, the door opened on the chain, framing a wan-faced girl whose straight black hair hung in her face. She was sucking on an electro-pop, little motor in the handle turning the sugar in her mouth so she didn't have to lick. She stared, holding the device to her mouth like a self-directed drill.

Sara showed the badge. "I'm looking for Lupé. She in?"

The girl nodded, stood there whirring.

"May I see her? Inside the apartment?"

The girl closed the door, unlatched the chain, and opened it again. Sara entered a cozy apartment rich with religious symbols. The tiny living room was devoted to several pictures of Christ, with and without Mary, and there was a small shrine in the corner, plaster Christ preaching from a heavenly blue shell on top of a cheap end table, numerous candles at his feet. The television was showing *The Powerpuff Girls*.

"Where's Lupé?"

The girl flopped down on some cushions in front of the television. It was a miracle she didn't drive her candy through the roof of her mouth. She gestured down the hall. "She's in her bedroom."

There were more posters on the door to the bedroom. The door was shut, quietly pulsating with music. Sara tried the knob. It was unlocked. Carefully, she swung the door inward. Lupé sat cross-legged on her bed, bopping to tunes playing in her head through a Sony Walkman. The walls were crowded with posters and pictures.

Sara let herself in and shut the door. Lupé's shoulders hunched. She turned. Eyes and mouth expanded into sinkholes. She snatched the headphones off and scrambled for the head of the bed, hand reaching beneath the pillows. Sara instinctively leaped after, both hands burrowing under the cushions after Lupé's. Sara's hands closed around Lupé's as it closed around a chunk of steel. Sara twisted the .9mm Ruger loose, tossed it over her shoulder. Her hand came back and struck Lupé hard across the cheek.

Sara hadn't intended to do that. It was the Witchblade.

Lupé crouched on her knees, hand to face, looking scared. Sara backed off, panting.

"Okay. Just so we know where we stand. I could bust you for attempted murder of a police officer. That's a lifetime term, little lady. But if you help me, I may not have to do that."

The girl stared at her with undisguised hatred.

"Is there a problem? You look like you hate my guts. What have I ever done to you?"

The girl's face twisted in outrage. It made her look even younger. "You take my boyfriend away from me, and you ask me *that?*"

"Your boyfriend? Are you referring to Jorgé?" Sara barked a rueful laugh. "I have nothing to do with him! I *have* a boyfriend. Girlfriend, you must be dreaming. Only reason I talk to Jorgé is to get him to lay off the residents. So far, he's risen to the task. He might be a lot better than you think." Too good for you, she thought.

"So what? What you want with me?"

"Estrella told me that you sometimes see future events, that you have precognitive ability."

Lupé drew herself up with newfound dignity. "I got the power, if that's what you mean. Sometimes I can see things before they happen."

"Do you know what a séance is?"

Lupé nodded.

"Have you ever conducted one?"

Lupé's young face clouded with blood. "Once, I try to contact my brother Enriqué, who was killed by some Jamaicans 'cause they wanted his corner. He tell me he in a strange place now, neither here nor there. It made me cold . . ." The girl grabbed herself around the arms and squeezed, as if trying to hold in heat. It was very warm in the bedroom.

Sara reached into her pocket and pulled out the troll. "My hair. It must have come from you. Where did you get it?"

Without looking at Sara, Lupé said, "The garbage chute."

Sara held up the drawing of her surrounded by wolves. "And this?"

Lupé bit her lip, eyes wide, and nodded. "S'posed to make you scared."

"I see that you're an enterprising young lady. It's too bad you haven't found something constructive in to which you can channel your energies. But if you help me, and keep your nose clean, maybe I can help you."

The girl said nothing. Simply stared at the floor and pouted.

"How old are you, Lupé?"

"Fifteen."

"You go to school?"

Lupé shrugged. "Sometime. Malcolm Shabazz Middle School."

"You gonna help me with this séance?"

At last the girl looked up. "Who are you trying to reach?"

"A Japanese samurai who was forced to commit suicide eight hundred years ago."

"Close the door," Lupé said.

Sara shut the door. "You going to help me?"

The girl nodded, swallowing. "You got something that belonged to this samurai?"

Sara produced the *tsuba*, black iron in the shape of a lotus blossom, and handed it to the girl. Lupé set it on the bed, went to the window and shut the blinds. "Works better if there's less light." She took a towel, wadded it up, and spread it at the base of the door.

"How often have you done this?" Sara asked.

"Twice. Once to find *mi hermano*. Once to talk to Selena."

"How'd it go?"

"I tol' you 'bout Enriqué. I never could get in touch with Selena 'cause I don't got nothin' of hers. Maybe I buy something on eBay one of these days."

Sara looked around. She hadn't seen a computer. "How do you know about eBay?"

"I learn about it at school. They sellin' all sorts of stuff used to belong to Selena. There's this statue of her in a black leather jacket, but that wouldn't help me get in touch with her. In order to reach someone who's dead, you need to have something that used to belong to them."

The *tsuba* had belonged to Muramasa, not Udo, or Shiegeyoshi. But if Udo had killed Muramasa, perhaps the swordsmith's ghost was in touch with that of the warrior. Perhaps they took tea together. Sara didn't know what she expected, but she was out of leads on the earthly plane. Time to cross over. She tapped the disc on the bed.

The girl took it, held it up to the light, looked as if she were about to take a bite out of it. "What is this?"

"It's a *tsuba*, the hilt from a samurai sword."

"Who we reachin' out to?"

Sara smiled. The girl had unconsciously invoked cop talk. "The sword's builder, Muramasa. He lived in Japan in the thirteenth century."

She nodded. "Hesh up now, I got to concentrate."

The girl set four large candles around the room, at the four corners, and lit them. They sat cross-legged on the bed, facing each other, with the black metal disc between them. Lupé instructed Sara to rest her fingertips gently on the edge of the *tsuba*; Lupé did likewise. Outside, they could hear traffic swooshing by a block away on Atlantic Avenue. The sound seemed to recede as Lupé bent forward and began to speak in a low voice.

"Muramasa, great swordmaker, you who wander in the void unsatisfied, unrequited, without rest, hear us. Speak to us. Tell us what you seek."

Nothing. Nothing save the distant swoosh of traffic, like an angry sea, the hiss of water moving through the pipes, the muted glee of the *Powerpuff Girls* from the television in the living room.

They sat awkwardly for five minutes. Lupé looked up from beneath her black bangs. "Sometimes it takes a while. Sometimes the spirits are busy."

"How often have you done this?"

"Twice, I told you. Hesh up. I got to concentrate."

The girl dropped her voice an octave as if speaking in

a patently fake tone would convince the spirits of her sincerity. "Muramasa, great swordmaker . . ."

Sara's hand began to tingle, an instant before the gauntlet arrived with a clank. A cold wind blasted through the room, making the blinds buzz and blowing out the candles. The room grew dark, as if someone had set a bell cover over the entire building, blocking out the sun. The Witchblade yanked her hand outward and held it there, as if to ward off a blow.

The voice emanated outward, in ripples, from somewhere within Lupé, but did not issue from her mouth. Her lips moved, but the sound came from everywhere and nowhere. It was a man's voice, harsh and guttural. It spat forth the words, *Washi no katana, kaese!* in a dialect that hadn't been heard in seven hundred years.

A tendril of burning chemical fiber wound through Sara's sinuses like a bramble. She looked down. The *tsuba* was glowing red hot, igniting the cheap bed cover. Instinctively, the Witchblade swooped down, picked up the glowing disc and tossed it in the girl's metal wastebasket. The trashcan was empty. The *tsuba* glowed dull and began to fade. Lupé's eyes rolled up into the top of her head and she collapsed sideways on the bed.

Sara looked down. The Witchblade was gone, replaced by the costume bracelet. Her palm tingled, from the heat of the disc. Leaning over, she straightened the girl out, thumbed open her lids, looked at her eyes, felt her pulse. Sara let herself out of the bedroom, down the short hall to the tiny bathroom, where she found a clean washrag and soaked it in cold water. At the end of the hall, the younger sister remained sprawled on a cushion watching the Cartoon Network.

Lupé opened her eyes as Sara applied the cold cloth to

her forehead. She blinked a couple of times. "Wow. I guess we made contact, huh?"

Sara had been repeating the strange words over and over in her head until she found the mnemonic key, which she used to lock the memory. "Are you all right? Wait, don't try to sit up yet. Tell me what happened."

"You know what happened, lady. I made contact. I wasn't there. I got displaced. Only you saw and know what happened."

"You don't remember the words?"

"No. What's that smell? Is something burning?"

"The artifact I brought became red hot and set the bedclothes on fire. Don't worry. It's out. There's no danger."

Lupé sat up. "Wow. Did that really happen?" She stared at the charred disc in the middle of her bedspread.

"Why are you surprised? You believe in witchcraft, don't you?"

The girl nodded.

"You have extraordinary abilities. How are you doing in school?"

The girl drew her knees up beneath her chin. Suddenly, she looked twelve years old. "You ain't my mother."

"That's right, I'm not. When someone expresses interest in you, the least you can do is be polite. Let me guess. You don't attend regularly. Can you read and write?"

"Of course I can read and write. I'm not stupid." Sara just stared at her with limpid green eyes. Lupé squirmed. "Okay. I'm sorry. Maybe I made a mistake 'bout choo. Maybe you ain't evil. But you a witch, I seen that for myself!"

Sara winked. "Takes one to know one."

Lupé gaped. A guffaw escaped her reluctant lips. "Okay. We just a couple a witches havin' a coven."

There was noise outside the room. A moment later, the door swung inward, revealing a rail-thin Latino woman, her long black hair streaked with gray and fixed atop her head in a bun, wearing a coral-colored waitress uniform. "I thought I heard voices. Who is your friend?"

Sara stood. "Sara Pezzini, Mrs. Guttierez. I live on the fourth floor."

"You're the policewoman." She offered her thin, strong hand, quizzical expression on her face. "Is Lupé in trouble?"

Conspiracy, incitement to riot, illegal possession of a firearm, driving without a license. "No, ma'am. Not at all. We just discovered we have a few things in common."

More quizzical.

"We both have precognitive abilities, Mama," the girl said.

Mrs. Guttierez nodded, smiled. "Would you like some coffee, Miss Pezzini?"

"No thank you, ma'am. I have to be going. But if there's anything you need, that I can help, here's my card."

She scooped up the nine on her way out the door, gave mamacita a smile. "It's mine. I just set it down for a minute."

SEVENTEEN

Sara had three hours before she was to meet David for the mayor's reception. Ralph Munster was not in the Manhattan phone directory, but Sharpe had written Munster's home and cell phone numbers on the back of the card. She tried the cell phone first.

"Munster," he answered quickly with a hint of impatience.

"Mr. Munster, this is Detective Sara Pezzini, of the Eleventh Precinct. I wonder if I could see you for a few minutes this afternoon."

"What's this about?"

"Homicide investigation."

Beat. "I'm golfing."

"I won't take more than a few minutes. I can come out to where you're playing, if you like."

"No." Sigh of exasperation. Hand over the receiver while he explained to his foursome. "I can meet you briefly at three-thirty."

"Where?"

He named a tavern called J. Pierpont's on Route 29, near Danbury.

She carefully packed her bike with all necessary items. It was a tight fit, enough to make a girl wish for saddle-bags. She'd been thinking of investing in a pair of Corbin Beetle Bags, but they weren't much larger than her compact, and cost eight hundred bucks. Between her tank bag and the strap-on overnighter, she got it all in: the dress, the shoes, the makeup, even the hair dryer.

It took her just over an hour to make the run up to Danbury, dicing with semis and brain-dead hausfraus in SUVs. She found J. Pierpont's on a frontage road between Schulman's Wholesale Furniture and Curtis Chrysler/Dodge. It was one of those faux folksy fern bars with a polished brass rail and an eight-page menu, from Mexican to Thai. She made a bet with herself that the BMW 5-series with the WALL ST license was Munster's.

He was in a window booth, scowling at a copy of *Barron's*, iced latté at hand. He had the lean, tanned good looks of a surfer or professional politician, wore a coarse-weave ecru cotton jacket over a white golf shirt, looked surprised when she slid in across from him. Surprised at her. He wasn't expecting this.

"How do you know me?" he asked at once.

She slid the card she'd taken from Sharpe's place across the table. He picked it up, examined it, put it back down. "Where'd you get it?"

"Never mind where I got it. Nobody knows that I have it except you. Nobody has to know. I'm in the middle of a homicide investigation and I need answers fast. It's possible the killer will strike again."

"What's this got to do with me?"

"You're a close personal friend of Derek Sharpe, aren't you?"

The waitress came. Sara ordered an iced tea.

"This is about those damned swords, isn't it?"

"What makes you think so?"

"Derek. Thinks he's the reincarnation of Toshiro Mifune."

"Toshiro Mifune has only been dead a short time. Does Derek really believe he's a reincarnated samurai?"

Munster offered a wry grin. "I was speaking figuratively. He is a great admirer of their culture, history, and tradition. He speaks Japanese, you know."

"I didn't know. Look, it's none of my business, but are you Derek's . . . gentleman friend?"

He frowned. "I'm his lover, okay? I'm not butch, and I'm not a drag queen. My partners know I'm gay, but they don't mind because I don't mince around in a pink tutu demanding money for AIDS research. Derek's situation is somewhat different."

"That's why I'm being discreet."

"I appreciate it. Not that he makes a secret of it."

"I'm actually surprised he was hired."

Munster shrugged.

"Mr. Munster, is Derek the samurai killer?"

"How would I know?"

"I figure if anyone would, you would."

"Well, I don't. We have a complicated relationship. He's a very private person. So am I. I do know he went native in a big way, and now he's back. Certainly he's physically capable of these deeds, but not mentally, or spiritually. Derek is a very spiritual person. I just can't see him murdering anyone."

"He's a former SEAL."

"He's changed."

"Has he ever experienced blackouts?"

"What do you mean?"

"Periods of time for which he can't account."

"Not that I'm aware of."

Sara handed Munster her card. "If you think of anything, please call me."

Munster tapped the card against the tabletop. "There *is* one thing . . ."

Sara leaned forward. "Oh?"

"He did tell me, he'd gone on a joint operation with Japanese special police after some terrorist, one of those charismatic monks in a mountain stronghold in Hokkaido. Something happened, something that frightened him badly. He cut himself . . ."

"Cut himself how?"

"On a sword. That's all I know. He won't talk about it."

"Do you know what happened to the sword?"

"No. But he worries . . . that he's been infected. Some poison."

"Has he had himself tested?"

"Everything. He gets a clean bill of health. I asked him what made him think so. He said, 'I just don't feel like myself.'"

"That's it?"

Munster shrugged. "I'm sorry."

"You'll call me if you think of anything."

"Sure."

She arrived at the precinct house at ten of five. Hers was the only bike. She sat at her desk and wrote out the phonetic statement she'd heard, as accurately as possible.

DEMONS

WASHI NO KATANA, KAESE!

She knew enough about Japanese to recognize the word for "sword." She phoned the Asian Languages Department at Columbia and got a recording. It was, after all, Saturday afternoon. She couldn't hope to connect with any scholars. She searched the central roster for Japanese-American cops, came up with a couple, tried reaching out to them. Nada. She ended up e-mailing the phonetic phrase to the foreign language departments at Columbia, CCNY, SUNY, and the Japanese Consulate. Any luck, she'd find an answer waiting Monday morning.

Who had spoken through Lupé? Muramasa? Oji? Shigeyoshi? She knew so little about any of them, she felt lost. The *tsuba*'s maker was not necessarily the speaker. Any powerful spirit would seize on the opportunity Sara and Lupé had provided. Sara was convinced that whoever had spoken, it was the driving force behind the murders. Forget the ex-wives. Forget the business rivals. It was another monster chase.

"Lord," she said to herself, "couldn't you send me a nice, simple, live human suspect? Just one."

Her phone rang.

"Pezzini."

"Detective, it's Norm Hansen with Panther Security."

Sara's heart did a one-and-a-half gainer. "Yes, Mr. Hansen. It's about a device I found across the street from Bachman." She described the device, and how she had traced it back to Panther.

"I don't know about that, and I should. We were all shocked at Mr. Chalmers' death. I knew him—not a close

245

friend, but we were friendly. Let me look into this and get back to you."

"I'll e-mail you the serial number."

"That would be helpful."

At 5:30, she packed it in and headed downtown to change at Dave's place. She could have used the women's room at the station house, but she preferred David's commodious bathroom. It was more private. She'd phoned David ahead of time so that he was standing by the open door in the alley when she arrived. He wore a pair of loose-fitting heavy black cotton pants with elastics at the waist and ankles, Chinese kung fu slippers, and a gray T-shirt that said FOURTH ANNUAL PRIDE CLASSIC. He was dripping with sweat.

"Hi! I was just working. Make yourself at home while I take a quick shower. Won't be more than ten minutes."

"Just a minute," she said, grabbing him before he bolted. She drew him close and kissed him on the mouth. "Okay. You may go."

The swordpolisher clasped his hands together next to his tilted head, a moony expression on his face. "Whoo! Whoo!" he sang like the wolf in a Tex Avery cartoon, spun around, leaped in the air, clicked his heels together three times before he landed and sped off. Sara laughed.

She set her bike in a corner and unpacked her bags. She looked around for the sword on which he'd been working, but couldn't see it.

Toting her bags, Sara went through the workroom, down the hall, into the living room where she set her bags down, sat on the folded futon opposite the television, and flicked it on. It took her a second to figure the controls.

She cued in WKAX, the all-news Fox affiliate. Not a blip about her set-to the other night at Hecht Gardens.

She could thank Hecht for that. The man had an aversion to negative publicity.

She turned off the television and turned on the radio. It was on a jazz station, Rahsaan Roland Kirk blowing three horns at once. Sara stretched supine on the futon, feeling safe and cozy for the first time all week. No one knew where she was. David made her feel secure, which was funny, because she generally felt superior to the men around her.

It was she who made them feel secure. Or scared them to death. Between the end of Rahsaan and the beginning of Art Blakey, she heard the shower running. She dozed. The next thing she knew, David was tapping her on the shoulder. He'd covered her with a Navajo blanket.

"It's seven, Sara. You probably ought to start getting ready."

"Oh my gosh, the reception's at eight!"

"Plenty of time. We'll take a cab."

Sara sat up and blinked. For a moment she thought she was still dreaming. The young man before her was a far cry from the sweaty smith she'd first met a week ago. This David Kopkind appeared to have stepped from the pages of *GQ*, in a cream-colored, French-cut Pierre Cardin over a coarse beige peasant shirt with the top button undone.

"David, you look like a great big vanilla sundae. I could eat you."

He blushed charmingly. "We don't have time. You can't be late for the mayor. He won't invite you back."

Sara got up. "Ha. As if. The only reason I got this invite is because he wants to hear firsthand what I've got on the Chalmers investigation. Which is bupkus."

"And maybe, just maybe, he's been told how beautiful you are?"

"I doubt that." With a toss of her head, Sara headed toward the bathroom. "You'll have to wear a tie with that!" she shouted over her shoulder.

"I know."

He'd even straightened out the bathroom, clearing out the used laundry, providing enough fluffed cotton to dry a buffalo. She emerged a half-hour later in a white St. John shift by Marie Gray and a pair of white Dolce and Gabbana heels with straps. David did a double-take and flopped over backwards on the floor in a perfect judo drop.

"Get up!" Sara said, laughing, pulling on his hands. "You'll ruin your suit!"

David got up, took off his jacket, and used a lint roller to remove cat hair.

They caught a taxi right in front. The Egyptian driver had decorated his cab with an ostentatious show of patriotism, red, white, and blue bunting draping the interior like a campaign car. A small photo of George Bush was affixed to the dash next to a Yankees button. He whisked them uptown toward Carl Schurz Park and Gracie Mansion. A uniformed cop checked Sara's invitation at the gate before admitting them to the mansion grounds. The circular driveway in front of the mansion was bumper-to-bumper with limos. The house itself was gaily lit, highlighting its wedding cake regency style.

Only when they stepped inside did Sara realize David had chosen a tie the exact color of her eyes. They joined the reception line. A dozen people ahead of them, Sara spotted Adrian Hecht and his date, the supermodel Katrina. A liveried waiter offered them champagne from a sterling silver tray while they waited in line. As they approached the mayor, an aide whispered their names and why they were there.

"Detective Pezzini," the Mayor said, shaking her hand solemnly. "I'm so glad to finally meet you. You're a folk heroine in the police department."

"My escapades have been greatly exaggerated, Your Honor. This is my friend, David Kopkind."

David and the mayor shook, the mayor introduced his wife, a bubbly lady with pink cheeks and silver hair, and then they were through the line and mingling with several dozen other swells in the ballroom, its main features a parquet floor and oak paneled walls hung with paintings of past dignitaries. A string quartet in the corner played a Brahms concerto.

They drifted toward a buffet set up under a large painting of "The Deal for Manhattan": Dutch settlers handing over trinkets and beads to pipe-smoking Indians, at a time Manhattan was a cow pasture. Sara observed Katrina carefully inspect the shrimp before choosing one, eating it with the delicacy of a cat. Hecht was jawing with another square-shouldered mover and shaker.

"Detective Pezzini," he said, extending his hand to include her in the conversation. "Want to thank you for looking out for my property. Barry Gower, Sara Pezzini. Barry's a developer. Sara's a detective."

Gower, with an obvious rug, a chin the size of New Jersey, and a shark skin suit, shook her hand. Then he excused himself, leaving the foursome. Katrina dabbed at her lips with a monogrammed napkin.

"Sara and David—is that right?"

David nodded and shook the model's hand. She was taller than him by at least two inches.

"Detective Pezzini," she said with a faint East German accent. "You could be a model."

"I've had offers, but I'll stick to police work. It's less dangerous."

"You're coming to our soiree Monday night," Hecht said.

"I wouldn't miss it. A little bird told me you're going to unveil something special."

Hecht stared at David for a hard instant, looked at her, gave a slight nod of the head. The two of them drifted off, leaving David looking up at Katrina's famous features.

Hecht and Sara stood beneath a portrait of Willem Van Der Koot, an early Dutch settler. "What did you hear?" Hecht asked, just loud enough for her.

"You've got it. The Holy Grail. Muramasa's last sword, Skyroot."

Hecht's eyes and mouth were slits. "Who told you that?"

"Hunh-unh. Is it true?"

"I don't know. It hasn't been verified."

"Oh, come on, Adrian. This is what you've been waiting for. If it is true, you're in danger. The samurai killer is after that sword. And he has a nasty habit of decapitating whoever's got it."

"Trust me, the sword is safe."

"Unless they get to you."

Hecht turned his body so his back was to the crowd, opened his jacket just enough for Sara to see the butt of an automatic pistol riding in a custom leather holster. "I'm aware of that, and before you start squawking, I've got a permit to carry."

"How did you get that by security?"

"Be cool. I'm an ex-Marine officer."

"I'm not worried about you shooting someone. I am worried about you defending yourself. If you think you're a match for this nut, you're mistaken. Why don't you have bodyguards?"

"What makes you think I don't?"

"Do you?"

"Yes, I have security here. But, as always, Detective, just seeing you around makes me feel safer." He grinned, pleased with himself.

Sara spotted the Japanese consul across the room, clutching a drink in a tumbler with fruit. "We'll be there, Adrian. In the meantime, be careful. I mean it."

She excused herself and made a beeline for the consul, joining the group as Mr. Harushi explained economic policy to three Wall Street heavyhitters. Noticing her, Harushi excused himself. They had met at several functions where Sara was often chosen for parade duty. She was the type of face the department liked to feature in public relations campaigns.

"Detective Pezzini. How can I be of service to you?" Hana Harushi was a short, middle-aged gentleman with huge rectangular glasses and a shock of gray black hair.

"Good evening, Mr. Harushi. Would you be so kind as to translate for me a Japanese phrase?"

"If I can."

Over Harushi's shoulder, an intense, balding young man in oval designer glasses was heading her way like a torpedo, mouth set in a grim line. Brandon Stern. As soon as he saw her looking at him, he forced a wan smile.

"Good evening, Mr. Harushi. Good evening, Detective Pezzini. When you have a minute, the mayor would appreciate your company in the den."

Sara raised her eyebrows. "Brandy and cigars?"

"I'm sure those are available if you wish."

Stern hovered. Apparently, she had a moment now.

"Mr. Harushi, will you excuse me?"

"Certainly."

She accompanied the aide toward a hallway beneath a carved oak lintel. Looking back, she saw Harushi staring after them, playing with the plastic sword in his cocktail.

The mayor was all smiles as he greeted Sara in his private study. He was a jovial, pink, pear-shaped politician with a fringe of curly white hair. A moderate Republican, which, of course, meant his policies were indistinguishable from those of any urban Democrat. The library had a sixteen-foot ceiling, wall after wall of oak shelving laden with red-leather bound books, all softly glowing in the light of a green-shaded banker's lamp on the mayor's Federalist rosewood desk. A fire crackled in the marble-framed hearth, surmounted by a slab of Vermont granite the size of the Queen Mary, above which a portrait of Jimmy Walker twinkled with a hint of mischief.

"Detective Pezzini! Thank you for coming. I've heard so much about you! I'm sorry it's taken us this long to meet."

She shook the mayor's hand. His palm was surprisingly moist for a politician. Maybe he needed to warm up. "We've been on the same podium several times, Your Honor."

"Is that right? Can I get you a drink?"

"Just water."

The mayor went to a sideboard, opened a camouflaged refrigerator, and removed a bottle of designer water. He twisted off the cap, poured water into a tumbler, added ice with a pair of silver tongs, and a twist of lemon. He indicated a wing-backed red leather chair, brass studs gleaming softly in the firelight.

The mayor sat opposite, resting his drink, Scotch and water, on a small round rosewood table. "Is that young man your boyfriend?"

A hint of blush crept into Sara's cheeks.

The Mayor laughed. "I think that says it all. The Commissioner tells me you're quite a detective."

Sara sipped water and offered a Mona Lisa smile. "It runs in the family, Your Honor. As you know, my father was a cop."

"Yes, indeed. Vincent Pezzini, one of the brave heroes who gave their lives protecting the citizens of this great metropolis." The phrase tripped off his tongue. "Brandon told me about your involvement with the Russian Mafia a couple months ago. You're a brave young woman. I'm putting you in for a mayoral commendation."

"That's very kind of you, your honor, but a lot of the credit goes to my fellow officers, and my partner, Jake McCarthy."

"You're too modest. I guess you know Scott Chalmers was a friend of mine."

She nodded. *Here it comes*, she thought.

"As is Adrian Hecht. The problem is, some people look at these crimes, including your donnybrook the other night at Hecht Gardens, and think it's part of a terrorist plot to discourage developers in lower Manhattan."

Sara tried not to do a double-take. "Sir, with all due respect, that's ridiculous. The killer is clearly after ancient Japanese swords."

"Have you heard of a group called Black September?"

"Yes sir, and I'm aware that members of the Japanese

Red Guard participated in an airport massacre in Rome in 1984. But as far as I know, they haven't been active since."

"I received a report from the State Department yesterday. They seem to think the Red Guard branch of Black September may be in the country."

What do you want me to do about it, she thought? *I'm dancing as fast as I can.* "I'd like to see that report, if I may."

"I'll have it sent over. If there's any chance you can wrap this up before Hecht's wing-ding Monday night . . ." The mayor must have seen something in her eyes because he quickly back-pedaled. "I know . . . I'm sorry. I know that's unreasonable. But it would be helpful if you could announce that you've got a suspect, or even some new leads."

"Your Honor, all I can tell you is that I do have a promising lead, and I'm close to cracking the case. But the answer isn't simple."

The mayor stared with pursed lips a moment, sipped his drink. He sighed. "I was afraid of that. I'd appreciate it if you'd keep me posted."

"Of course. Will you be at the party Monday night?"

He nodded.

"I'm not sure that's a good idea."

"I really have no choice. I said I'd come, and Hecht is a major campaign contributor. Whoops. A gaffe is when a politician inadvertently tells the truth. How about you? Will you be there?"

She nodded. The mayor stood. The interview was over. "Then I'll feel safer."

They shook hands, and she showed herself out.

Harushi was waiting for her in the ballroom. "What did you want to ask me?"

"I'd like you to translate a Japanese phrase for me."

"If I can."

"*Washi no katana, kaese!*" Sara snarled.

The consul blinked. " 'Give me back my sword.' "

EIGHTEEN

Sara gazed down into David's sated eyes as he lay on his back on the futon in the living room.

"Wow," he said. "Wow wow wow."

"Was it good for ya, baby?" Sara asked, batting her eyes.

"Tell me again what the Japanese consul said?"

" 'Give me back my sword.' " She said it again in a campfire scary voice. "*Give me back my sword!* Vince sent me to summer camp when I was eleven. The counselors used to tell us scary stories at night, around the campfire, and the one story I always remember—that everybody always remembers—is about the corpse searching for his heart/slash/hand/slash/kidneys. And he creeps right up behind you and crowls in your ear, 'Give me back my kidneys!' The Polish variation is, 'Give me back my kischkes!'"

"What's a kischke?"

"I don't know, and I don't want to know." She slid off and snuggled under one arm.

"Don't get too comfortable because I have to go work."

Sara looked up. The digital clock on the VCR said 11:15. "It's Saturday night. What kind of work?"

"Polishing, that's all I do."

"Tonight? Saturday night?"

"I promised the client it would be ready on Monday. I have to put in twelve hours a day."

"Can I see it?"

"Nope. I promised the client I wouldn't show it to anybody."

She ran her nails lightly across his smooth, hairless chest. She didn't like hair on a man. On top of the head, that was okay. Maybe a well-trimmed mustache. But none of this hairy ape stuff. "Come on, David. You can show me."

He hoisted himself to one elbow and cradled her head in one hand. "Baby. I promised. And when I make a promise, that's it. If I made a promise to you, I wouldn't break it. The client asked for absolute discretion. This is absolute."

She gazed into his aqua eyes for a minute, heart swelling. At last. One true man. "I understand. You mind if I just curl up here and sleep?"

She was rewarded with a lupine grin. "I was hoping you would."

She heard him pad lightly down the hall, the key in the lock, the swing of the workroom door. He kept it locked? The door shut, the lock latched faintly shut. A few minutes later, she heard the steady swoosh of steel on stone through the vents. She plunged into sleep.

Sara awoke a few hours later. She'd kicked off most of the bedcovers, and lay tangled in the sheets. She extricated herself. It was 3:30 in the morning, and the swoosh through the vents was as steady as ever. Had he been at it for four hours?

She rose, grabbed a terry cloth robe, went into the bathroom, and took a quick shower. She doubted she'd get back to sleep. She dressed swiftly in blue jeans, cotton shirt, cotton sweatshirt. Yoshi came into the room, yawning and snarling.

"C'mere, cat," she said, scooping him up, falling into a sofa and cuddling. Yoshi clawed his way loose. Sara put on her high-top Reeboks and began to pack up. She would have liked to have spent the day in bed with David lingering over the *Times*, maybe going down the street for breakfast, flipping through the news shows. But clearly, he had other priorities.

Problem. Her bike was in the workroom. She'd have to disturb him to get it. Oh well, she thought, hoisting her leather overnighter and the tank bag, both of which she'd lugged into the living room. She went down the carpeted corridor past his library, his Spartan bedroom, to the workroom door, constructed of heavy-gauge steel, closed and sealed with a Dunwich deadbolt. The steady swoosh of steel on stone issued faintly from within.

Sara listened for a moment, loath to interfere with his concentration. But if she wanted to leave, there was no getting around it. She had to have her bike. She knocked lightly on the door. There was no response. The swooshing never stopped. She knocked harder. There was a break in the swooshing for an instant. Absolute silence, save for the constant susurrus from the street.

"David?" she said tentatively.

The swooshing began again, a little more intently. She

rapped hard on the door. No response. The swooshing continued. This was ridiculous. She had to have her bike. What was the matter with him? Maybe he was wearing a set of headphones and couldn't hear.

Sara hauled back her foot and kicked the door robustly several times. The swooshing stopped. An instant of silence, followed by a scraping sound and then the thick click of the lock unlatching. The door opened twelve inches to reveal David, flushed, without his glasses, sweating profusely, with a silly grin on his face.

"What?"

"David, I'm sorry to bother you, but I need my bike."

"You're leaving?"

"I'm done sleeping. I'd love to stay . . . " If there were an invitation. "But I've got work to do. No rest for the wicked."

"I understand. Hold on one minute and I'll let you in." David shut the door and slammed home the deadbolt. She stood for a moment outside the locked door, feeling foolish. Surely he realized she would never violate his sanctuary if he requested privacy. She heard him scuttling around, some scraping, then the door swung open.

"Sorry about that," David said, grinning foolishly.

"It's okay. I understand." The polishing stone was wet, the odd apparatus surrounded by splattered water. She couldn't help wondering where he'd stashed the sword. The workroom was a museum of oddities, with hundreds of concealing places; among the old cabinets, beneath stacks of packing blankets, in tons of boxes arranged against the wall, in any of several old steel and wood cabinets. She forced herself to stop looking, and concentrated on fixing her bag to the back of the bike. When she finished, she turned, and David was waiting to take her in his arms.

"I'd love to have you stay. I really would. But I promised the client . . ."

She put a finger to his lips. "Hey, it's all right. I understand. Work's work. Call me?"

"Count on it."

She put her helmet on, got on the bike, and walked it out the door into the alley. He'd shut the door and locked it even before she got the engine started.

It took Sara slightly over an hour to cover the sixty-five miles from Manhattan to Upper Salem, where Murray Rothstein resided in a twenty-two room, Richard Neutra-designed, retro-futuristic monstrosity that was meant to suggest a Superchief. Sara had ignored the PRIVATE ROAD signs and rolled up the seventy-five-yard red brick drive to the parking circle in front of the white and stainless steel house. A white XK8 and a Lexus sedan were parked in front of the square glass entry. Sara wheeled her bike up to the glass wall and left it there, beneath the stainless steel portocochere, while she rang the buzzer.

A moment later, the speaker grill snapped. "Yes?"

"Mr. Rothstein? It's Sara Pezzini. I'm a New York City Police Detective. May I speak to you for a minute?"

"Just a minute."

Five minutes later, Rothstein approached the door grumpily, clad in a white terrycloth robe loosely fastened at the front so that Sara had a better view than she wanted of his blue Speedos, a slight roll of fat spilling over the rim. He was damp, and his dime store flip-flops left a trail on the Spanish tile floor. The glass door opened, releasing an exhalation of chill air.

"Come in." He turned, oblivious, and marched back down the hall. They emerged in a gleaming stainless steel kitchen, stovetop a single smooth surface, glass patio doors looking out on the pool area, which Rothstein seemed to have to himself that morning. He wheeled on her.

"Well? Who did I kill?"

He was a bantam rooster with tufts of white hair behind his ears. Sara bet they stood out like bird's wings when they were dry. His beak-like nose and crane legs did little to erase the impression of some exotic bird. He crossed his arms.

Sara gave it a hint of blush. "It's not about murder, Mr. Rothstein. It's about a property you own: Waubeska Place in Brooklyn."

"What about Waubeska Place? Christ, I got so many properties I can't keep track of them all. Are you really a detective? You look like a chorus girl, please excuse my impertinence."

Sara held up her badge, directing light from the extensive skylights into Rothstein's eyes until he put a hand up.

"Okay! Okay! You're a cop! What about Waubeska Place?"

"I have friends in that building. They were being harassed by a group of Puerto Rican kids. I got to know the gang members, and far from being hardened criminals, they're just a bunch of kids who are at a loose stage in their lives. Three of them are carpenters. You have a couple unfinished apartments in that unit . . . "

Rothstein held up his hands and signaled like a railroad flagman. "Wait a minute. Wait a minute. Now I remember. Waubeska Place! I hadda give up forty percent of that building 'cause I got this furshtunker bleeding heart liberal judge, who thinks the world owes blacks a living! Excuse my harsh language, Detective, but I'm an old man, I been around, and I know how things work. Can I help it if the onsite property manager lets in some jerk, her second nephew twice-removed turns out to be a crack dealer? You have no idea the *tsuris*, being a landlord."

Sara let him ramble. When he paused for air, she resumed. "Sir, I understand how frustrating it must be, but surely, at this stage in your life, you've reached a level of success that keeps you insulated from the daily grind."

Rothstein looked around, as if to reaffirm his wealth. "You might say so. So what's your point, young lady?"

"I would like you to let the Romeros use those apartments while they fix them up. I know these boys. They know what they're doing. Instead of the property standing vacant, you could be renting it out. In the meantime, they'll fix it for free, if they can stay there while they're doing it."

"The reason those apartments are vacant is because they're in the part of the building controlled by the federal government. If they were in my sixty percent, I'd fix 'em up."

"Then what have you got to lose?"

Rothstein raised his eyebrows. "What, indeed? If you're asking for my permission, go ahead. But don't come crying to me if they knock you on the head and attack you behind locked doors."

"I appreciate your frankness."

"All right, enough, already! It's Sunday. I don't want to hear business. You're welcome to join me. My daughter Roberta is about your size. I'm sure we have a suit somewhere."

"Thanks, Mr. Rothstein, I'll take a rain check. I have to get back to the city. I'd appreciate it if I could use your phone."

He pointed to a wireless on the counter. "Don't call Singapore."

The meeting between the residents of Waubeska Place and Los Romeros took place at one P.M., in the lobby and on the front stoop of the building. Jorgé wore a three-piece suit like something out of *Saturday Night Fever*, with a long, pointy, open collar, and a snap-brim fedora. Hector wore white linen pants and a silk shirt. Mrs. Finkelstein made raspberry strudel that disappeared faster than free beer at a ballgame.

There were five Romeros present, the core homies, and a dozen residents, including Ben and Mrs. Milman from the third floor. Jorgé brought two cases of Tecate. Ben offered him sips from a bottle of Peppermint Schnapps he kept in the pocket of his heavily pilled Cardigan. Lupé did not attend.

Ben, Howard Lubar, Frank Hernandez, and Mrs. Finkelstein discovered that they shared a passion for baseball with Jorgé and Hector. None of them could fathom how Robert Ruiz, an up-and-coming rookie with the Yankees, could have thrown his career away by stealing teammate Derek Jeter's glove and bat, which he sold for a fast twenty-five hundred.

"One of my homies did that to me," Jorgé said, "I'd light him up."

"Light him up?" Lubar asked.

Jorgé made a gun out of his right hand and picked off a few ghost targets. "You know. Blam blam blam."

"Are you carrying a gun now?" Lubar asked.

Jorgé made a pained expression. "No, ése. It's just an expression. I ain't never shot nobody."

"But do you have a gun?" Lubar persisted.

Jorgé made an expansive sweep of the room with his arm. "Man, we all got guns. My choice is the Glock nine, even if it does that have that stupid trigger safety. You?"

Lubar looked startled, as if he'd discovered a spider in his cottage cheese. "Me what?"

"You got a piece?"

"A piece of what?"

"Howard!" Ben snapped. "He's asking you if you own a gun!"

"Certainly not! Why would I need a gun? Why do you need a gun, if you've never shot anybody?"

Jorgé looked surprised. "Man, are you for real? If you're a man in this country, you have a gun. I don't mean to insult you, dude, it's a cultural thing. I come from a culture of machismo. I had a gun for ten years now, ain't shot nobody yet. Ain't sayin' they ain't a lot of punks packin', that maybe shouldn't. All I'm sayin', a man should have a gun."

Ben looked like he was about to volunteer something.

Sara stepped to the center of the foyer and waved her arms. The front door was propped open with a rubber wedge, admitting warm afternoon air, circulating lazily up through the building and out a skylight, courtesy of a large ceiling fan.

"Hey, listen up, everybody!" The hubbub immediately stilled. "I want to thank the residents, especially Ben

Weiskopf and Mildred Finkelstein, for pitching in and providing refreshments. Thanks also to Jorgé for bringing the beer. You all know we've had trouble with gangs in the past. My friend Jorgé assures me those days are over."

Jorgé raised a clenched fist. "Power to the people!"

"You got that right," Hector said, not so loud.

"I spoke with the landlord, Murray Rothstein, and he's agreed to let the Romeros have the two vacant apartments on the second floor in exchange for fixing them up. As most of you know, three Romeros work as carpenters, and they assure me that they will finish the job in two months. Those two months will be a trial period to see if we can coexist."

"Time we done with them, those apartments will be like a palace," Jorgé stated. "Donald Trump will be standing in line." He said it again with a carnival barker's conviction. "Standing in line!"

"Rothstein!" Ben spat like a piece of bad fish. "That goniff!"

"Mr. Rothstein was very nice. He didn't have to do this. Let's give it a chance, shall we?" She gave Ben a dazzling smile.

He nodded and smiled back. "Yeah, you're right. You know what you are, Detective Pezzini? You're a fixer-upper. You find problems and you fix 'em."

"She's a saint!" Mildred Finkelstein said.

Sara laughed. "And on that note, I gotta go."

When Sara knocked on the Guttierez door, Syreeta answered, electric swirling lollipop drilling into her teeth. She stood there, mouth buzzing, staring over the chain. Sara showed her the badge. "May I come in?"

The girl closed and unlatched the door, opened it, and returned to her place in front of the color console, as if she hadn't a care in the world.

"Is your sister in?" Sara asked.

A shrug, without looking.

"Hello!" Sara sung. There was no answer. She went down the hall to the closed bedroom doorway and knocked on Lupé's door. She felt, rather than heard, a subtle bass line and figured Lupé was plugged in. She tried the door. Unlocked. She swung it open. Sure enough, Lupé was seated cross-legged on the bed, back to the door, big pair of earphones clamping down on her glossy black hair, bouncing slightly to the bass, surrounded by CDs.

Sara moved into the girl's line of sight. Lupé lurched once, as if zapped, and whipped off the headphones. "What are you doing here?"

"You know the Romeros are in the lobby."

"I know."

"Where's your mother?"

"How should I know?"

Sara snagged a folding chair, the only piece of sitting furniture in the room, and sat on it backwards, arms on top of the back. "Only reason I'm here, girlfriend, is to see if you're okay. I understand why you don't want to run into any Romeros right now."

"I hope you're happy with him, 'cause he dump you in a New York minute."

"I told you, Jorgé is not my boyfriend. You're young. You're very pretty, smart as a whip, and you have special abilities. The whole world is yours, Lupé, if you'll give it a chance."

"Here it comes," the girl sneered. "Stay in school, don't be a fool."

Sara stared at her, unblinking. The girl fidgeted, shuffled CDs. "How you get that power?"

"Excuse me?"

"You a for-real witch. I saw you fall from that crane. All of a sudden, your whole body zipped up tight in some kinda armor. Then you bounced. How did you do that? How did you get to be a witch?"

"I'm not a witch."

Lupé looked bemused. "Hokay. I see where you goin'. What are you then, a mutant?"

Sara gave a tight little smile. As good enough an explanation as any.

"How can I help you?"

"You remember that little séance we had here the other day."

"I remember you comin', I don't remember what happened."

"You were possessed. It's okay. He's not coming back." *Not here, at least.* "See, I dig the way you do that. Maybe we can trade secrets."

Lupé shrugged. "I don't know how I do it."

"That's all right. We'll figure it out."

Sara let herself out. The party was still going on in the lobby so she took the stairs four flights up to her unit. The air conditioner was going full blast in her bedroom. She went inside, shut the door, and phoned Leesha Bachman in Newton. The woman answered on the first ring.

"Miss Bachman, it's Detective Pezzini."

"Have you caught my father's murderer?"

"Not yet. But I expect something to break soon. There have been several promising developments."

"I heard somewhere that if you don't catch a killer in the first twenty-four hours, the odds against catching him increase astronomically."

"Well, those are the statistics, but every case is different."

"Well, who do you suspect?"

"I can't tell you that."

"Then why did you call?"

Sara could sense Bachman's anger and impatience, although she'd kept her voice neutral. Why *did* she call? Out of guilt, perhaps, for initially leaving Bachman out of the loop? Out of genuine concern? To cover her ass? "I'm calling to tell you that I'm confident we're going to find the person who did this."

"Well, I appreciate that. The next time you call, I hope you have better news."

Click.

I deserve that, she thought. Before she could set the phone down, it rang.

"Sara, it's David."

He sounded breathless. Her heart did a stutter-step and dove for daylight. "Hello! I was just thinking about you!"

"Yeah, well, about tonight . . ."

For one awful second she thought he was going to cancel. Her brain turned into a strobing file search as she sought the reason why. Came on too strong? Another girlfriend? Not ready to commit to a serious relationship? Freaked out she was a cop? "Yes?"

"Is it all right if I meet you at the party? I'm really sorry, but I'm working on a rush job that has to get done, and I still have a little ways to go. It's going to take me right up to party time. So I thought I'd just meet you there, and we'd take it from there."

Her heart performed a complex series of aerial maneuvers. "What kind of job do you have to do on a Sunday night?"

She could hear the grin through the phone. "A lulu. I'll tell you all about it. Tell me what you're going to wear so I can wear something complimentary."

Dreamboat, she thought. "Emerald sleeveless dress, one over-the-shoulder strap, and matching heels. And a jade necklace."

"You look beautiful already. The other women will hate you."

She sighed theatrically. "That's the burden I have to bear."

"Okay. I should be there by seven-thirty. Love you."

Her apprehension gone, Sara let the receiver float back into the cradle while she floated into the bathroom. Pause. She'd planned taking the bike to Manhattan and stashing it at Dave's place. That was now out. The journey by bus and subway would take at least an hour, and she did not relish doing it in her little green dress. On the other hand, if she threw on black leather jacket, *de rigueur* for residents of Manhattan, she could project enough attitude to keep the creeps at bay.

Or, she could pack her tank bag and overnighter as cunningly as a Chinese chess master, and use the facilities at the station house. She might even luck out and cop a ride with a patrol. That way, she'd have her bike in the morning when she went to work.

All righty then, she decided. By motorcycle to the world. She took a shower, hair down, and spent a half hour drying it. She pulled out the cheap, motley-patched leather overnighter she'd bought for seven bucks in Playa del Mar and cunningly packed it with her green Jil Sander—it really was wrinkle-proof—her green Louis Vuitton high-steppers, a hair dryer that resembled a radar gun so much she'd used it to freak speeders, and her makeup kit. She'd ride clean and make up at the station house. Last but not least, the little bottle of Hugo Red. She pinned her hair up and slapped a Yankees cop on top. One bag looped over her shoulder, gripping another in one hand and her helmet in the other, she made her way down the stairs, let herself out the back door, and ambled across Prospect Place.

The newly installed and vigilant security cop waved to her. He looked like a native of Central America. Sara hoped he at least spoke English. It was nearly six when she hit the Brooklyn Bridge, and traffic was light. The motor pool at the station was jammed tight, but hers was the only bike. Of course. Sharpe had told her he'd be working security tonight.

Bernadette Goines was ending her shift as Sara applied makeup in the women's locker rest room. She'd let her hair down and tied it loosely at the nape of her neck with a black velvet ribbon.

"You like to start a riot the way you look, girlfriend," Goines told her, dabbing at her face with a piece of brown paper towel.

"Thanks, Bern. Rough night?"

"John comes at me with a Swiss Army Knife. 'Gonna put my brand on you, honey,' he says, right before I clock him between the eyes with my leetle brass fran'." She held up a set of brass knuckles that must have weighed a pound.

"Nice."

"Then some sheik wants me to join him and a few other select buddies on his yacht. But by then, the sun was comin' up and I was NOT goin' down, no more, not today. I'm headin' home, I'm catching some shuteye, and then Waggles and me are headin' upstate to a little B&B and some R&R."

"That that cop from the Two-Seven you've been dating?"

"A-huh. Saw your little honey bunch in the dock t'other day. Don't he look like a vanilla parfait. Where you off to, dolled up like that?"

"The Hecht Center for the Performing Arts. Adrian's throwing a party to celebrate the sublime beauty of his Hechtness."

Goines laughed. "Really? What's the occasion?"

"Getting the Hecht Center ready in time, I guess. And he might be announcing a new acquisition to his collection. Big deal, huh?"

"What's he collect?"

"Japanese swords."

Goines closed her large black leather bag with a snap, tossed her processed curls. "Well why not. I knew a guy collected insects. Y'all have a swell time."

"You too, Bern."

NINETEEN

The Hecht Center for the Performing Arts was situated kitty-corner from the excavation where Sara had confronted Los Tecolotes. It was also separated by its own eight-foot hurricane fence topped with concertina wire. Contractors had been working around the clock to finish it off in time for the Big Event, and it looked like they'd pulled it off. Sara exited the taxi directly in front of the main entrance, a cascade of crescent-shaped steps in front of the arched entrance. Security in suits greeted each vehicle at the main entrance on Liberty Street. A number of cars were parked directly on the spanking new concrete that would eventually become Hecht Plaza.

A number of thin-blooded saplings were held in place by guy wires. The building itself suggested concrete sails, with great, soaring abutments and tiny cube windows punched into its side like player piano tape. At its base, valets in green jackets were busily parking large cars inches from each other, slotting them in like so many dominos, leaving barely enough room to squeeze out the doors. As Sara approached the main entrance, invitation ready, she glimpsed a flash of chrome between the cars. Someone had parked a motorcycle in an alcove too small for a car. She walked back to take a look.

A bronze and black 1100 Shadow rested in the penumbra, fitted with crenulated Roadhouse pipes and a fishtail tip. This was Sharpe's other bike. He'd told her he had a Shadow for cruising. And suddenly it all came together.

Akira Kurosawa had directed a film called *Kagemusha*, which meant, literally, "shadow warrior." Chalmers' rival for the online sword had signed his e-mails "Kagemusha." Sharpe was the shadow warrior. Sharpe had beheaded Chalmers and taken the sword, because he'd cut himself on a Muramasa, and in that instant, the warrior's restless spirit had entered.

But which warrior? Which blade?

There wasn't a lick of proof. It was all circumstantial.

Sara joined the knot of swells waiting to be admitted by a body builder in an Armani suit, carefully examining each invitation before dropping the red rope. Sara was just about to show her invite when three limos whipped up to the curb, nearly clipping a valet. From the front and rear limos, two well-dressed flunkies sprang into action. A tall young man with styled blond hair opened the rear door of the middle limo, and extended his hand to New York's junior senator.

The gatekeeper's eyes were on the senator.

"Excuse me," Sara said, flashing her invitation. "Excuse me."

"You'll have to wait. The Senator's here, and she doesn't like to stand in line."

Sara caught a glimpse of the frosted blond hair as the senator stalked past, surrounded on all sides by expensively-clad bully-boys lest one of the hoi polloi try to touch her garment.

There was a great deal of cooing and the pop of flash-bulbs as the Senator entered the building. Only then did the gatekeeper turn his attention back to Sara. He looked like he was from the Caribbean somewhere, with a slight lilt to his voice.

"I am sorry about that, but we have strict orders to move the Senator to the front of the line. Always to the front of the line."

"She *is* the smartest woman on Earth."

"That's right." He examined Sara's invitation and let the red rope drop. "You enjoy yourself," he said with a smile.

The lobby of the Adrian Hecht Center for the Performing Arts resembled a high-tech cathedral, with a peaked ceiling displaying bones, and immense steel girders with oval cut-outs. The floor was an intriguing mix of circles, squares, and triangles set in marble and granite—a patchwork of contrasting textures. Huge crimson rugs with the Hecht logo endlessly repeated provided a jolt of color. There were at least a hundred guests wandering the lobby, *ooh*ing and *ah*ing over Hecht's art collection, which hung from walls, from ceiling beams, were mounted on plinths, or crouched in corners. There was a set of sixteenth century samurai armor mounted on a mannequin, enclosed in a Plexiglas display case. Another case displayed a dozen of the rare blades, naked steel reflecting a thousand little lights. Several waiters in black tie circulated with trays of champagne, and there was a buffet in the corner, presided over by a chef in a white toque.

The gently curved glass front wall arced thirty feet to

the ceiling. Sara scanned the crowd for David, but couldn't see him. She made a beeline for the buffet table. Might as well eat something while she had the chance. She was on her third bacon-wrapped shrimp when she sensed a presence at her shoulder. The smart young thing with lank white hair, pierced chin, and silk jacket over black silk T looked familiar.

"Hi," he said, flashing high-priced choppers. "I'm Rondo."

She shook his hand. "Sara Pezzini."

"You don't know who I am, do you," he said with an air of jovial expectancy. He had a strange, toothy, East Coast accent that sounded made-up.

"Sure I do. You're Rondo. You just said so."

"Maybe you've heard of my band, Flying Stankfish."

Sara paused. If he were trying to be witty, he was incredibly dry. He wasn't trying to be witty. He was some self-involved rock star who expected her to know who he was. "Sorry. Your fifteen minutes haven't come up yet."

"Excuse me?"

But she was already cruising toward the front entrance, where James Bratten had entered with a tall, thin model on his arm. His gaze fell on Sara and he headed her way, towing the model like a skiff. "Offisa! Arrest this woman! She incitin' indecent thoughts!"

"Hello, James."

"Sara, Celque. Celque, Sara." Sara recognized the Somalian model. She was six-feet-two, and weighed one hundred and twenty pounds, with Nefertiti cheekbones and cinnamon skin.

A string quartet in some distant corner dove into Vivaldi with a small splash.

"Have you seen our host?" Sara asked. "You probably have a better view from up there."

Bratten looked around with the slightly self-conscious profile of the well-known celebrity. He was gratified by the subdued murmuring of his name. "Nope. Tha's all right, though. Adrian's always late. You still seein' that sword polisher?"

"Yup. I'm supposed to meet him here."

"Tha's good. David's a fine lad. Hey! There's my man Calvin!"

Bratten veered off like a fighter jet going into combat, moving to intercept his teammate Calvin Broadbent. Celque gave an indulgent smile. "He's like that. Always rushing off, every second, a new interest. He sees life like a child."

"I envy him."

"Me, too. Sometimes I think I am too sophisticated to enjoy life."

Sara scanned the crowd for Hecht or David. There were at least two hundred people now swirling across the cubist floor, jumbles of voices rising like startled pigeons. "How so?"

"I have had nothing to drink, nothing to smoke, nothing to snort, and nothing to shoot now for two weeks. Can you believe it?"

Sara reapparaised the ectomorphic model. There had been rumors of drug use, but who cared what a bunch of overpaid models did in their spare time? Celque looked serious, with a sober gleam in her eye. "I'm sorry, I have nothing to compare it to. You seem perfectly normal to me."

The woman's face split in a supernatural smile. "Thank you," she said warmly, extending her hand.

A steady clinking penetrated the throng, and conversation gradually slipped away. All heads turned toward a cantilevered balcony extending over the lobby like the prow of a ship. There stood Hecht, striking the metal rail repeatedly with a silver spoon. Sara wondered if it had been in his mouth when he was born. Behind him, at a slightly lesser elevation, stood a flush-faced David, grinning like an idiot, light striking his glasses in such a way that the lenses appeared to be a field of white. He was clutching a long narrow objected wrapped in newspaper.

"Greetings!" Hecht boomed from the bottom of his diaphragm. "Greetings and salutations from Hecht! Thank you for honoring us with your presence on this, our inaugural night, the Official Grand Opening of the Hecht Center for the Performing Arts!"

The crowd applauded enthusiastically for such a well-heeled bunch. Sara noted the imperial "we." She tried to catch David's eye. And there it was. He took the glasses off, winked, blew her a kiss. As she responded, Celque nodded approvingly. Bratten returned and took the model's hand.

"I had planned to treat you all to a performance of *42nd Street*, but the auditorium isn't finished. In fact, only this room is finished, so we're having the party in here. In a little while, Mama Digdown's Brass Band will walk among you, along with some of the more energetic members of the Peach Haddison Dance Company.

"As some of you know, today's my birthday . . ."

"Happy birthday, you old weasel!" cried a drunk.

"Thank you, Cyril. And don't let go of that young man you're leaning on."

Laughter. Other comments. Hecht made a gesture for silence. "I didn't tell you, because I didn't want you to bring me gifts. I have everything I need tonight. Many of you know I have a passion of samurai swords and have, in fact, made my own modest contribution to the art and hobby. Some of my pieces are on display in the lobby tonight.

"I'm proud to announce a new addition to my collection, and something that should create a bit of a stir in the world of collectors." He turned and David handed him the package, then stepped crisply off the balcony and disappeared from view. Hecht held the long, narrow package before him for a moment, as expectations built.

Here it comes, Sara thought. *Skyroot.*

"As aficionados know, a debate has raged about the two swordmakers named Muramasa. No one doubts the existence of the latter, and his sons and cousins. But of the former, there has been much doubt. Until now. With the aid and assistance of many people, including the Hon'amis, I have acquired and authenticated the first Muramasa's last and greatest sword . . ."

The newspaper came off. It was already loose. The slender, curving, lacquered black sheath emerged. Gripping the sheath in one hand and the handle in the other, Hecht slowly drew the blade, extending the shimmering sliver toward the ceiling. Someone started clapping, Bratten joined enthusiastically, then everyone. A triumphant moment for Hecht. As he expertly slid the blade back into its sheath, tracing an ellipse in the air, jugglers, dancers, and acrobats appeared, and a nine-piece brass band, lean young men in hip-hop clothes, chugged out of an alcove pumping "When The Saints Go Marching In" on trombone, trumpet, tuba, and snare drum. Chiseled young men and glamorous young women wearing discreet Navy HCPA jackets released confetti and glitter from the upper decks. Something for everyone, including the unions, who would clean up in the morning. Heck, Sara thought. They're cleaning up right now. She spotted the local Teamsters' president yukking it up with the Junior Senator.

Warm breath gusted Sara's cheek. David put an arm around her and pulled her close. "Sorry I'm late," he whispered.

"You're just in time," she whispered back. "Was that your rush job? That sword for Hecht?"

"Yes. Sorry I couldn't tell you, but I was sworn to secrecy."

Sara closed her hand around her tiny suede Luis Vuitton purse, feeling the hard outline of the .25 auto. David had had Skyroot in his house while they'd made love. Why hadn't the Witchblade said something?

White hot pain flooded her right arm from the tips of her fingers to her shoulders. Dipped in acid. Her forehead scrunched, and she bit her lip.

"What's wrong?" David asked, immediately sensing her distress.

A force rippled through the crowd on her right. The pain went away, replaced by a relief that made her gasp with gratitude. She staggered. The gauntlet appeared. David gripped her arm, startled.

"What is that?"

Sara looked up. No good. She was too short! But she knew what had happened. Sharpe had passed her, heading for the stairs. Suddenly, the Witchblade was doing its job, sensing danger, putting two and two together. Sharpe and the sword. Or, more accurately, whichever of the samurai ghosts was most fierce and the sword.

She took off, threading through the throng. The crowd

thinned behind the buffet, toward the broad, curving stair leading to the balcony. Sharpe was halfway up the stairs, just as Hecht appeared on the landing halfway down.

"Sharpe!" Sara yelled. He did not respond. Hecht paused at the landing, holding the sword in both hands.

Sara saw Hecht form the words. "Sharpe. What is it?"

Sharpe never slowed. His left hand shot out, clipping Hecht on the chin. His right hand grabbed the blade, and he kept on going. A few others saw what happened and gasped.

David appeared at her elbow. "What the hell was that?"

She turned and grabbed him by the arms. "David, listen. Find the chief of security and tell him to meet me here."

"What's going on?"

"Just do it!" She raced up the steps, cursing herself for not alerting security as soon as she'd arrived. But it was all circumstantial! Until Sharpe hit Hecht, there had been no proof he'd so much as jaywalked. Hecht was sitting on the marble landing, legs splayed, feeling his jaw.

"Are you all right?" Sara snapped.

Hecht goggled. She'd forgotten the Witchblade, encasing her right arm to just above the elbow. "Don't look at me! Are you all right?"

"Yeah, what the hell—"

Sara kicked off her shoes and sprinted up the stairs two at a time, feeling in her purse for the Baretta. Without breaking stride she hung her badge around her neck and tossed the bag over her shoulder. Twenty feet ahead of her, crimson arced across her path, hit the gray marble. A security guard, pale blue shirt drenched crimson, staggered backward from between naked iron girders, designer rusted to henna. He collapsed, half turned toward her, one hand extended. He'd been nearly cleaved in two with a horrendous slash from shoulder to waist.

Confusion mixed with calliope music drifting from below. Sara could sense men running, weapons being drawn, but so far she was alone. She stepped to her right, back into the shadows where the girders created a separate gallery. Sharpe stood with his back to her at the end of the corridor, facing the wall, the blood sword in his right hand. He'd discarded the sheath.

Sara went into a shooter's crouch, both hands cupped around the tiny Baretta. At this distance, she doubted she could hit him, much less bring him down. And she didn't want to get any closer.

"Sharpe! Police! Drop the sword and get down on the floor!"

She heard someone running up behind her, the quick slap of leather on stone.

"David, stay back!" she hurled over her shoulder.

"Are you all right?" he said from right behind her.

"David, go downstairs. You're not helping." Her eyes never left Sharpe, who still stood with his back to her. He turned, chin buttoned to his chest, regarding them through loony, hooded eyes.

"Sharpe!" Sara snapped, hunkering lower into her stance. "Drop the sword and lie down now! I will shoot you!"

"He's not Sharpe," David hissed. "Look at him." Abruptly, he fired off staccato Japanese, the only word of which Sara recognized was "Shigeyoshi."

At the mention of that word, Sharpe snapped into *chu-*

dan no kamae, holding the blade in front of him with both hands, the point directed at David's throat. Sara heard the *zing* of metal on metal. David stepped forward, holding one of the long swords from Hecht's exhibit in two hands, like a batter warming up.

"David! Stop it! Get the hell out of here!"

"I know what I'm doing," he said through his teeth. Holding the pistol in her left hand, she reached with her gauntleted right, grabbed him by the collar of his jacket, and pulled him forcefully backward. He twisted loose, leaving the jacket behind.

An elevator *gong*ed. Hushed voices, the quiet mutter of dispersal. Two men in the pale blue of the security force dashed around the corner, gripping riot batons, and ran smack into a propeller. Sharpe took one step, shifted his shoulders, and sliced through the first one's neck like a cheese log, continuing the motion downward at an angle as the second guard ran into the suddenly inert body of his companion.

David stopped when the men had appeared, giving Sara an opportunity to catch up with him. Her gauntled hand shot out, striking him just above the elbow. The sword fell to the floor. David looked at her with surprise, mingled with pain.

"Don't make me handcuff you. Go downstairs now." She shoved him forcefully, and he grudgingly retreated a few feet, hurt expression on his face. The last thing she needed was a distraction. Sharpe/Shigeyoshi had just killed three men.

He advanced, blade like a dousing rod, speaking Japanese. Sharpe wore a black silk T-shirt beneath a silver jacket, loose-fitting black cotton trousers. His sneaker-clad feet edged forward without leaving the floor. He looked demented, mouth a slash. Sara was ready to shoot. She braced herself, cupped the pistol, aiming at his thigh, knowing she shouldn't play around, especially not with a .25, knowing she should let him have five right in the torso, and then the Witchblade tossed the gun away.

It flipped the gun off at an angle like a Frisbee. Sara stared at her hand like it was an alien thing. It *was* an alien thing. Betrayal. Sharpe was upon her. The blade whistled, a silver blur. The Witchblade twitched, subtle as a hummingbird's wings, and caught Skyroot in its center, closing around the blade. Sara was too astonished to move, right arm extended, feet in a combat stance. Sharpe froze, too, a ghostly expression on his face, as if he were emerging from a long sleep. His muscles remained fully engaged, thrusting forward with all his strength. Sara slid backwards in her stockinged feet, but she did not yield, nor did the Witchblade, its grip complete and unbreakable.

Sharpe stopped and reversed direction, drawing the blade out of Sara's grip. A synapse-popping shock whipcracked up Sara's arm and burrowed down into her center. Her arm was numb to the shoulder, but continued to move, controlled by the Witchblade. The volatile mix of emotions left her shaken. Sharpe looked confused as well. He withdrew, sliding backwards.

The Witchblade pulled her forward. The blade came alive in Sharpe's hands and appeared to be struggling.

Sharpe gripped the blade in both hands like an aluminum baseball bat and dragged it backwards. It appeared to have great weight. Sara glanced behind her. David was gone, thank God, but Hecht had rallied two NYPD blues from out front and were directing them toward Sara.

Sara turned to consult. The Witchblade yanked her back, drew her after Sharpe, hand clamped in an iron grip. She turned the corner just in time to see the elevator doors shut, in a bank of four leading to the unfinished ballroom on the fifth and top floor. Like the Flying Fickle Finger of Fate, the Witchblade's index finger beelined to the button. An elevator opened, and the Witchblade dragged Sara inside, just as the two cops skated around the corner, guns drawn, one high, one low.

"Hold your fire!" the high one cried, as the elevator doors slid shut.

Kenny G played softly on the sound system. It was only audible in the elevators. Sara stood with her back against the wall and watched the digital display count up to five. The doors dinged and slid open. Sara crouched, ready for anything. The door had opened on a broad area of indeterminate depth, lit only through reflected light streaming through the immense arched windows that encircled the ballroom like a crown.

The Witchblade was inert, awaiting her command. An instant ago it had been alive, dragging her along. "What do you want?" she snarled. "Help me or get lost."

Witchblade leading, Sara came out of the elevator fast and low. She was behind a collonade marking the grand ballroom, with its inlaid wood floor, cut into a vast map of the world. America was oak, South America was mahogany, teak from Thailand, cedars from the Middle East. The oceans were alternating strips of ash and maple, cut into a wave pattern.

Sharple knelt on the Canary Islands, sword thrust before him.

"Help me," he groaned.

"Derek?" Sara asked, cautiously edging forward. She

did not regret the loss of her gun. It wouldn't have done any good. "Derek, can you understand me?"

He looked up with haunted eyes. The mask of death was gone. "Sara, stay back. It's the sword. It wants me to kill . . ." The thing twitched, gleaming in the city light. Sharpe looked like he was trying to hold it still. It vibrated, casting off shimmering rays of light.

Sara stopped ten feet away, Witchblade held placatingly forward, inert for now. "Who? Who does it want to kill?"

His eyes were pleading. "Everybody," he said in a hoarse whisper. His face twisted, mouth a grimace, some internal struggle taking place.

"Run!" he screamed, rising, struggling with the blade, gripping the handle like a mountain climber at the end of his rope. It turned toward her, dragging Sharpe like a pull toy. He was trying to hold it upright, but the blade bent in a tight little curve. It yanked Sharpe along like a kid on water skis. It dragged him across the polished hardwood floor, his heels emitting a rodent-like screech.

"Let go!" she barked, backing up, feet describing alternating crescents, never leaving the ground. "Let go of it!"

"I can't!" Sharpe wailed in a voice frayed with pain. Skyroot flicked, a god's eyelash. The Witchblade rose to meet it. The impact caused a crack to appear in one of the glass arcs overlooking Battery Park. The very air seemed to come alive and punch her, everywhere at once. Sara was deaf. The mask descended on Sharpe's face, and he and the blade were one, attacking with savage fury, leaving a quicksilver figure eight in the air. Sara was forced backwards by the overwhelming attack. She had no chance to think, to plan strategy. The Witchblade thought for her, parrying, trying to hang on. As Sharpe withdrew his blade, Sara could actually feel the metal splitting. Not deep enough to reach her hand. But it was parting before the samurai sword, acknowledging a superior force.

Her head was filled with buzzers, fire alarms, tinitis, black noise. Her eyes were filled with tears of rage and frustration. She cursed the Witchblade, and in that instant it sprouted a scythe, index and middle finger blending into one. Sharpe reversed direction and thrust forward like a fencer. The Witchblade rose. It made a faint metallic whisper as it cut through Sharpe's arm above the wrist. Sword and hand fell heavily to the floor, dappling the finely finished ash with the suggestion of a chrysanthemum.

Sara panted, supporting herself with her hands on her knees. Her blade was gone, faint afterimage of a quicksilver loop. Skyroot lay on the wood floor, still in Sharpe's grip, blood spreading, tip of the blade thrust skyward. Ever so slowly, it began to descend, a recalcitrant lever, until it touched the ground. One by one, the fingers of Sharpe's hand let go.

Sharpe had staggered back until he hit one of the iron girders, slid to the floor clutching his pumping stump. The sight of his blood gouting forth snapped Sara out of her trance. She was on him in three steps, had his belt off in three seconds. It was narrow, made of some kind of lizard skin, and had probably cost more than her entire wardrobe. Sharpe was going into shock. She got the belt around his forearm below the elbow and drew it tight.

"You're going to be all right, Derek. I have to stop the flow of blood. You're going into shock, okay? That's normal. Breath deep, from the pit of your stomach. There's an ambulance on the way."

Was there? Where the hell was everybody?

Her hand blazed. The Witchblade flowed over her hand again, from the tips of her fingers to her shoulder.

And then the power went out.

Not just in the building. All of lower Manhattan. First the Woolworth Building. Then every light on every wall in the canyons of Lower Manhattan. The elevators wouldn't be operating. But somebody should have shown up by now. Maybe they were waiting to hear from the SWAT guys. Why weren't they coming up the stairs? Where *were* the stairs?

The gout of blood from Sharpe's cleanly amputated arm had stopped. The wound was grotesque. Sharpe sat with his knees up, his head resting against the wall, eyes shut, slowly counting out his breath. It was an impressive display of self-control.

Sara crouched next to him. "Derek, you're doing great. I have to leave you for a minute to get help."

"Cell phone," he rasped. "Jacket pocket."

Sara felt in his jacket, found the plastic clam, flipped it open. Dead. It wasn't a natural blackout. Something was sucking the juice out of every battery in Lower Manhattan, not just the grid. She looked at her watch. Not long enough.

"I was . . ." Sharpe croaked. "Water," he gasped.

Sara rose. She remembered passing a water fountain by the elevator. She grabbed an Etruscan style vase off a plinth, rinsed it out, filled it with water. Outside, the city breathed in fear, wondering what had happened. Millions would assume it was another terrorist attack. They'd rush to the televisions but receive no solace. The cars were dead. Nothing was moving. For the first time ever, Sara couldn't hear any sirens.

She heard voices, howls of confusion, anger, paranoia, floating up from below. Cries of fear, questions hurled into the night. She ran back to Sharpe, knelt, helped guide the vase to his mouth. He drank greedily, Adam's apple bobbing.

"This time," he said, "I could feel what was happening. Spirit of a dead samurai, fierce. Fierce spirit. Chose me! Because of what happened over there . . . "

"What happened, Derek? What happened over there?"

"Joint exercise . . . with Japanese Anti-Terrorist Police. Charismatic shintu priest named Osagi, holed up in a mountain retreat in Hokkaido . . . He attacked me, I took a cut in the shoulder, was wearing a vest. I shot him, but it was too late. When he cut me, the spirit of the sword transferred from him to me. It was a Muramasa. The spirit belonged to a samurai who was forced to commit seppuku . . ."

"Shigeyoshi?" she asked in surprise.

"How did you know?"

"It doesn't matter." Where was the damned ambulance? She forgot. Nothing was running. No help was coming. Sharpe looked pale, and had slumped down. The best she could do for now was to make him comfortable. She looked around for something to cover him, to keep him from getting cold, found an Oriental rug on the wall in a side room, tore it down.

Taking a cushion from a sofa near the elevator, she covered Sharpe and made him as comfortable as possible. There was nothing more she could do. She turned to examine the sword.

Sharpe's hand lay on the floor, empty.

A scraping sound from the shadows, a gleam of reflective light from the three-quarter moon as the blade emerged, seemingly suspended in midair. Then she saw the man, short blond hair, moon in glasses.

"David," she said in an eerily calm voice. "Put it down."

But he was not David. The creature that shuffled into the moonlight wore David's clothes, his body, but it belonged to another era. Death lurked in its eyes, no longer hidden. The thing that was David spat guttural Japanese and attacked. He did not seem to lift his legs. He skated forward, seemingly exempt from the laws of physics, the glittering blade held overhead like an ax. Sara had always been quick, but were it not for the Witchblade, her reflexes would have failed.

Her arm didn't raise the Witchblade. The Witchblade raised the arm, meeting Skyroot's downward stroke six inches above Sara's head. The shock compressed her nearly to the floor as the Witchblade instinctively closed on Skyroot. It was like catching a Lincoln Blackwood with a razor attached. For an instant they remained frozen, the un-David bringing all his weight to bear on the blade, Sara struggling, free hand bracing the Witchblade inches from her face, as Sharpe struggled feebly to distance himself.

"Who are you?" Sara demanded.

With both hands, the creature withdrew the blade. There was a sound like exposed nerves, fingernails on chalkboard, yowling cats, screaming children. Skyroot sliced through the unknown metal of the Witchblade, scoring Sara's palm. She could feel the blood flowing down her wrist.

Skyroot cut Witchblade.

The creature backed off, an unknown expression subtly rearranging David's features so that he resembled a bad wax image of himself, or the way he might look after an undertaker had done his work.

Slitted eyes beamed hate. Clenched jaw spat forth a stream of jagged-edged consonants like tobacco juice. One word was recognizable.

"Udo," she hissed.

The creature smiled grimly, a smile of death. She recalled the story—how once he had slain his rival and his lady love, Udo had gone on to kill hundreds of innocent men, women, and children. His malignant soul had come to roost in sweet, innocent David. How could that happen? How could she fight him?

Crunching sounds from below, as someone tried to batter their way through a locked steel door. Hecht was concerned about security, all right. He'd made his performing arts center a fort, an elegant pillbox with a wig and makeup. The glass was three inches thick, optically perfect, impervious to armor-piercing rockets.

Hand burning fiercely from the blade, Sara leaped to her feet, hunkered into a combat stance, most of her weight on her left leg, the right ready to kick. She couldn't compete with the heavy sluggers. She had to rely on her speed, agility, and the Witchblade.

"I know you can understand me," she hissed, speaking not to the young man she'd come to love, but to the warrior spirit lurking like cancer behind him. "What do you want?"

"*Blood.*" Voice like buckling metal, like white noise, like screams in the night.

"Why? You're not human. You came from up there." She nodded toward the ceiling. "You fell from the sky, a lump of metal. Where do you come from?"

The thing that used to be David grinned, glanced briefly upward. "*Up there.*"

It attacked, fusing supernatural strength with skill and cunning, a dragon's tongue, leaving a gleaming retinal silver trail. Sara had no time to anticipate. The Witchblade was in constant motion, intercepting each blow, describing a series of arabesques. The stone glowed like a red dwarf with each contact. If Udo killed her, nothing would stop him. Skyroot had proved a match for the Witchblade. Would the police be able to gun him down in a fusillade of lead? Would he spin the sword like a propellor, repelling each shot?

A bolt of white-hot fury ignited in her gut and flushed through her system, indistinguishable from the Witchblade. Her fingers fused into a twenty-six inch blade of a delicate curving nature. The metal itself was not smooth, like the katana. It was a crazy quilt of textures that never settled. Only in motion could Sara get a sense of shifting patterns, rune-like, a ghost finger writing on the wall of some long-forgotten tomb.

The non-David grinned and pressed his attack. Sara gave herself to the Witchblade, moving through a series of complex steps designed to provide maximum mobility, thrust, and defense. The non-David relentlessly circled, slashing, stabbing, seeking an opening with terminal fury. It drove her across the inlaid ballroom floor, across the North Atlantic, East to West, almost faster than she could shuffle on the balls of her feet. She stumbled at Hudson Bay. The thing coiled like a serpent. She saw death in its obsidian eyes. She remembered that David's eyes were hazel.

For a nanosecond, she saw the way things might have

been: the split-level in Westchester, the two moppets—one boy, one girl, some kind of pound puppy, spreading waistlines and happiness. All futile. Not for her. Never for her. Not for Vince's little girl. She had her own curse to bear.

The malevolence shrieked with all the bloodlust in the jungle and slashed downward in a killing stroke. Sara skittered forward, ducking inside the slash and inserting her knife arm at the hip, drawing across his body toward the opposite shoulder, feeling the meat part, the scrape of the bone, the tensile snapping of connective tissue. The Witchblade was out the other side, flicking blood as far as Rio de Janeiro. David looked down in astonishment.

"What—?" he said, before slipping in two. He was dead before his torso hit the floor. His guts splashed in righteous display. A man of honor forced to commit seppuku would welcome such incontinence. Sara remained in a combat crouch, but the Witchblade had withdrawn into itself, leaving only the bracelet. A massive scraping sound issued from somewhere close, followed by matter-of-fact murmuring. Hecht must have rallied his troops and broken through. Or maybe the police department.

Trembling, she sank to her knees and crawled forward, cradling David's lifeless head and torso in her arms, soaking herself in gore. Skyroot lay inert, temporarily sated. Her tears dripped onto his lifeless eyes.

"Oh, David," she moaned softly. "I'm so sorry . . ."

The black bone snouts of assault rifles poked around the corner, followed by Kevlar-clad SWAT guys in fiberglass helmets.

"It's okay," she tried to say. It came out a croak. She waved her hand. She remembered the shield around her neck and held it up, dripping blood.

"I'm a cop," she gasped.

EPILOGUE

She wouldn't let go of David. Siry had to pry her loose, finger by finger, while talking to her in a low voice. He rode with her to the Emergency Room at Cedars/Mt. Sinai, where a woman doctor examined her for damage. Only shock, the doctor declared, and gave her a sedative.

Siry drove her home and tucked her in. "I'm putting a guard out here, just in case."

Sara rallied. "You don't have to do that, Joe. I've got Los Romeros."

He wondered what she meant, did it anyway. She hated the fact they'd put her under, hated that she wouldn't be in on the cleanup. She fell through warm gauze toward a feather bed.

When she woke, Raj was seated in a kitchen chair he'd brought into the bedroom, and was sipping tea from a cup, Schmendrick perched contentedly on his lap.

"Greetings. It is I, Raj."

"I see that. What are you doing here?"

"I am protecting you from the press and seeing you do not choke on your own vomit."

Sara sat up, feeling woozy. "What time is it?"

Raj set his teacup down in its saucer on a tray on a TV table, and carefully lifted the cat to the floor. "It is just past noon on Tuesday, and even as we speak, the Mayor, the Commissioner, and the Chief are proudly declaring that the case of the samurai killer has been solved."

Memory caught up with Sara in a great, walloping smash and took her breath away. A sob clawed its way unbidden from her lips.

Raj rose. "I shall get you some tea."

Sara fumbled for the remote and keyed on the little Sony that perched on her dresser. There was Joe, reading from a teleprompter in a monotone. ". . . responsible for these murders. He had all the missing blades, hanging on the wall of his studio."

Coiffed heads bobbed for attention. An especially shrill reporter drowned out all others. "Chief, Mr. Commissioner, wasn't Detective Sara Pezzini involved in this case? Didn't she, in fact, shoot the alleged perpetrator?"

"I have no comment."

Sara switched it off.

Oh, David. First decent guy she'd dated in years, and he turns out to be the samurai killer. A case could be made that David was innocent, being possessed by a thirteenth century samurai at the time of the murders, but this was small comfort to the victims' families.

Sara held her right hand up and stared at the swirl of silver orbiting her wrist.

Raj returned to the room with an old tray he'd dug out of her cupboard, a silver pot of tea, and a plate of Pepperidge Farm Bordeaux cookies. "Feeling better?"

"A little," she lied. "Thanks for baby-sitting, but I'm all right now."

"The chief told me in no uncertain terms to stay here until I was relieved."

"I'm relieving you, Raj. I'll take full responsibility."

"You are certain?"

"Want me to throw you out?"

"That will not be necessary."

She padded after him and made sure the door was locked and the phones were off. She took a shower for fifteen minutes, toweled herself off and put on a set of workout fleece. She sat in the middle of the living room cross-legged for a while, staring out the window at a high cloud in the west. Sometimes the cloud resembled a horse, sometimes a man. But when all was said and done, it was just a cloud.

She stared down at her wrist.

"Did you have to kill him?" she sobbed. She was overwhelmed with such a feeling of loss and regret, it was like a physical blow.

The chittering voices of the Witchblade—voices that never seemed to stop babbling in the back of her mind—suddenly fell silent. If she hadn't known better, she might have taken it as a sign of respect for her grieving.

But she did know better.